Acknowledgements

I wish to thank my entire family for their encouragement and support while I was writing this novel: my husband Peter, my three grown-up children Rachael, Ruth and Anthony, my granddaughters Sophia, Giorgia and Harriet, my brother Owen, and my cousin Brian. I also appreciate the support of my friend Diane, for her interest and encouragement. I was also heartened by the faith shown in me by pupils at school and my colleagues, when I told them I was going to write a novel.

Series Destroying the Light:

1. Destroying the Light
2. Destroying the Light 2: The Invisible War
3. Destroying the Light 3: Has the Invisible War Returned?
4. Destroying the Light 4: Is Invisible Death Still Stalking?
5. Destroying the Light 5: Is This the Beginning of the End?

First Edition

Contents

1. A New Beginning

Does life always turn out the way we hope, dream and expect?

I had previously been a career girl and had expected to work full time with a family, however, having a family changed all that! Before I left to go on maternity leave, Alex Wynn, the headteacher of Turnerlane School, told me, "I hope you have a happy and safe confinement; you've been worth your weight in gold to this school." My classes sat GCSEs early at the end of year 10 for the first time in the school, and passed with higher grades than previous years had, when they had sat their exams in year 11! Turnerlane School was in the city of Sealand and was the best school in the area, at that time! Alex was the youngest headteacher in the Local Education Authority (LEA) and was often on the local news for all of his many accomplishments in the school! He was short, assertive and called a spade a spade! He was very slim, with short brown hair and was certainly in control of the school! The assemblies were unbelievable! In assembly, all of the staff sat on the stage and rules, expectations and routines were very clear and easy to follow, for everyone.

My friend, Beatrice Milton, who worked in the school we had both gone to as pupils, was asked by a member of staff who had taught us both, Mr Green, "How did Ellie get a job in Turnerlane School? It's the best school in the whole area!" Beatrice was very slim, with short, curly hair and we'd been friends for years. Beatrice was also in her early twenties; she'd always been quite shy but was now slowly crawling out of her shell. Mr Green was tall, chubby and friendly, with short, wavy, auburn hair and in his late forties.

"Her dad saw a job advert in the paper, so she applied."

"She was lucky to get that job!"

I really had only applied for a post in this school because my father had seen an advertisement in the local newspaper and I hadn't wanted to let him down! I had been very happy doing supply teaching at Leggepool High School, where I was valued and very happy. The headteacher, Michael Miles, was a pleasure to work with every day! When I told him I'd applied for this post, he told me, "I will write your reference and if you don't get this post, I'll want to know why!"

At the interview, for the permanent post, the headteacher, Alex Wynn, told me, "We have three different posts going at the moment, and you are the best for them all! Which post would you prefer?" Wasn't I lucky? However, after having had a family, I was no longer the career girl I had been before I had a family. My life shattered before me when I had a baby; I was no longer the career girl I had been!

I later rang the Sealand English Adviser, Philip Handy, "I thought I'd be happy working full time as a new mother, but I'm not! I just can't manage to work full time with a baby, and I'm going to resign."

He advised, "Don't resign. Let me arrange a part-time post for you. I have another teacher who is in the same predicament as you; you could both job share, if you want to."

"I think I could manage two and a half days"

"You'll be able to return to full time teaching whenever you want to. Just let me know."

We agreed I would work two and a half days a week, Tuesday, Wednesday morning and Thursday. Philip told me, "I am going to go into Turnerlane School to ask for a favour. I'm going to ask if the headteacher knows anyone who might be interested in working part-time for the LEA. When someone contacts you from the school, you must say you will transfer to part-time supply, without resigning. You could then return to full time work, when you want to, around your family. Do not tell anyone that you've rang me first." I was currently on maternity leave, after just having had a baby.

May Elliott, the deputy headteacher, rang me and asked, "Do you know anyone who would be interested in working part-time, for the LEA, on a Tuesday, Wednesday morning and Thursday?"

"I'd love to volunteer to transfer to part-time supply, without resigning; working on a Tuesday, Wednesday morning and

Thursday would be great!"

"That's great! That's exactly what the LEA is looking for."

This was ideal, as it was only two and a half days, which was much better for me than full time!

I was incredibly happy working part-time, doing supply. I was on the same payscale and was treated with respect and equality in every school. I worked in a number of schools and was incredibly happy. I even went back to my original school to do supply teaching. When I left to work in another school, Alex, the headteacher asked to see me and asked, "Why are you leaving? What can we do to keep you here?"

My reply was amazingly simple, "I'm sorry, but I'm still keeping the days and hours I'm working now, for family reasons."

"We're incredibly sad to see you leave, again."

"I really don't want to work full time, with a family."

"We're always here for you when you want to return to full time teaching."

Wasn't that lovely? I continued to work part-time, being a supply teacher. I was paid by Sealand LEA, so there was no difference in my payscale and holiday pay.

Philip Handy rang me later, saying, "There's a school that would love you to work there on a permanent basis, and you can keep the hours and days you're already working, and there would be no pressure for you to work more hours, unless you want to. Would you like to look at the school, as a favour to me, to see if you would be happy there?" I went to Firlane School, and the headteacher and the head of department were a pleasure to meet.

When I first went to Firlane School, it was a pleasure to go into the staffroom, which was friendly, happy and very welcoming. Everyone was so happy when I first went to the school, I couldn't believe the amount of laughter and smiles in the staffroom. Breaks and lunchtimes were very friendly and full of happiness. This was a new beginning and I was filled with love, happiness and trust. Firlane School was in a built-up area, in a concrete jungle. It had many children living in challenging circumstances, which knit a close staffroom community. As a student, I'd thoroughly enjoyed working in small groups, role play and drama and had expected life at work to be an extension of my student days.

Andrea Tweed was one of the first teachers I met, in the

staffroom. She was slightly older than me, in her early 30s, and impressed me with her friendliness, her big smile and her infectious laughter. She was smartly dressed in a lilac suit, had fashionable light grey hair and was extremely pretty; she was also very popular and had a word for everyone. I was then 27. When I first went to Firlane School the staffroom was happy, laughing and friendly!

It was Opportunity Week when I first went to visit the school, and Andrea told me, "My sister's ill! I'm going to have a word with the head, as he's usually very good over things like this."

The headteacher, Keith Stephenson, told Andrea, "You can have the week off, with pay, so you can spend time with your sister!"

Wasn't that lovely? He later did the same thing when Dawn Sinclair's father was dying too! I was totally impressed and felt lucky to work in such a kind, caring and supportive school! It was the headteacher's kindness that I couldn't believe! Keith was in his late 50s, was tall, slim and smoked enormous cigars, every day! He also always drank a glass of red wine, daily, at work, in his office. His door was always open, so it wasn't a secret. Dawn Sinclair was my neighbour at school and was slightly older, but very friendly, caring and welcoming! She had worked at Firlane School for a number of years and was a well-established member of staff.

Mary Evans, an older teacher and a head of department, was always laughing and made our whole group of friends laugh at breaks and at lunchtimes. Mary was in her 50s, had natural grey hair, which was always perfectly styled, and was pretty, slim and well dressed. Mary was a head of department and always sat with the same group of friends. Everyone was always happy, kind and supportive. This reflected the expectations of the headteacher. Everyone was important in the school, no matter what their role was in the school. Everyone was valued, everyone was happy and everyone was kind. What a marvellous school! It seemed like Leggepool High School!

Mary was always laughing when Susan Stone and Krystal Welsh bought flowers for Margaret Crow (the deputy headteacher)! Susan Stone was also in her early 30s, with dark brown, curly hair. She was of stocky build and wore clothes to match her frame. Krystal was also in her early 30s, and was extremely slim (some would say skinny), with long brown hair and was always immaculately dressed. However, Mary told us, "Buying flowers for management has worked for them!" Mary was very astute and, time showed, she was always right! She identified the people who had nothing to learn from Machiavelli! "If you notice, they don't give flowers to everyone, just to the people in power!"

There were many departmental lunches, Christmas staff meetings and end of term staff meetings, all characterised by humour! The speeches at the end of term were full of laughter; the staff leaving speeches were well planned and funny! Laughing at staff meetings was frequent and expected, a happy time was had by all, with wine at the end of term gatherings. I had everything! I had my family, which was then two children and I worked two and a half days in the career of my dreams! However, my husband's job was no longer safe, as there were many closures in the industry across the country, so I worked part–time for family reasons. This was a happy compromise; I was happy every day; my family was happy every day too. What more did I want out of life?

Opportunity Week was a revelation and tutor group days out were happy, full of fun and fantastic; this was always in the last week before school broke up for the summer holidays that year. What a marvellous school to work in! I had many days out at Lipton Wafer Valley, Flamingpool, The Main Centre, Southern Bay and the beach! This gave me plenty of time for shopping, buying gifts and enjoyable days out, with friends and pupils. Dawn and I enjoyed sitting in the café in the train, The Mystery Tour; we were the teachers on duty, in case anything went wrong, so pupils knew where to find a teacher. It was fantastic! Pupils did come to find us, so we were doing an important role, and we solved all problems, so all pupils felt safe and thoroughly enjoyed their day out. This was the last week before school broke up for the summer holidays! I also bought treats for our family on the day trips out and presents in the shops, as the sales were on! Life seemed perfect! Ellie Grainger always justified this by saying, "I encourage all staff to patrol the shops, to avoid problems such as shoplifting, on days out with Opportunity Week." Perfect! (Ellie Grainger enjoyed shopping in Opportunity Week as well!)

Dawn was happy and friendly every day, and our group met at breaks and lunchtimes, and laughed whenever we met! Everyone looked forward to going to work; everyone felt valued as an individual, as part of a department and as part of the school. Staff meetings were always characterised by jokes, laughter and enjoyment! The staff was happy, relaxed and optimistic. The laughter grew from the concrete jungle; it was better to laugh and survive! If people hadn't laughed so much, they would have found themselves trapped and ill! Together, everyone had a good job, a good life and a good future. Everyone cared about each other; everyone was expected to help each other; everyone was a valued member of a team. The headteacher's vision was firmly that together a team achieves more; the headteacher expected everyone to be kind to everyone on the staff; the headteacher regarded every single person in the school as an important member of the team. This simple strategy made the school successful and a pleasure to work in!

The caretaker was also treated with the greatest of respect by the headteacher and the senior leadership team. The caretaker was an older person, in his late 50s, and was a gentleman! Sam Jones was small and very slim, with grey, short hair. He always treated me, and everyone else, with the greatest of respect. He was always polite to the pupils, even when they did something which caused him more work, by their negligence! I had been in such a school before! Michael Miles had been an outstanding headteacher at Leggepool, but he now had competition! It was actually very close! Michael Miles was always excellent and I had been valued every day in his school, on both sites of the school!

This headteacher, Keith Stephenson, passionately believed that a happy staff produced higher standards of work and was totally committed to everyone being pleasant, polite and supportive, so all staff had an environment they could work in, and so did the pupils! Once he called an emergency staff meeting. "Have you heard the tannoy?" Dawn asked me. "It must be important as everyone not on duty must attend!"

I didn't know anything about the problem. The head was furious, "I'm going to make this perfectly clear to everyone! Every single member of staff is a valued member of this team! Permanent staff are not more highly valued than supply staff! Supply teachers are fully qualified teachers, or they wouldn't be working in this school, would they? Every member of staff in this school is expected to be kind, helpful and supportive. A supply teacher came to me today, very upset, at some comments that were made about her being a supply teacher! I am making it absolutely clear to every member of staff in this school: we are all a team and every member of the team is valued, respected and important!"

It never happened again to another supply teacher in Firlane School! I totally agreed with the headteacher, Keith Stephenson! I now knew this was excellent management! I knew a happy staff was more productive and this headteacher allowed everyone to be valued and to reach their maximum potential! This was the type of environment I had as a student, when I had been so happy and had accomplished so much!

I totally agreed with Keith Stephenson, as I had done supply teaching at the beginning of my career and had been treated as an equal by everyone! Years ago, when I worked at a school in Leggepool, the headteacher, Mr Miles, always came and talked to me! I hadn't passed my driving test for very long, when I did supply teaching at Leggepool. I had to transfer to another site at break, as the school was on a split site, only to find someone had blocked me in, in the car park! I had to ask someone to move their car! This took time, but I still managed to arrive at the second site on time!

When I arrived back at the main building of the school, a member of the office staff told me, "Mr Miles has been looking for you and has something to tell you. He said he wouldn't tell us, until he told you first." As he was a gentleman and a pleasure to work with, I went straight to find him! Michael told me, "Something dreadful has happened and I wanted to tell you first!" I wondered what it was! He told me, "The problem was all my fault! Straight after you had asked someone to move their car, because you were blocked in, I had to go to a meeting in another school. On the way to the meeting, I didn't look right properly, at the roundabout, and I pulled out! I collided into another car and it was all my fault!" Wasn't that kind of him to tell me, the supply teacher, first? He was a diamond and a pleasure to work with, every day! I was teaching in one of the best schools in Leggepool and the headteacher always treated me with respect, as though I was an important person on the staff! I expected teaching to be like this forever. Would my dreams, hopes and expectations come true? Was I right?

We were all happy and everyone supported each other with disruptive pupils; we were all valued and part of a successful team at Firlane School. I expected Firlane School to be as happy as Leggepool High School; I had loved doing Teaching Practice as a student; I expected Firlane School to follow on from my previous happy and successful experiences in schools!

It was the teamwork and the support of the staff that made the job a pleasure! If there was a problem, we discussed it in the staffroom and someone would always have a witty answer! That was how we solved all problems with the pupils, so we were happy, every day. The happier we were the more productive we were and the school obtained our best! It wasn't rocket science but it worked! Teamwork worked with the pupils too! We supported each other and acted as witnesses for each other; the pupils knew this, so they didn't push their luck! This had been exactly the same as at Leggepool High School! I had also taught in their Behaviour Unit at Leggepool High School and I didn't have any problems with any pupil! Not a single one! Michael Miles had told me, "Tell them I want to see anyone who does not do as you say in the Behaviour Unit!" Guess what? No one wanted to see him!

An ordinary day at work at Firlane School was enjoyable, with friends, a group of friends and going out on a Friday; the end of term gatherings were fantastic and fun. We used to sit in the staff room, at different times of the day, and laugh! Mary Evans always knew what was going on in the school and made jokes about everything, so everyone laughed, then worked hard as a team. Smiling, being happy and good times were the norm. Mary made us all laugh at every problem in the school! Mary was witty, no nonsense and called a spade a shovel! We worked well together for years; we laughed together for years; we talked about our families for years too. Feeling part of a group, being incredibly happy and laughing lots meant we worked together as a team, for the benefit of the pupils. I thought life at school would stay as happy every day. Was I right?

Mary always made us all laugh, every day! Mary always cheered us up with her witty conversation. She continually laughed at how Krystal Welsh and Susan Stone ingratiated themselves with the senior leadership team (particularly Margaret Crow, the deputy headteacher), by buying them presents. "It's a constant array of flowers. I wonder if they have shares in the flower shops?" Mary asked us. We all laughed. Margaret Crow seemed to appreciate the flowers! Margaret was a friendly woman, in her 50s, who was approachable and supportive; she made no bones about the disruptive pupils and also called a spade a shovel! Margaret made us all laugh, as she told staff nightmare stories about her day! She often made everyone laugh, when she ended with, "If anyone hasn't had a nightmare day like me, they mustn't be doing their job properly in this school!"

Krystal and Susan were a similar age to me. Krystal was tall and slim, with shoulder length, brown, curly hair. Susan was well built, with short black, curly hair and wore glasses. Were they both best pals with Machiavelli? They always bought Margaret flowers!

Angela Rivers did the same as Susan Stone and Krystal Welsh; she also bought flowers for Margaret Crow. She ingratiated herself with management. Most people regarded her as a liar, untrustworthy and manipulative; I gave her the benefit of the doubt and treated her the way I would like to be treated. Everyone told me, "She tells lies about herself, her family and her career. How can all she says possibly be true?"

Angela told me (the first day I met her), "I've been married twice and there was something wrong with both my husbands! One ran away and the other wasn't interested in women!" I just listened. Angela was a similar age to me and I was then 31. I didn't know anyone else who had had two husbands and had both marriages annulled. No one else believed her stories, but I gave her the benefit of the doubt. Who was right about Angela Rivers? Angela Rivers made many enemies at work (including the dinner ladies)! She always defended herself and blamed others but smiled at the people who she classed as friends. She always smiled at me! Who was right about Angela Rivers?

For years, we'd been happy at work and had laughed every day! We enjoyed our positive, problem solving conversations. We had a group of friends at work and were incredibly happy. Alex Yates, a deputy headteacher, and others referred to our large group as the scone making/ knitting circle. Alex was tall and broad, in his 30s, and still enjoyed teaching PE. Everyone laughed lots and we were all happy and all enjoyed going to work; we were able to do our best at work, because we all felt happy and supported. Dawn told us, "Happy workers equals more productivity; unhappy workers equals the bare minimum." We had been incredibly happy and phenomenally successful, working in a challenging concrete jungle.

We all had a fantastic night at the prom with Andrea Tweed

and Ellie Grainger, our head of year. Ellie was in her late 30s, was tall and stocky, with light brown hair. We laughed all night and Andrea Tweed sang to year 11, and they loved it! I will never forget Andrea's singing and the silence and rapture of everyone at the prom, as Andrea sang, "If you need me, call me, no matter where you are. Just call my name, I'll be there. There ain't no mountain tall enough, there ain't no valley low enough, ain't no river wide enough, to keep me from getting to you." It was an unforgettable night! Year 11 were enthralled and couldn't believe how much of a professional singer Andrea was! No other year 11 had ever had a year 11 tutor who could sing like Andrea!

I really appreciated the cards and presents I received when my tutor group left, before the prom. My tutor group had received the best references from employers on their work experience in the whole year! Hadn't they done well?

We had had an amazing time in France, on the week long school trip during the Easter holidays. It was an extremely happy environment to work in, so my family came too! The best thing about Firlane School was that my family was always welcome too! I was able to combine being a mother with being a teacher! We were all happy and the pupils on the school trip all made my children and husband very welcome too! Life was great! We were all happy! I was happy! My family was happy! The pupils were happy!

We went to Disneyland, Paris, Notre Dame Cathedral, the Champs-Elysees and ate ice cream up the Eiffel Tower. I was good friends with other members of staff, and we all had a great time. Andrea Tweed, Laura Harper, Molly Newsome and Martin Smythe all came! Laura was tall, slim and lively, with blonde hair. Molly was older, in her 40s and married with a grown-up family. She wasn't very tall, had black curly hair and was of average build. Martin was an older supply teacher, in his 50s, married with a grown-up family. He was tall and slim, with brown/grey hair. All three were a pleasure to work with and to go on holiday with. It was great! However, Pauline Steel seemed to be in a clique, with Susan Stone, and they both stayed up drinking all night, with a group of other teachers. Pauline Steel was in our year group and had organised this trip and organised the trip every year. She was an assistant head of year, which was why I'd gone, along with Andrea Tweed. Susan Stone also went on this trip every year.

None of my other group of friends went on this trip every year. I could see Susan Stone putting ambition before her family. This clearly led to tensions with Susan's husband, as he went to bed early with their son, while she stayed up drinking all night! It was apparent for us all to see! He was clearly unhappy and miserable. Pauline Steel babysat, so they could try to solve their problems. When we returned to school, the teachers who stayed up drinking all night looked shattered at school! The rest of us were happy, refreshed and rejuvenated. Hugh Percy, my head of department, asked, "How do you and Andrea look ready for work but every year teachers come back, from France, looking as though they need a holiday?"

I took our children to school discos and we always had a great time! I had taken my daughter to Flamingpool and to discos at another school before Firlane School and everything was great, so I did the same at this school too. Our group supported each other with problems in life, as well as at school, which was why we were all so happy and healthy. There was good management and Continued Professional Development for all! Staff development was expected and staff felt happy and valued. All staff were sent on courses, so each person was an expert in an area and reported back to the department, so best practice was shared across the department.

2. Teamwork

Gradually, the atmosphere in the school changed, as the school was worried about the new style inspections. It was a war: the whole school was against HMSI (Her Majesty's School Inspectors). Everyone supported each other: we were a team; we sank or swam together! I had a change of family circumstances, as did many others, when jobs were destroyed across the country, so I worked full time, to protect my family from adversity and change.

There was a Sealand LEA inspection before HMSI, and I was excellent in this, as usual. I didn't tell anyone what the Sealand LEA inspector had told me. Then followed our first HMSI inspection. HMSI, 1992, reported, "The success of the school is based on good relationships." Unexpectedly, the whole staff laughed when Keith read their report out, in the staff room; it had been the whole staff supporting each other against HMSI, and that was what they'd liked the most! The headteacher, Keith Stephenson, was praised by HMSI, but his reply was: "It was a team effort; it was the whole school."

The head of department, Hugh Percy, was so pleased he called an emergency meeting at lunchtime, telling us, "I was so pleased with the HMSI report I went out at lunchtime and bought champagne and cake for the whole department." Hugh had been so worried about the HMSI's visit that he looked as though he'd lost weight! He was already tall and slim! He was married with grown-up children, in his early 50s. The whole department was successful, and I was identified as "best practice" by HMSI. Even HMSI had found, "The good relationships in the school are a strength of the school", which made everyone laugh, because the war had been the whole school against them and they'd seen this as a strength! When Keith received a letter from Sealand LEA praising him, he put the letter on the school notice board and his reply on the school noticeboard. He had written, "It wasn't just me, it was a team effort!" The surprise was that HMSI had loved the whole school being a team against them! The only time I told anyone what HMSI had told me was when I applied for a post in management. After this, I received a management post, to extend best practice across the department, so it could be extended across the school.

Then, there was another Sealand LEA Inspection and I was excellent in this, as usual. Hugh Percy and Susan Stone made comments, within my hearing! Hugh Percy told Susan Stone, "She came out better than us!" I had before, so what was the change? I hadn't told anyone what had been said to me in this Sealand LEA Inspection either. What crime had I committed? Susan Stone replied, "We are the management. We show what we can do, that she can't." Why would she say this? What had I done to annoy them so much? Had I met Ruthless Ambition?

Was Susan Stone jealous? I had a family and I wasn't looking for further promotion, but she was! This wasn't how I'd been treated at previous schools! I'd always been valued, but now I felt threatened, uneasy and afraid!

In the second HMSI Inspection I was told by HMSI, "You are the type of teacher the government wants to value and part of HMSI's remit is to tell teachers like you that you are valued by the government." I was also excellent in Sealand LEA Inspections. Also, in the HMSI Inspection in 2000, I was praised by HMSI and Firlane School was officially a good school. HMSI continued to identify the good relationships in the school as a strength of the school. When Keith Stephenson received another letter from the LEA praising him, he put the letter and his reply on the school noticeboard again: " … it wasn't just me, it was a team effort!" Everyone was highly motivated and wanted to be excellent teachers! As the staff was happy and highly motivated, everyone was happy to work above and beyond the call of duty, for pleasure.

However, there was no champagne and cake this time. Why not? What was changing in the school? Why wasn't the management as pleased?

Where was the happiness in the school? Where was the teamwork?

3. Leaving

Martin Smythe left. He was the first member of staff to leave under the change of atmosphere. Martin told me, "There's a change in the attitude of the management." At the time, I didn't understand what he meant but his words were prophetic. He told my whole group of friends, "It's a pattern of behaviour; you'll see the management change!" Martin left Firlane School, where he'd been so happy for years!

Dawn's daughter, Jane Sinclair, a year 11 pupil, was bullied by pupils in her tutor group and subject classes. Dawn later told me, "Jane was also bullied by Pauline Laserton, her tutor, and even her GCSE grade A coursework was stolen from the teacher's filing cabinet, from Mr Smythe's filing cabinet, after school. Mr Smythe told me he'd put the work in the filing cabinet and Jane's work was the only piece taken, so it's been done deliberately."

"Jane's work has been stolen! She'll have to do it all again and it will be incredibly stressful."

"As you know, Pauline Laserton's her tutor. Jane asked Mr Smythe to tell me, because she was too frightened to!" Pauline Laserton was a married woman in her late 50s, who wasn't very tall and was extremely stocky. Previously, she had been friendly, but I knew before I came to Firlane School that she'd been accused of bullying staff at Firlane School. I could now see a more ruthless side to her. While I had been at Firlane School she had argued with Angela Rivers, in the staffroom, for all to see! Were they a match?

Dawn continued, "You're right! Jane will have to do all her coursework again, in a few weeks, for English. Jane told me she was being bullied; she's an outstanding pupil, and was also bullied by her tutor, as Pauline Laserton put her on the "naughty table". Jane was terribly upset! Jane's often in tears over other pupils. She's a teacher's daughter and she's being bullied."

Later, I arranged for other pupils to speak to Jane whenever they could, so she was happier, and wasn't isolated. This worked. The pupils I'd spoken to, John Jenkins and Graham Arnold, told me, "We knew something was upsetting Jane but we didn't know what it was! We told Jane you'd asked us to be friendly to her, to be kind to her and to talk to her on the corridor. We all laughed about it, together, and now Jane seems much happier in school. We always speak to her, whenever we see her, so she doesn't feel isolated." This solved the main problem. John and Graham were two of the most outstanding, kind and considerate boys in their year group; I knew they would support Jane, because they knew how cruel bullying could be. A smile, a wave and a kind word saves people!

Dawn continued to be upset as her daughter, Jane, continued to be upset by staff! "Jane has also been upset by Marion Sales, her subject teacher, asking questions about what the form is doing after they leave school." Marion Sales was in her late thirties, with an adopted son. She was tall and of medium build; her husband was one of the school governors. "I knew Jane had been set up by Pauline Laserton, because subject teachers don't have the right to humiliate pupils." The pattern was: identify a problem to management, management then blamed the person, because they wouldn't blame themselves! "Pauline Laserton will not accept that Jane is being bullied in the school. Marion Sales also upset Jane as she asked everyone what they were doing when they left school. Jane said she was going to Queen's College; Marion Sales' reaction upset Jane, as she implied, by her looks, that it was too expensive for her to go.

"Marion Sales then asked everyone: What are you doing after you leave school?" Jane was devastated and I felt this was done to embarrass Jane, as she was wanting a clean break from the bullies, without them knowing what she was doing or where she was going. Marion Sales was a subject teacher and this question had nothing to do with the lesson, which was an important exam revision lesson!"

Jane told her mother, "I'm too frightened to go to school to collect my GCSE results this summer! What can I do?"

"I'll go to school for you and I'll collect them for you! Don't worry about a thing! No matter what the results are, I'm going to have the biggest smile on my face!" Jane was glad they were nearly all grade As, including the subject where her work had been stolen!

Jane Sinclair later changed schools and with supportive management from her new school, blossomed, far away from the hostile environment of Firlane School. Dawn, her mother, needed a bank loan to send Jane to a private school, and she told the senior leadership team at the new school the whole story, and they gave Jane the positive support she needed to succeed. Dawn told the headteacher and the deputy headteacher at Queen's College, "Jane was very upset by bullying in her previous school."

"We promise to keep her safe," they told Dawn, which they did. They were as good as their word. Dawn outlined the problems to Queen's College and this school did not upset Jane; in fact, she blossomed in this school and even played her violin in St Petersburg, Russia, when Queen's College went on a music concert to St Petersburg.

What a contrast to Dawn's worries and nightmares, about her going to a sixth form with the people who had bullied her. Dawn was really pleased with Jane's four A Level results, particularly her grade A for English Literature. Dawn published the photograph of Jane with her A level results in the local newspaper and praised Queen's College; she also wished Jane well, in her new venture at Law School. Jane flourished and went on to become a highly qualified, successful lawyer, after an extraordinarily successful university career.

Pauline Laserton went on to bully all of our group at work, one by one, in any way she could! What a difference a private school had made to Jane! Jane had just been very frightened in her previous hostile environment; Jane wasn't the only one!

School shows and the school drama productions at Firlane School had been fantastic over the years! Andrea Tweed and Simon Coyles organised them and rehearsed with pupils; they were the motivational forces behind it all! It was great and an absolute pleasure to be part of it all! I helped after school with the makeup and the prompting of lines. Andrea Tweed, Dawn Sinclair and Rebecca Appleby dressed up as The Supremes, singing "Baby Love"! Rebecca sat with us every break. She was tall and well-built, with black, straight hair. Dawn made all of the jewellery out of Aston's Christmas decorations. We were a team together, and we all enjoyed working on the school productions! The staff enjoyed it and so did the pupils too! Susan Stone played an important part in the shows and productions too, which was greatly appreciated.

However, a chink in the light was when a disruptive pupil swore at Simon Coyles, when he was lining the pupils up, outside of the main hall. Simon told me, "I reported this through line management, but the pupil was never reprimanded! Instead, I was blamed!" Simon also sat in our group of friends (it was a large group of friends). Simon was also married, with two children still in primary school. He was tall, slim and friendly, with auburn hair.

"I'm shocked to hear how you've been treated! Sarah Jones is a nuisance around the school! She's always telling me she's put out of lessons around the school!" I had supported productions in a previous school, school excursions and discos and I had never seen such unacceptable behaviour being ignored! The instruction to all pupils was to line up, in a single file! This was the beginning of the end for Simon Coyles.

Andrea Tweed worked well with Simon Coyles, so her life began to change for the worse too. Susan Stone stopped supporting the dramas and school productions too. Jacqui Ayre told me, "I've noticed that Simon Coyles is no longer popular in the staffroom." Jacqui sat near the group with Susan Stone in it; I didn't know what she meant, because Simon was part of our group. Jacqui later moved from this group and joined our group, because she felt she couldn't join in with their views anymore. Jacqui was also in her 30s, with two children in primary school. She had done her degree later in life and was very pretty, confident and slim, with long, black, curly hair. I soon found out why she couldn't sit near Susan Stone and Krystal Welsh anymore!

Ellie Grainger left, through ill health. What a pity! Why were so many people leaving the school? She was our friend, our colleague and our head of year and a strict disciplinarian. She was a total pleasure to work with; she was not fooled by anyone either! Ellie saw things as they were. She was totally supportive, and pupils knew exactly what was expected! Was this the problem? Was she no longer flavour of the month? I had some of the most disruptive pupils in the school in my tutor group, but they were a pleasure to have in the tutor group, because I was totally supported by Ellie and the school. The problem in the year group began after Ellie left.

"Ellie's been given a good leaving deal, so long as she can prove she's ill! If she can't, she has to get a job, like the rest of us,"

Burt Haswell, a member of the senior leadership told me, a group of my friends and anyone else who wanted to listen! Why wasn't that kept private, for Ellie's sake?

Pauline Steel, the next head of year, was not so supportive and didn't share the same high expectations of behaviour as Ellie, as I soon found, and so did others! Pauline Steel was an excellent assistant head of year when Ellie Grainger was head of year. Pauline Steel changed once she had power and she was head of year. Susan Stone, Krystal Welsh and Deborah Lashley also became heads of year, but they didn't share the expectations of behaviour as the previous heads of year, who had all left very quickly. Why did they leave? Were they no longer flavour of the month? Why did they all look upset to leave?

Alan Buxton left. Alex was an older teacher, who was small and slim, but had been an amateur boxer all his life! Keith Cool then told Dawn, "I'm leaving as well; I've seen it happen before; no one can win against them, once they start on a victim." Keith was also an older teacher, in his late 50s. He was tall, broad and well built, with curly, grey hair. Two strict, supportive heads of year left. Dawn told Keith, "I have nightmares about coming to work now! I feel frightened every morning. Why are the strict teachers leaving? The high expectations of behaviour were always supported in the school previously, but the change, and lack of support, by management now gives me nightmares."

Keith Cool advised Dawn, "Leave, because I've seen this before. No one can win against them. Do supply while you still can." One day, after work, on her way home, she saw Keith Cool again and told him what was happening at work, "I'm being undermined at work every day now! The disruptive pupils now seem to be supported by management. They're all making my life a misery."

"That's why I'm leaving as well; you can see the same as me!" Keith soon left, following the supportive heads of year! Susan Stone and Krystal Welch became heads of year and so did their friends. They supported each other and their friends, but not the older, experienced and expensive members of staff! It was appearance and reality. They appeared successful by worldly values but they were morally corrupt.

Colin Glass also left, after he'd told me, "I've seen it all before as well! I've seen this pattern of management before! They don't support staff with disruptive pupils, then the member of staff becomes ill, then they leave!" Colin was in his early 30s and was not very tall, with straight, black hair. He was kind, thoughtful and considerate. He wasn't ruthless or ambitious at all! Colin told me, "One member of staff left heartbroken by management and then committed suicide! This was ignored at school and no one went to his funeral!"

"How awful! They make themselves out to be so caring and supportive."

"Don't be fooled by them."

"I think everyone should care about everyone else! No one should be leaving school and committing suicide! I'm totally shocked!"

Colin later told me, "They're doing it to me now! I'm no longer being supported with disruptive pupils and I'm now very unhappy in this school. I'll have to leave, before they make me ill as well! They're obviously telling the disruptive pupils to tell their parents to ring their head of year to complain about me! I've seen them do this to others before: the disruptive pupils just laugh when I give them detentions and they all say they'll get their parents to complain! It's the same pattern!"

"That's terrible! I hope they start supporting you with disruptive pupils!"

"They won't! I've seen them do it before."

Colin later left. At this point, I still hoped for the best!

Keith Stephenson, the good headteacher retired. What would happen in the school now?

Pauline Lane left. Pauline Lane was an older teacher, who was single and lived with her elderly father. Pauline wasn't very tall and had blonde hair and blue eyes. Pauline Laserton had made her life a living nightmare recently! Dawn told me, "Pauline Laserton makes people's lives a misery at work if she can't control them!"

"Years ago, Linda Bird left Turnerlane School to come here. Other staff told me she'd complained about being bullied by Pauline Laserton."

Pauline Laserton went on to bully all of our group, one by one. Dawn told me, "I saw Pauline Laserton bully Pauline Lane; she deliberately showed her up in front of other members of staff!

Pauline Laserton did this in the staffroom. She left Pauline Lane heartbroken. Pauline Laserton then went to Pauline Lane's classroom and rearranged the furniture without any discussion. Pauline Lane then put it back, to where she had had it in the first place. This pattern continued, of moving the furniture in the classroom, without any discussions at all. Pauline Laserton did this to Pauline Lane on numerous occasions. Pauline Laserton treated Pauline Lane unmercifully."

"That's totally undermining and soul destroying! No wonder Pauline was so upset and left. Linda Burn left as well, because of Pauline Laserton, and that was before I even came here."

What could we do? Who could protect us against Pauline Laserton, who was in a position of power in the school as deputy headteacher? What power did we have, to stop it? Pauline Lane left very quickly, heartbroken, very thin and extremely pale.

Gradually, we were no longer supported with disruptive pupils, in the same school, because of a change of management. Ellie Grainger, Andrea Tweed, Martin Smythe were all incredibly supportive and they all left, upset. Pauline Steel, Deborah Lashley, Krystal Welch and Susan Smith were not supportive, but all became heads of year! There was a change in support by the head of department and the head of year. Suddenly, the disruptive pupils were protected and their lies believed! Deborah Lashley was in their group of friends, what a coincidence! She was a similar age to Krystal and Susan; she wasn't very tall, like Susan, but was slimmer. She had auburn hair.

The problem was a change in management. Previously, we'd been happy at work and had laughed lots! Our team was being destroyed, one by one, deliberately. That was the bullying. The pattern was: identify a problem to management, management then blamed the person, because they wouldn't blame themselves! It was a pattern of divide and conquer! It was the difference between heaven and hell! It was the difference between appearance and reality!

This was where the school changed: there was a change of management, who did not value the staff who had done so well. They stopped valuing older, expensive and hardworking staff. The pupils soon realised they could be disruptive, and the staff would be blamed, as Simon Coyles found out!

Dawn told me, "I've been the victim of a sexual assault and it happened in front of a whole class; the head of department laughed!" Dawn had been the victim of a sexual assault! "I reprimanded the head of department by saying, "Would you laugh if someone sexually assaulted your wife? Would you laugh if someone sexually assaulted one of your daughters? How would you feel if someone sexually assaulted you in front of a whole class?" All Percy Banks did was laugh! What a head of department!"

The school was now changing beyond all recognition! I'd also been the victim of a minor assault (a pupil pushed me) and verbal assault, but all cases were ignored by management. This type of thing had not happened before! Dawn's sexual assault was laughed at! Dawn reported it to the police and a verbal warning was given to the pupil concerned, on the school premises; I reported verbal assault to the Civic Centre, which gave written warnings to the pupils concerned. Neither of us had been protected by the school. Why? What did the future hold?

The senior leadership team was furious that staff were reporting incidents inside of school to authorities outside of the school! What else could we do and what else were we supposed to do? I reported the assault, which was a mild knock on the arm (a push), but I was told there were no witnesses! No wonder a female teacher was later savagely beaten up in the school yard! The pupil who did it was in one of my classes; she was by no means the most disruptive pupil in the class.

Claire Marshall was one of the senior leadership team; she was tall and well-built, with short blonde, curly hair. Previously, Claire told me, "I've been working late at school, to get work done, and I'm now often the last person to leave the building." When I next saw her, she had two black eyes, an arm in a sling and bruises all over her body. She was off work for two weeks, but the bruises were still terrible when she did return to work! The senior leadership team kept that quiet too! Did they blame her, for working so late at school? Another teacher, Andrea Tweed, had money taken out of her coat pocket, which she had left in the classroom, but a teacher saw this pupil take it. It was the same pupil who had assaulted Claire Marshall. The pupil who had beaten up a member of the senior leadership team was in one of my classes and she was by no means the most disruptive pupil in my class! Why were pupils in Firlane

School now allowed to assault teachers?

Janette Chapman left. Janette, an older teacher, had always been happy at work and had always been funny and laughing with our group of friends, every break and every lunchtime! Janette had been working in Firlane School for years and was a head of department. She was married with a grown-up family; she was extremely short, smartly dressed and always wore cardigans, as she was in her early 50s. However, there was a problem of congestion on the stairs, so she told Terence English, as she was supposed to, and he turned the problem around and blamed her! She told me, "I'm not surprised, because that's what management does in this school! The problem on the stairs is a common problem all over the school." The senior leadership team then deliberately made her life more difficult; they didn't reinforce school rules about movement around the school but told her to change classrooms. Terence English was a member of the senior leadership team; he was tall, slim and handsome and always wore a suit for work. He was married with three children and was in his late 30s.

Janette told me, "The senior management team didn't give me a classroom on the ground floor. They gave me a classroom on the top floor, with more stairs to climb every day! When I asked for consideration, because of age and a weak heart, they told me I was obviously unfit for work! Don't tell the girls!" She left terribly upset too! They ignored her pleas to stay in the same classroom.

"I know what they've done! They've blamed you, not the pupils who weren't following school rules regarding movement around the school!" Janette Chapman left heartbroken and destroyed. Janette couldn't believe she'd been so upset in a school where she'd been so happy for years! Janette would never have treated anyone the way she'd been treated; the people involved in this wouldn't like to be treated like that either!

I had now met Power at work! Janette had been driven out because she'd complained about the crush of pupils on the stairs! She was an older teacher, and they then moved her to a classroom on the top floor. When she complained about that, saying she had a weak heart, they turned that against her, claiming she was unfit for work. The pattern was: identify a problem to management, management then blamed the person because they wouldn't blame themselves.

My mother had cancer and had an operation in which she could have either died that day or lived for at least another 10 years. If she didn't have the operation, she would die quickly, with the cancer! Instead of being supportive, the head of department, Hugh Percy, asked me, "Why do you have this problem in your life, when others don't?" That was the beginning of a change of attitude towards me! My mother survived the operation, but he kept asking me, "Why do you have this problem when others don't?" What a thing to say to someone whose mother had cancer!

He was lost for words when I replied, "Many people would love to be as lucky as me, because my mother has survived cancer." I hadn't made any unpleasant comments when he told me his wife had had a nervous breakdown when they had concerns about their daughters.

Ross Blythe left because they didn't give him enough support either! Ross was second in our department and was responsible for behaviour in the department. He was excellent! He was older, in his early 50s, and wasn't very tall. He wore glasses and always wore smart trousers, a shirt, a tie and a dress jacket for work. He was also married with grown-up children. He left with heart problems. When Hugh Percy was absent for a term, for an operation, Ross had had his job to do and Hugh's job too, without any additional support! No wonder he was ill! There hadn't been any problems with discipline when he'd been in charge of discipline in the department. However, he'd suffered with the change of heads of year too. Ross told me, "They want to molly coddle the disruptive students, not punish them! They're blaming the individual teachers and the disruptive pupils go running to them all! They always say they haven't done anything and the teachers are lying! How can anyone work with that attitude?" I knew Ross wasn't the problem! It wasn't Ross! It was the unsupportive change of management!

The younger person who replaced him didn't have the experience to do the post and made mistakes with standardising material for the exam board! They had to give the exam standardisation to someone else! However, because of how Ross had left, they supported the young, inexperienced teacher, who was obviously so much cheaper! They had two members of staff doing his job!

Ellie Wrightson was the young teacher who replaced him,

but she didn't have the same high expectations of behaviour as Ross Blythe. When Hugh Percy, the head of department, was absent for months, through illness, Ross had tried to do both jobs, without any additional support, which was why Ross became so ill, with heart problems! When Ross left, the behaviour of pupils in the department, and in the school, deteriorated. All of the teachers with high expectations of behaviour were leaving, either through illness or because they were so miserable they just couldn't stand it anymore!

Mary Evans retired! She was an enormous loss, because she always made us laugh about every problem, both in school and outside of school. She laughed about Susan Stone and Krystal Welsh buying flowers for the senior leadership team and ingratiating themselves with them! Mary noticed they were always smiling at the senior leadership team and always supported each other at meetings. Mary always told me, "If there's a problem in your life that you can't solve, you should concentrate on your strengths in your life, to cope." She made us laugh every day; we found that laughter was the best medicine! She retired saying, "I want to leave early, so I leave at the top and enjoy life."

However, when she returned for some social events at Firlane School later, she told me, "I can't believe the way I've been treated by some people. When I was a head of department, the same people were friendly, pleasant and couldn't do enough for me. These same people have now ignored me when I can do nothing for their careers." She was referring to Susan Stone and Krystal Welsh! Machiavelli had nothing to learn in this school! Before she left, Mary told me, "Don't be fooled by them or anyone else. They try to make it out as though they're everything in the world, but they're not. The pattern of management is: if there's a problem, they protect management and blame the person. I've seen them do it to people over the years. Someone will tell them there's a problem: they don't like that. Then they wait and blame the person. Always look after your family, and don't let them trick you into thinking they're everything."

Redundancies were offered at the school, for experienced teachers. At the time, no one in our group wanted to take their redundancy, as a permanent post was better for our families. Krystal Welsh, now a member of the senior leadership team told me, "Your position is safe in this school; no one has anything at all to say about how you do your job."

My family was the victim of a series of accidents, that were caused by other people's neglect! Again, Hugh Percy asked me, "Why does this keep happening to your family?" He didn't know what to say when we had a solicitor to protect us, for each accident. They were accidents because the perpetrators didn't intend them to happen! They were not our fault because other people are responsible for their own actions, not us! However, Hugh did become totally supportive when he knew we had a solicitor to support us, and that we didn't have to pay for the solicitor as the insurance companies paid for the solicitors, because the accidents weren't our fault. In addition to this, we had paid for unlimited free legal aid; if there was an accident and it wasn't our fault, we were entitled to free, unlimited legal aid! Hugh was then totally supportive over this and was genuinely pleased when they eventually paid us compensation. However, the pattern of management was there: if there's a problem, protect management and blame the person.

Andrea Tweed was bullied, but she didn't want to believe it. She confided, "I went to see my GP because I feel so unhappy at work! He told me to leave and find another job, so I'm now going to leave and do supply." Andrea had been happy teaching in her classroom, surrounded by supportive friends (like me!) so we couldn't understand why she'd been taken out of her classroom. Andrea Tweed was devastated but didn't think it could have been done deliberately. They put Susan Stone in her classroom, and they didn't care that Andrea was upset. It was a pattern of divide and conquer! It was the difference between heaven and hell! The laughter had stopped! I didn't want to believe what was happening either! My instincts told me there was danger ahead and something was terribly wrong in the school! Should I trust my instincts or wait for evidence?

Andrea Tweed was in tears and terribly upset every day in school. What a contrast! She'd always been bubbly, happy and full of life. Instead of teaching in the same classroom, where she'd been teaching for years, they moved her out of it, so she was no longer always in the same classroom. She became more upset every day, because she was treated less well than she had been over the years. The laughter ran away; the smiles followed; the tears remained. The doctor told her, "Look after your reference and find another job!"

Andrea Tweed told me she'd been to see Basil Wright, the new headteacher, and he told Andrea, "Leave, if that's what you want!" As a deputy headteacher in Firlane School, Basil had always been kind, thoughtful and approachable. He was tall and slim, in his 50s, with greying hair. We couldn't believe the change! We were all shocked at the way Andrea had been spoken to! We hadn't been treated like that before! Before, we'd been valued, but now, we were cannon fodder, and no longer valued, and it was a pattern of management!

How convenient, to force staff to leave by creating an environment they couldn't work in, and then save lots of money by getting rid of experienced but expensive staff! They knew what they were doing: it was the same pattern of management! They made Ruthlessness look like a saint! It was a pattern of deceit, manipulation, fear and misery, the symptoms of bullying. Pauline Laserton went on to bully all of our group, one by one. Andrea Tweed could not believe she felt so upset in a school where she'd been so happy for years! Andrea would never treat anyone the way she'd been treated; the people involved in this wouldn't like to be treated like this either. I still didn't really want to believe what my instincts told me! My instincts told me to run a mile, as this school was becoming unsafe and it was management behind it! However, the money protected my family! What could I do?

Andrea Tweed had been a popular, funny and supportive friend, colleague and team player. Everyone else was sad and devastated to see her leave! This left a big gap in our support group, where we'd supported each other for years, with problems outside of school and inside of school! This was a chink in my armour; my light was being destroyed. Previously, disruptive pupils hadn't been a problem, because our group saw them together, so we had witnesses, so lies couldn't be told. When Andrea Tweed left, a key member of our success team had been destroyed; our light was dimming. It was appearance and reality. They appeared successful by worldly values but they were morally corrupt.

Janette Chapman had left Firlane School broken hearted! She didn't live very long after she left either!

Pauline Laserton also went to Janette's funeral, but she went her way into the funeral and then Dawn, Andrea and Colin went their own way, in the procession into the crematorium. Why did Janette die so quickly after leaving Firlane School?

My memories came flooding back …

Dawn was told by one of the ladies in the school office, "Your reports for your tutor group, this academic year, are the best in the year!" Dawn was delighted.

Simon Coyles was bullied! He told me, "I just feel very unhappy and feel bullied, every day. I just can't stand it here anymore!"

Dawn confided, "I am a witness for the way Simon Coyles was spoken to by the headteacher, Keith Stephenson, before he left; I am a witness for the way he was spoken to by Hugh Percy as well." It was a pattern!

"Simon was unsupported by the senior leadership team with disruptive pupils and was taken out of the classroom he'd taught in for years, only to be given lessons in different rooms around the whole school!" I replied. This was how they destroyed our group. They divided us and upset us, so we couldn't support each other with problems and with disruptive pupils!

Simon informed me, "They were using you against me, as someone who is doing well in the school."

"They did this without my consent, because if you'd told me about a problem I would have helped you to solve it," I replied.

Simon admitted, "They gave me a timetable, around the school, that was impossible for anyone to do. I was in so many different classes they made it impossible for me to do my job. I was isolated from our group and had no one to support me with disruptive pupils, but when my classroom was near our group, I had lots of support, so there weren't any problems with disruptive pupils, because we all supported each other. Also, they gave me an additional GCSE subject, which was not my strength, on purpose, without our group to support me."

I also saw disruptive pupils ignore him and when I spoke to the pupils they shouted, "It's him! It's Mr Coyles! It's not us!" Pauline Laserton was often humiliating Simon in the staffroom and was obviously supporting the disruptive pupils against him! I saw her do it and I heard her undermine him in front of everyone! It was done in a full staffroom! Pauline Steel, the head of year, was also totally unsupportive!

Simon Coyles felt upset and told me, "It's a set up, as staff are not supporting me with disruptive pupils. I feel it's a vicious cycle because disruptive pupils feel empowered against the teacher! The teacher's the victim!" This was from a teacher who had been praised by two HMSI Inspections and Sealand LEA inspections!

After Simon Coyles left, I was at a meeting with one of the parents of one of the disruptive pupils, and she said to Pauline Steel, Head of Year, "You told the parents to complain about Mr Coyles, because the school couldn't do anything without the parents complaining. That's why all the parents complained about him. You told us to tell our friends to complain as well." I was totally shocked! I totally believed her because Pauline Steel just agreed with her. This confirmed what Simon Coyles had been saying to me. He told me, "It's the management! They allow pupils to chew chewing gum in lessons, and if I say anything, they blame me." Also, he confessed, "I was so very frightened for the safety of my wife, who is also a teacher, and for the safety of my children in schools. I was pleased my son got a job as a dentist, in Scotland, so he is safe, and far away from them."

However, this was part of a pattern, because Simon Coyles disclosed to me, "I've been threatened by Basil Wright, the headteacher, who told me that if I go to the newspapers he'd make sure I never worked again!" The pattern was: identify a problem to management, management then blamed the person because they wouldn't blame themselves!

Dawn disclosed to me, "I heard the way the senior leadership team talked to Simon Coyles. I'd been coming down the stairs one day but stepped back, at the turn in the stairs, just in time, before the senior leadership team saw me! I heard Simon Coyles being threatened by the senior leadership team and he was spoken to harshly, on the stairs. No one saw me, but I heard them."

It was a pattern of divide and conquer! It was the difference between heaven and hell! It was about capitalism, not socialism: they didn't care about the employees. Basil Wright was the headteacher who had replaced Keith Stephenson! He was in his early 50s and was tall and slim. Basil was also married, with two children. I'd taught them both and there were never any problems with them! They'd already left school. Pauline Laserton went on to bully all of our group, one by one. Simon Coyles couldn't believe he'd been so upset in a school where he'd been so happy for years and had been praised by both HMSI inspections and by Sealand LEA! The problems were power, money and ruthless ambition!

Hugh Percy left very quickly, after a Sealand LEA Inspection. While I was speaking to Jim Macey, the LEA adviser, a message came over the tannoy, "Could Mr Percy go to C24 immediately please? Mr Percy to C24 immediately."

Jim told me, "It's now 20 minutes into the lesson. I saw Hugh's name on the cover list; he didn't go to the cover lesson on time. We have discussed the management work you do in the department many times and it is always excellent! Other departments in Sealand would benefit from doing the same as you!" I had been praised as excellent in this inspection, again. Kim Macey, the LEA inspector told me, "You are excellent, as always. It is Hugh!" I had no doubt someone was trying to set me up, but the Sealand LEA Inspector had known I was not the problem. Hugh retired immediately after this inspection. Why did management look daggers at me? Had their plot backfired? Why did I feel so afraid to go to work every day, at a school I had been so successful in and had been so happy in for years? Was my name next on the list? How could I prove what I felt?

4. Why Do They Keep Leaving?

Dawn was the victim of a vitriolic attack by Pauline Laserton over the new dining hall; other staff were shocked, Dawn could see this on their faces. The pupils were in chaos; Dawn did go out to help, on her own. She made pupils line up and made it into a game. Anyone not following the rules of the game would be sent to the back of the queue. They went in like clockwork; this strategy was highly successful. Dawn was shocked to be on the receiving end of this vitriolic attack because she'd done nothing wrong. Pauline Laserton was complaining about something that she hadn't even seen for herself! Dawn just looked at her but didn't say a word. Dawn then saw Terence English, Assistant Headteacher, and told him the truth. Dawn asked him to explain what she'd been doing on duty, as Pauline Laserton wouldn't let her get a word in edgeways. Dawn heard nothing more about it after she explained, in polite terms, what she'd been doing.

Roberta Oliver and Susan Stone both arranged for Sealand LEA to do an inspection in our department. Roberta Oliver was the new head of department, after Hugh Percy left. She was small but well built. She had auburn hair and had started teaching later in life; she was married, with two children. Before he left, Martyn Smythe had told me, "I would've left anyway, if Roberta Oliver is going to be head of department. She's a ruthless bully. I've seen her make people's lives a misery, then they all left. If they're employing her, they'll know the type of person she is; this seems to be the way this school is going now. I don't want to be a part of what will be happening in this school. I've seen the changes in the attitude of management. It used to be a happy school to work in. You need to watch your back now." I still hoped for the best! Was I just being naive?

The LEA was coming in on a Thursday, which I didn't

mind. However, I knew something was very wrong when Susan Stones told me, "You are going to be observed with a year 7 class." I didn't even teach a year 7 class on Thursday, but their head of year was unsupportive and empowered the disruptive pupils in it. The problem with this year 7class was a change of management! The previous head of year had been excellent at discipline, but the new head of year, Deborah Lashley, supported the disruptive pupils! This head of year supported her group of friends, which didn't include me and my group of friends!

I suggested, "As I don't teach year 7 that day, why doesn't the LEA observe someone else in the department, who does teach year 7 that lesson?"

Roberta Oliver and Susan Stone were both furious and both told me, "It can be arranged for the LEA to see you with that class, that lesson anyway." This was extremely strange! This had never happened in this school before; I'd then been teaching in the school for about 10 years and I had a management post!

"Why don't they observe someone who does teach at that time?" and they were both furious beyond words! Roberta Oliver was spitting tacks when she answered, "I have a very difficult year 9 class then, so I obviously don't want to be observed with that class!"

The only person teaching that lesson time was Roberta Oliver, with a difficult, disruptive year 9 class, and she didn't want the LEA to observe her with that class! I felt this was an example of bullying and unwanted behaviour and that they were trying to set me up! I reported this to the headteacher, Basil Wright, who, to my face, was supportive. Basil told me, "If Roberta Oliver refuses to be observed with a class she usually teaches, you do not have to be observed with a class you don't usually teach on that day." The form of bullying, harassment and unwanted behaviour continued, but the form of it kept changing. I still kept hoping for the best. Was I still being naïve?

At Christmas, Roberta Oliver bought everyone in the department a Christmas present, except me! I'd never seen anything like it before in this school! I was shocked beyond belief and reported this to the headteacher too. I was deliberately being isolated in the department and I knew I was being bullied. Roberta Oliver was supported by Susan Stone and Pauline Laserton. I reported this to the headteacher too! The bullying continued but the form of the bullying kept changing. I still hoped for the best!

Changes: 2nd prom. It was unpleasant! What a contrast to the previous prom! Dawn and I sat down, and the rest of the department did what the head of department, Roberta Oliver, told them to do and moved away from us! Roberta Oliver was supported by Pauline Laserton, so she could do whatever she wanted! We felt hurt and shocked! We'd never seen anything like it in the school before! The other proms had been fun, full of laughter and a pleasure. Why was this one so different? Andrea Tweed had left but came back for the prom. Andrea came over to us and commented, "I saw what happened! Come and sit with me and the group of teachers who've left and have come back for the prom." Laura Harper was there, and our real friends, so we were incredibly happy there! Laura Harper had also left but had come back for the prom! Only the well- behaved pupils actually went to the prom, so the pupils weren't the problem!

The problem was the atmosphere and the feeling of uneasiness, unfriendliness and danger: this was from the staff, not the pupils. It was a total contrast to the previous prom, and I was shocked beyond belief at the change! Andrea Tweed and previous staff who came back just for the prom, saved the evening; however, the change in management was visible, open and threatening. I really appreciated the cards and presents I'd received from my tutor group. This tutor group had also received the best references from employers on their work experience in that particular academic year! Hadn't they done well? However, this head of year, Pauline Steel, was furious about that! What a contrast to the previous head of year, Ellie Grainger. Roberta Oliver was now head of department, and I had reported incidents of bullying to the headteacher, for over a year. I was not the only one! Things became worse by the day. I still hoped for the best. Was I still being naive?

Susan Stone became particularly unpleasant compared to previous years, to me and to all my group of friends! She sent Roberta Oliver a card saying: "I'll be there, right behind you, to help you with every problem!" When we went camping with the school years ago, Susan Stone had not been particularly friendly then, neither was Pauline Steel. Everyone else had been friendly! Susan Stone was unfriendly at this prom too! Also, when I went to a weekend conference, with the school, she was unfriendly to me and to others! Some staff were terribly upset with the clique in the staffroom! There had been a change in the friendliness of the school, which had once been praised by HMSI for its teamwork, strength and good relationships. Who had allowed this to happen? Why did they allow this to happen? Why didn't they keep this strength of the school?

It was now a cloak and dagger environment! The teachers knew the problem was disruptive pupils in the school and that the same pupils were creating conflict for staff. The management was not going to blame themselves, were they? The management was less friendly generally, not just to me, but to others in my friendship group! This was a group of experienced but expensive teachers, who had all been praised by two HMSI Inspections and a range of LEA inspections. What was the problem? Money? Ruthless ambition? Mary Evans had been right.

My tutor group was lovely at the prom that year! They told me, "We've waited to talk to you, away from the other teachers, because we don't want them to hear. We only came to the prom for you! We haven't come for any of them! What did any of them do for us? You looked after us, all the time: they didn't!"

Pauline Steel, the head of year, was a total contrast to the previous head of year, Ellie Grainger. The previous head of year had been a pleasure to work with and a pleasure to sit with at the prom! Pauline Steel was rude and ignored the tutors! Instead, she engineered the situation so that she became the centre of attention and made the prom about her, along with her friends Pauline Laserton and Pat Emmerson. My tutor group was disgusted! They told me, "That Mrs Laserton and Mrs Emmerson did nothing for us in five years! Mrs Emmerson wasn't even in our year group! We're shocked and disgusted at how Mrs Steel, Head of Year, has behaved at this prom! They've made it all about them and nothing about us!"

"I only came for my tutor group and the classes I taught too! I want you all to have a lovely time! This is the last time we'll all be together, so we now enjoy tonight, concentrating on our fun, dance and laughter!"

"That's a better answer, so we make the prom about us!" they replied.

"Exactly! I'll dance with you and so will our form tutors! That should make you all laugh!" My tutor group laughed and they, and other ex-pupils, kept coming up to thank me, which was lovely and greatly appreciated.

Some of the staff made it unpleasant and unfriendly, which was a total contrast to the previous prom. It was a symbol of the light being destroyed.

Dawn was often upset at work. A pupil told her, " I think Mr English's lost my music certificate for Grade V1 theory of Music, from the Associated Exam Board."

Dawn asked Terence English, "Do you have David Marrs' certificate in music? He says he gave it to you."

"No one gave it to me." Dawn knew fine well this certificate had been given to Terence English because she was present when the certificate was given to him and he'd put it in a blue folder, on his wall! Dawn also believed the pupil and knew the pupil had been awarded this highly treasured certificate. Dawn also knew this pupil was one of the most outstanding pupils in the school, at that time, and was proud of receiving this certificate, a grade V1 theory of music from ABRSM, post GCSE and a step towards A Level work, and would not just throw it away. Dawn went back to Terence English and asked, "Have you found the certificate yet?"

He was openly annoyed with Dawn but continued to repeat, "No one has given me a certificate." Eventually, Terence English "found" it, in a blue folder stapled to the wall in his room. He tried to smile and laugh about it but Dawn was just relieved the boy had his certificate in his own safe keeping.

Dawn later complained of cruelty, injustice and bullying. She told me gradually. At first, I couldn't believe what was really happening! It was a number of small things at first. Dawn told me, "Terence English keeps giving me cover, more than any other member of staff. He says it's because my name's at the top of the list, so every cover lesson I'm the first person to be given cover!"

"How strange! It doesn't happen to anyone else, does it? Your classroom is on the top floor, the third floor, of one block, but you're always given covers on the top floor of other buildings!"

"This means I have to walk down several flights of stairs, across an excessively large yard, only to go up a number of flights of stairs again! No one else is being treated like this. I did all of this, only to be reprimanded by Carole Miller for being late, in front of a large class of pupils who gave this incident their full, undivided attention! What else could anyone expect, from any member of staff?"

"Who's organising this cover?"

"Terence English."

At the time, I didn't noticed the link to how Simon Coyles had been treated with classrooms. At first, I couldn't understand why Dawn was being singled out and treated like this. Was this Terence English's revenge about the pupil's certificate he lost? Was he really going to blame himself? Was he really this ruthless? Can people be fooled by good looks, power and ambition? Dawn felt as though she needed a panic button in her classroom, which could be pressed if needed! Her unhappiness at work was characterised by blatant unfairness and mental cruelty. The perpetrators of the grossly unfair regime made working life extremely difficult. It was appearance and reality. They appeared successful by worldly values but were morally corrupt. Dawn would never treat anyone the way she'd been treated; Terence English wouldn't like to be treated like that either.

As well as teaching Music at Firlane School, Dawn organised several musical activities at lunchtimes and ran the school orchestra after school, one evening a week. Dawn also played the organ at several churches on a weekend in the surrounding area. Sometimes, Dawn's head of department, Percy Banks, sat in the congregation at one particular church, even after bullying Dawn during the week at school. Dawn left that particular church and wouldn't go back to play the organ on a weekend. One day, there was a knock at Dawn's front door and who should be there, other than the minister of that particular church? "Why have you stopped coming to my church?"

"I'll explain everything when I no longer work at Firlane School." The minister was an intelligent lady, so she had words with Percy Banks. Dawn later found out – quite by accident - that Percy no longer attended that church, so Dawn thought he'd either stopped going there or had been asked not to go. Anyway, he left that church and never went back.

Pauline Laserton was angry with Dawn, shouting, "Leave them up there!" She told Dawn to leave her posters up on the wall, but the posters didn't belong to the school. Dawn had bought them, and they belonged to Dawn. Pauline Laserton was playing mind games, to upset Dawn. She was undermining Dawn, making her afraid at work. Dawn told me, "They belong to me! She made me feel like a thief!" Pauline Laserton started moving the desks in Dawn's classroom, along with Percy Banks! Pauline Laserton had moved Pauline Lane's desks in Pauline Lane's classroom, before Pauline Lane felt she could no longer work in the school!

At the same time, Dawn told me, "Pauline Laserton is always with Carole Renwick. Carole Renwick now always makes comments to upset me." This implied line management was using our friend, Carole Renwick, to upset Dawn. Dawn knew Pauline Laserton was behind it.

"Carole's being used and doesn't realise what's going on! She's thinking she's doing what management is telling her to do."

"I can't understand why she'd do it."

"Ambition! She can see what's going on and wants to keep her job and get promotion."

"We can't even say anything to her about it, or it could make things even worse."

"They do it to one person at a time, so her turn will come, eventually."

"Unfortunately, I think that's true."

Angela Rivers had arguments with Pauline Laserton and others; they both argued with each other and with other members of staff! Angela had needed my friendship then. She was extremely glad to talk to me then! However, she tried to manipulate me into going to a deputy headteacher and telling her anything anyone had ever said about her to me! I declined the invitation and replied, "If Margaret Crow wants to do an investigation, and asks all staff about this, I will answer her questions."

Margaret Crow later came to me and told me, "I would've said the same as you; I wouldn't have gone knocking on someone's door either!" Were both Angela Rivers and Pauline Laserton ambitious, manipulative and ready to attack others?

Derek Mildew upset Dawn by making untrue comments. Dawn felt set up, as staff were not supporting her with disruptive pupils. Dawn felt it was a vicious cycle because disruptive pupils felt empowered against the teacher! The teacher was the victim! This was from a teacher who had been praised by two HMSI inspections!

Percy Banks monopolised the use of the keyboard room, and Dawn hadn't been allowed to use it with her classes. One family complained, because the class didn't have access to the keyboard room. This complaint was passed on to Pauline Laserton, who blamed Dawn; Percy Banks was there, but he didn't tell the truth! Percy Banks was Dawn's head of department and our neighbour. Over the years, he'd been friendly and supportive. He was tall, in his early 40s and married, with two daughters. This was a change in his behaviour. Why was he changing? What pressure was being put on him? Pauline Laserton did her best, along with Percy Banks, to make Dawn's life a living hell! Dawn asked, "How am I was supposed to take my classes in, when Percy Banks is in all the time?" Percy Banks was the head of department, so Dawn was powerless. This was just one, in a long line of things, where Pauline Laserton supported Percy Banks, leaving Dawn feeling upset and powerless. Dawn knew she was being bullied. Dawn defended herself saying, "I've offered classes lunchtime use of the key board room. The pupil whose family complained didn't go to the extra sessions in the key board room," so Pauline Laserton's plan had failed miserably. What more could Dawn do, if the head of department wouldn't allow her to use the key board room in lesson time and the pupil wouldn't go after lessons?

However, the bullying just continued. Percy Banks, supported by Pauline Laserton, made Dawn's life a living nightmare at work. Percy Banks and Pauline Laserton emptied Dawn's classroom of some stock, while she had classes in front of her, so she couldn't say anything about it. Although Dawn was terribly upset, she gave Pauline Laserton a broad smile. Management looked after itself, not its employees! Then, Dawn's worksheets were criticised, even though Percy Banks used the same worksheets! Management tried to drive Dawn out without any compensation, but she knew she needed some compensation, to complete the payment of her mortgage. This was a stressful, worrying and anxious time for Dawn! Percy Banks kept making many direct, upsetting comments to Dawn, such as, "When are you going to hang up your boots?" He kept repeating the phrase; he kept up the broken record treatment.

Dawn eventually replied, "I will retire on the same day you do."

Once, when Dawn told Percy she was upset, Percy Banks replied angrily, "It's about time you grew up!"

Dawn's doctor saved Dawn, "Stay with the people you trust, who make you happy; keep away from the others." Following this advice, saved Dawn and everyone else she told! He told her she was showing the classic symptoms of being bullied. He saved her from being tricked by worldly values! Dawn's doctor was delighted when she applied for redundancy and was accepted!

3rd prom: I was really pleased to go to this prom, at Langley Castle, with my husband and friends, Dawn and Richard and Gail and James. We'd put our names on a seating plan, to sit together, but when we arrived, we'd been split up! This was upsetting, unacceptable and done deliberately, to hurt us. The intention to hurt is bullying. I felt much better when my husband came too, but he'd not gone to previous proms, because in the past, we went as individual teachers, because we weren't frightened at work. Again, this was a symbol of change and an acute feeling that something was not right in the school. Unfortunately, I was placed near Susan Stone, who was supporting Roberta Oliver, and both were being supported by Pauline Laserton. Susan Stone was now unfriendly and made unpleasant comments, which were directed at me; she had never treated me like this before. However, this was how Simon Coyles had told me he'd been treated before he left!

My tutor group had received excellent references from me, because they had been a pleasure to teach over the years (I'd taught most of them over the years) and as a tutor group in year 11. This head of year, David Wilson, was also excellent and a pleasure to work with, which was a contrast to the previous head of year, Pauline Steel. David Wilson was in his early 40s, tall and well built. He was always smiling, laughing and friendly. Why did I feel the floor shaking, quivering and broken hearted beneath my feet?

At the prom, the problem was not the tutor groups, but the way we (Dawn, Gail and I), and our partners, were treated by staff, who were in management! The prom felt unfriendly, threatening and dangerous and that was just by some of the staff. Our head of year, David Wilson, was friendly, sociable and welcoming.

My new tutor group was an absolute pleasure! I took the tutor group over in year 11, but it was lovely because I'd taught them all, when they were younger, and they'd all been a pleasure to teach. I really appreciated the cards and presents I received. The head of year, David Wilson, was a pleasure to work with, and so was the assistant head of year, so they weren't the problem either. The problem was Pauline Laserton and others, in line management, who were supported by her. We later told David Wilson, the head of year, "We put our names on the seating plan to sit together, but we weren't sitting together."

"Someone must have changed it, without consulting me." This could only have been done by the senior leadership team, because it had to have been done by someone higher than him! David Wilson was a pleasure to work with, so we knew it wasn't him. Who could have done that? Pauline Laserton and Susan Stone were the only two who could have authorised that, as they were both deputy headteachers now. Why would they do this without consulting our head of year? None of us had any problems, at all, with our tutor groups.

Percy Banks was then off ill, due to a physical injury, not connected with work; he'd been involved in a road traffic accident, outside of work. Dawn told me, "It's a relief he's off; I'm much happier at work now, as a result. It had got to the point where we no longer spoke to each other at work, unless it was absolutely necessary. Unfortunately, it made coming to work, with only two full time members of staff in the department, a living nightmare!" This meant that Dawn had peace and quiet at work; this worked to Dawn's advantage.

"You look much happier and years younger overnight!"

"I feel it!"

"It shows he's been upsetting you!"

"They've now employed a retired head of department, from Sunnyton School, to do supply work; he was absolutely appalled at the behaviour of pupils in this school. Clearly, I'm not the only one who can see the school's falling standards!"

"The management won't blame themselves, will they? Is this the real problem? Are they always looking for someone to blame, because they won't blame themselves?"

"I think you're right!"

"How can we prove it? I know how I feel."

"I know how miserable I felt and I dreaded coming into work every day! Percy's off and I suddenly feel much happier!"

"You look much happier."

Fear, misery and despair lodged in my heart. I kept thinking:

fight or flight; how could I fight what I can't see? I wanted to protect my family and my wages kept them financially safe. What could I do?

"I've been supporting the supply teacher (a retired head of department) as much as I could but I refuse to be blamed by the senior leadership team for the state of Percy Banks' classroom, because I don't have a management post. I told Terence English, "I've done everything I can to support Music staff so now it's up to the school to support the teacher covering for Percy Banks as well!" I know, that legally, they can't blame me for the state of his classroom."

"It's still very stressful because look at how Terence English treated you before."

This was just another symbol of the light being destroyed. Dawn never used Percy Banks' classroom at any time for teaching purposes. This meant she was not responsible for the untidy state it was left in, every day. "They've put pressure on me to mark and assess the GCSE coursework and exams, but this is not my responsibility either, as I've never been allowed to teach the pupils in these classes. This would have meant extra work for me, on top of my full-time teaching workload, so I suggested that the management of the school bring in an external marker."

"This will mean more cost to the school. If you hadn't suggested it, they would only keep asking you to do things and wouldn't have appreciated it anyway! I can see why you want to leave."

"I can't stand the way I've been treated any more! Working in this school is now a living hell! My doctor's told me he'll give me a sick note any time I want one, because he knows I'm being bullied at work!"

Why did Dawn say exactly the same as Simon Coyles and Andrea Tweed? Simon had told me, "I'm so unhappy working in this school now that I can't stand it another day! They have me, a head of department, working in different classrooms every lesson, away from other teachers in my department! They're doing it deliberately to make my life a misery! They've made me worry in case they now get other schools to pick on my family!"

Andrea had told me, "My doctor's told to leave and find another job, because I'm so unhappy here now, since they turned me out of my classroom and gave it to Susan Stone! Heads of year never have their own classrooms, but they move around. Classroom teachers are the people who have their own classrooms, not heads of year!"

"You're right!"

"I never thought I'd ever want to leave here but every day makes me more unhappy! I'm going to take my doctor's advice and get another job. I'll have to leave and do supply because I just can't stand another day in this school now."

It felt unfriendly, dangerous and unsafe in Firlane School! I was trapped in a tunnel of fear, anxiety and misery; where was the light, so I could escape? I felt afraid to go to work, every day. How could I prove what they were doing to make me feel so afraid? Clearly, I wasn't the only teacher who felt like this! Dawn and I met in my classroom at breaks and lunchtimes and no longer went into the staffroom as often! We talked less to other people and concentrated on our jobs, to avoid conflict! What a change! How had it come to this? How had they destroyed a happy, successful and friendly staff? How could they sleep at night? Did they care? Why were they destroying the light of truth, goodness and developing all staff to their maximum potential? Why was the soul of the school being destroyed? Why was life being sucked out of older, experienced and expensive teachers?

Dawn felt that GCSE Music was dying in the school. Her GP had offered Dawn a sick note, but with Percy Banks absent, the school bullying stopped for Dawn, because they needed her, so Dawn felt she could manage until the end of term. She had already handed her notice in; she was just working until the end of term. Percy Banks was off ill and Ben Hudson, the deputy headteacher, commented on the grossly untidy state of the classroom of Percy Banks, in Percy Bank's absence. Dawn was not head of department, so she told him, "It isn't my responsibility to do everything if Percy's absent."

Ben Hudson tried to intimidate Dawn, "I'm going to check on the state of this classroom every day and I expect you to do something about it. When are you going to start marking the work for GCSE?" This deputy headteacher tried to intimidate Dawn into taking responsibility for Percy Banks' GCSE classes.

"I refuse to do this extra work because I've never taught

these classes and I'm not paid to do it. Why don't you employ someone to mark this work? I have a fulltime teaching workload and I just don't have enough hours in the day to do extra." Dawn was trembling with fear and indignation after he left! Dawn was relieved that she'd already handed in her notice and had a job as a supply teacher to go to!

Percy Banks was absent, which took pressure off Dawn, but it was only less pressure because he was absent and he wasn't in school to bully Dawn! This proved it was management, because Dawn's doctor knew about it and he told Dawn, "I know you're being bullied at work because you show all the symptoms of being bullied. You are able to stay off work, through illness."

"I only have a few weeks to work now; just this last term and then I leave."

"You must promise to come back to see me again if the conditions get worse at school." However, so long as Percy Banks was absent, they needed Dawn at school and Dawn was much happier! This proved the problem was line management, not Dawn! If Percy returned, Dawn knew she had to go back to see the doctor. Again, Dawn's doctor told her, "You're showing the classic symptoms of someone being bullied." Dawn would never treat anyone the way she'd been treated; the people involved in this would not like to be treated like this either. Dawn told me, "They can't have a conscience!"

I was continually reporting incidents of bullying to the headteacher, who did nothing about it. I felt very unhappy in the school too; I kept feeling ill on school days; I started to have pains in my stomach. This had never happened to me before! My GP told me, "There is nothing physically wrong with you; work is causing your pain and symptoms! Find another job." Firlane School was drowning and was strangling its older, experienced and expensive staff to save itself!

It had not been us, as individuals, it was the way Dawn, Andrea, Simon and I had been treated by management. They came close to making us all extremely ill. Unfairness, bullying and manipulation were deliberately cloaked in veils of respectability. How could I escape? If I left, my family wouldn't have my secure income …

Jacqui Ayre was also bullied at work, at Firlane School!

Jacqui also had a family member, a pupil, who had been bullied at school. Pauline Laserton went on to bully all of our group, one by one. Jacqui Ayre was very upset and told me, "Our Janet is often in tears over other pupils, in her school. She comes home in tears, as a group of pupils are awful to her." It was the teacher's family member, a pupil, who was being bullied. "We can't stand this anymore so we're changing schools! It's no use when the fun, happiness and laughter have gone. There's more to life." Jacqui Ayre was only bullied at work, at Firlane School, after her relative (a pupil) had been bullied at school; she hadn't been bullied at work before this! There were now three members of staff (all teachers) who had family members, pupils, being bullied at school. Jacqui was then continually reporting incidents of bullying about herself at work, as a teacher, to the headteacher, who did nothing about it. She changed school for her relative (a pupil).

Later, I asked, "You look much happier than you did; is Janet settling in at her new school?"

"She is, thank goodness! The head of year has told Janet that she knows what's happened and there won't be any bullying in that school. That made Janet feel much safer and happier." The school stopped the bullying for the pupil, but no one stopped the bullying for Jacqui, as a teacher, at Firlane School. Fortunately, Jacqui found another teaching post, but comments were continually made in the next school to upset Jacqui, so she left that school as well!

Bullying at work was the hidden enemy. It was exactly the same pattern now for three members of staff, in a short space of time. The pattern was: a relative (a pupil) was bullied at school, then the family member, who was a teacher, was bullied at school too. The management of Firlane School was not supporting its staff when it should have been! It was left to the police, the medical profession and the new schools to stop the bullying for the pupils of family members at school. The teachers could only leave Firlane School, to stop the bullying in Firlane school.

Aidan Watt also left, because he couldn't stand the lack of support by management in the school, including Pauline Laserton, Susan Stone and Krystal Welsh! Aidan Watt had been the second in the department but told me, "It's Roberta Oliver! I can't stand being undermined and unsupported by her any longer! Krystal Welsh always supports disruptive pupils and my life is unbearable here!

Every day's a living hell! The problem has been the change in the heads of year! They are a clique and they support each other with disruptive pupils, but they definitely don't support the rest of us, with disruptive pupils. I've talked it over with my wife and I'm just going to retire. I can't stand it anymore! She's a nurse and she'll keep working full time. We can manage on her wages and she's totally supportive of my decision to leave this hell hole, before they make me ill. I just can't stand coming into work any longer!"

"Why don't you do supply? Andrea did supply when she left."

"I feel so upset I can't even think about going for another job. My wife doesn't mind if I don't work at all. I just want to be happy and my wife just wants me to be happy as well!" Aidan told me. Aidan was short, well built, with dark, curly hair; he was about the same age as me.

"Your wife sounds lovely!"

It was a common pattern! Pauline Laserton went on to bully others, outside of our group, one by one. Aidan Watt added," "I still can't believe I've been so upset in a school where I've been so happy for years and have been praised by two HMSI inspections! I've tried working part-time here, but I'm still unsupported by management with disruptive pupils, so I'm going to leave, years early, because I just can't stand it any longer!"

"Your wife sounds wonderful! Hopefully, that'll be the end of the problem and you'll feel much happier. I hope everything works out for you Aidan. I'm really sorry it's come to this! It's the way we're being treated."

Sharon Humphreys left too. Sharon also felt the effects of the lack of support by management! Sharon was tall, slim and very pretty, with long, brown, straight hair. Sharon had come to Firlane School as a student teacher and was appointed to a permanent post in the school. As a manager in the department, I had observed her in lessons, when she had been a student. I knew she was an excellent teacher too! She had been friendly with Roberta Oliver but had been dropped by her! Sharon also left, upset by Roberta Oliver and the lack of support with disruptive pupils. Sharon told me, "I'm just glad to leave now! I've been lucky enough to get another job. They told me at the interview, " Firlane School is behind you now and we've made up our own minds about you." They want me in their school and they aren't bothered about anything this school says about me at all!"

"That's fantastic Sharon! I hope everything goes well in the new school. They seem lovely!"

What a lucky escape Sharon had! Pauline Laserton went on to bully all of our group, one by one. Sharon couldn't believe she'd been so upset in a school where she'd been so happy for years and had been praised by HMSI!

It was about appearance and reality, because Pauline Laserton didn't care about anybody in our group. What a sad reality! To reinforce the message of no longer being on the team and being forced out, Dawn found the new headteacher (the third headteacher), Derrick Tusk rude, disrespectful and intimidating. He was short, stocky and very well built! He looked angry and had a massive chip on his shoulder! Her crime? "I introduced myself to Derrick Tusk, as he was near the door to the headteacher's office, as it was the last day of the summer term, before the school holidays. It was also my very last day in the building, but he didn't know that! I could've been anyone on the staff. As I approached him, with my hand out to shake his hand, I commented, "You must be the new headmaster. I'm Dawn, Music Department." He totally ignored me and, deliberately, refused to shake my hand. He looked down at his feet and breathed menacingly, with intense, intimidating and alienating body language, which was all done in total silence. After a few uncomfortable moments, I withdrew my hand, and walked away, extremely glad I was leaving that day!" This was another nail in the coffin of Firlane School; many staff were dying with the school!

"He didn't look very friendly at all, when I saw him on the corridor. He was with Pauline Laserton and both were trying to stop staff from walking along the corridor."

"How rude! That's the corridor to the staffroom as well!"

"What a contrast to the first day I came here, when it was a friendly school."

"We all used to enjoy Opportunity Week, the last week of term."

"We all went out on day trips, nearly every day."

"Everyone enjoyed the last week of term, every year."

"I bet you're glad you're leaving."

"I wish you were leaving with me. I'm worried about leaving you in this hell hole now"

"I just hope it'll get better."

"If it doesn't, you must leave and do supply, if you can't stand it anymore."

"That's why so many experienced teachers are leaving."

"Why are they treating experienced teachers like this?"

"We've all been very successful as well."

"I'm only staying until the end of term because Percy Banks is absent, and Richard persuaded me to keep going, to obtain a good reference for any future supply teaching work. I didn't want to attend the end of term leaving event, but was persuaded by Richard to go."

"Just as well Percy's off, so you can manage to work until the end of term."

"I comfort myself by playing "The Great Escape" theme tune, over and over on the record player."

At the leaving event, Pauline Laserton pretended to be pleasant to Dawn, as she shook her hand in front of the whole staff; Dawn smiled and told Pauline Laserton, "I hope you get what you truly deserve in life." Pauline Laserton was furious, but then she pretended not to be able to hear Dawn. Why would she pretend not to hear? Dawn had hoped Pauline Laserton would get what she truly deserved in life. Pauline Laserton had bullied all of our group over the years. It was really about power, appearance and reality.

At the end of term charade, where the management pretended to value the staff they had intimidated into leaving, Dawn even thanked the retiring headteacher, "Thank you very much for getting me out of this hell hole." She already had another post to go to, so her references had already been written. Unexpected situation irony! However, this headteacher's eyes glistened with rage; the outgoing headteacher, Basil Wright, was incandescent with anger!.

It was all about truth and lies; they were never going to admit what they'd done. The pattern was: identify a problem to management, management then blamed the person concerned because they wouldn't blame themselves! Pauline Laserton went on to bully all of our group, one by one. Dawn couldn't believe she'd been so upset in a school where she'd been so happy for years and where she'd been praised by HMSI! How would Pauline Laserton and Basil Wright take their revenge? They were beyond furious! Who was left behind?

On that same last day of the school year, the day Dawn retired, Carole Miller asked Dawn questions about Jane, so she could gossip about something Dawn was upset about! Carole Miller was also a teacher who had worked in the school for years! Why did she choose the day Dawn was leaving to say something to upset Dawn? She hadn't done it before! What had been said about Dawn, behind her back? This was the pattern of the bullying, finding an area the victim was upset about! Dawn was annoyed and asked her, in very strong terms, "Have you got nothing better to do than dredge up past events on the day I'm escaping from this valley of death?" Carole was flawed by Dawn's response and didn't expect this.

Dawn felt they had seriously underestimated her strength and resolve; she felt she had left at a time of her own choosing. Dawn removed the weeds from her backyard; Dawn removed the nettles from her life; Dawn removed the rubbish that had been destroying her life.

After she'd left Firlane School, Pauline Lane was seriously ill. She'd left frightened, distressed and broken hearted, like others. Before she died, she told Dawn, "I don't want Pauline Laserton to go to my funeral." Pauline died quickly, days later.

"Once she had died, she had no power to stop Pauline Laserton from going to her funeral!" Dawn told me.

"How sad!"

"Pauline Lane couldn't believe she'd been so upset in a school where she'd been so happy for years!"

"I don't know how Pauline Laserton had the audacity to go to Pauline's funeral! Pauline Laserton only went to the funeral for the sake of outward appearances; she ignored us all at work and was very uncaring and unsupportive to all of our group."

"Outside of work, none of our group wanted any contact with Pauline Laserton, not even the dead! Even those who'd died didn't want contact with her ever again. Pauline Lane's sisters knew Pauline hadn't wanted Pauline Laserton at her funeral, but the funeral was in a church, so they felt powerless to stop her from going to the funeral."

"Why was Pauline Laserton allowed time off work to got to Pauline Lane's funeral, when I was her friend?"

"Because she's in a position of power!"

"Of course! It was a terrible thing for them all to allow that, after what happened."

"Pauline asked me, on the last day of term, to help her to take her things home! Pauline Laserton was so awful that Pauline Lane simply resigned on the spot! She told them she wouldn't be going back! She told me she would just stay on the sick, because she couldn't work in the school for a moment longer, without being seriously ill."

"This is terrible! We'd all been very happy and highly successful! They haven't valued their staff!"

"They certainly haven't!"

I wasn't the only one to feel trapped in a deep, dark tunnel of never ending fear and misery.

Andrea and Dawn both felt upset to see Pauline Laserton at Pauline Lane's funeral and wondered how she could possibly have attended this funeral as well as Janette Chapman's funeral. Pauline Laserton had bullied them all at school, ignored them all them all at school and had created fear and misery for them all at school! Colin said he wouldn't go to Pauline Laserton's funeral! Andrea and Dawn both agreed with him. Pauline Lane's family knew Pauline didn't want Pauline Laserton to go to her funeral but felt unable to stop her. Pauline Laserton was still able to upset these people, even outside of work.

At Pauline Lane's funeral, Dawn was there, along with Andrea Tweed and Colin Glass. They were working at other schools and were all much happier.

Martin Smythe left, Janette Chapman left, Pauline Lane left, Ellie Grainger left, Andrea Tweed left, Simon Coyles left, Dawn Simpson left, Jacqui Ayre left, Aidan Watt left … and many others left! It was a pattern of divide and conquer! It was the difference between heaven and hell! They all felt very frightened, afraid and full of fear and misery, in this hostile environment. Management had created an environment of fear and misery. They hurt the staff, one by one, so staff felt it was in their best interests to leave. What are fear and misery the symptoms of? What possessed them to ruin a good school, which had been praised as "Good" by HMSI and the LEA, and which provided pupils with good examination results, based on their point of entry to the school? No wonder Firlane

School was dying!

"After I'd left, I was told by various members of staff that they were afraid of the new headteacher, because he was a bully. That was what I saw when I met him in the corridor. I went over to welcome him, to shake his hand and to congratulate him on his new job and he gave me a withering look and refused to shake my hand. What a pity there were no witnesses, but the whole thing was done so it was difficult to prove," Dawn told me.

"Individual staff were undermined, then felt ill, so they could no longer work in that environment, so they were forced to leave. The pattern was: identify a problem to management; management then blamed the person, because they wouldn't blame themselves! It was a pattern of divide and conquer! It was the difference between heaven and hell! It was about capitalism, not socialism; they didn't care about the employees. It was appearance and reality. They appeared successful by worldly values but they were morally corrupt."

"I couldn't have put it better myself. I feel really worried for you, going to work in that environment! I won't feel happy until I know you're safe and happy at work; it might mean you need to find another job."

"I shouldn't be forced to leave a job I've been happy in for years."

"No, you shouldn't but it will be very difficult to prove what they're really doing."

"That's the problem."

5. Who Would Believe It?

Who would believe it?

I was continually reporting incidents of bullying to the headteacher, who did nothing about it. Management waited … management waited … and management waited … It was appearance and reality. They appeared successful by worldly values but were morally corrupt. I didn't want further promotion, for family reasons, but I even applied and went to interviews for subjects I wasn't a specialist in! One headteacher told me, "Your problem is your own school, and how they've treated you!" He was certainly correct, wasn't he?

My new year 7 tutor group was excellent and a pleasure to teach, because I had known their brothers, sisters and older relatives for years. The new head of year was lovely but what a surprise! She was only there for a short time, then she went off on the sick, and left within weeks! I wonder why?

There was now a clear pattern of management: they tried to blame each individual and defend themselves! They caused conflict and distress and destroyed a team which had been praised by HMSI for working together! There was a clear pattern of Pauline Laserton supporting line management against each individual; it was all cloak and dagger! Clearly, the light was being destroyed in the school! Everything that HMSI had praised in the school was being destroyed! All management was doing was blaming each individual; Macbeth had nothing to learn in this school, neither did Machiavelli!

Pauline Laserton had been supporting Percy Banks, then Hugh Percy, then Roberta Oliver. Susan Stone was also working with Pauline Laserton, supporting line management against each individual teacher! Each individual teacher was picked off, one by one! It was all done by manipulation, power and deceit, so they thought they could get away with it! In reality, they were defending themselves and their own reputations; any individual would have found it incredibly stressful, because they wanted to go to work to earn a living and to make a positive contribution! No one wanted such conflict! All management was doing was destroying others and defending their own reputation. It was appearance and reality. They appeared successful by worldly values but they were morally corrupt. Why was it older, experienced and expensive teachers who were forced to leave, as they could no longer stand working in a cut throat environment?

Everyone had been highly motivated and had continued to strive to be excellent teachers! As the staff was happy and highly motivated, everyone was happy to work above and beyond the call of duty, for pleasure. What had happened to this staff? How had their light been destroyed? Who would want to do this? This staff had achieved a "Good School" award from HMSI; this staff had achieved good GCSE exam grades and had a happy, healthy staff.

The common problem was that each person was not treated the way other people would like to be treated themselves. Each person should have been treated as a professional and treated with respect and valued, with effective Continued Professional Development; each person should have had an environment where each person could reach their maximum potential. Instead, an environment of fear and misery was created; an environment of not being valued was created; fear and misery are the symptoms of bullying. There was not a feeling of teamwork; there was not a feeling of effective Continued Professional Development for all; there was not a feeling of us against HMSI! That was their mistake! HMSI had appreciated that it had been the whole school, united, as a team, against them! Why did they ignore the praise by HMSI? Why did they lose the plot?

Why hadn't management listened to HMSI? Why hadn't management learned from HMSI? Why didn't the management in the school keep doing the things they'd been praised for, by HMSI? Was all of this because of a change of management? How could we find the strength to survive this bitter conflict and bullying? Didn't they know there would be an eventual day of reckoning? Why were they too blinkered to realise the eventual outcome of their malignant scheme? How many teachers' lives did they destroy? How many pupils' lives did they destroy? How did they affect the community?

It was the wearing down of staff's mental health; it was the distribution of wealth; it was feeling powerless, worthless and unvalued. Was there a financial crash coming?

Bullying is the intention to hurt and management did it deliberately, with force. They were unsupportive and against us, one at a time, so it was planned. Thank goodness our doctors saved us, and so did the Occupational Health! The symptoms were fear and misery; what are they the symptoms of?

This form of management, I and others found, was not merely confined to schools. I, and others, could see sights now that we'd never seen before; unfortunately, it was now regarded as normal for people to be homeless! The reports showed that 1 in every 200 people in England were now homeless. There were many homeless people in the world. Do they know many people really are driven to suicide because of the way they'd been treated by others?

Jim Macey, a Sealand LEA adviser, who had also always told me I was excellent in every inspection, told me to leave, as did my GP. Jim told me, "All you can do is to leave! I will act as a referee for you."

"I feel bullied and afraid to come to work every day. The doctor has told me to find another job."

"It's not you. All you can do is to leave." Jim was slightly older than me, of average height and was truthful and honest! Was a cause austerity: getting rid of expensive teachers, to save money? There was clearly a problem: lack of support by management. I was afraid to go to school but felt unable to prove why. If I had told anyone else, who would believe it?

Opposing Worlds. A new world descended: there was now a change of management, causing destruction, devastation and manipulation. This destruction of a happy, efficient and effective team of teachers was caused by a change in the people in power, with a lack of support with disruptive pupils. I knew something was very wrong in the school when Krystal Welsh kept far away from me and was no longer friendly, at all. I hadn't done or said anything at all to Krystal to cause this change, but I felt something was wrong, something was terribly wrong and I felt I was in danger. Both Krystal Welsh and Sharon Stone kept way from me on duty; years ago we had smiled while on duty! I saw their faces and I now felt afraid!

Unfortunately, many lives (not just the lives of teachers) have been destroyed as many people felt vulnerable; the systems in place failed to support many, even though England had a welfare state, and many were left homeless and destitute. Where could these people go? Who could they turn to? If the problem was drug addiction, how could they access support? Why did I keep thinking and caring about others, who were even worse off than me? I knew many people were now less well off than years ago.
Why was it happening to so many people?

6. <u>Who Was Next on the List?</u>

The change of management led to the destruction of the health of individual teachers; psychological bullying had been the result of power and a looming financial crash! The mental cruelty and torture were characterised by a lack of support with disruptive pupils, which created a climate of fear and misery. This caused stress and a souring of the atmosphere in the staffroom and around the school. People began to be afraid to go to work. I met Fear and Misery in the staffroom. Staff were left feeling undervalued and worthless; they would have been ill if they'd stayed. It was clear people felt on the edge of a possible nervous breakdown, which could have led to suicide. People left to concentrate on being happy and healthy and to get another job! My doctor's advice was, "Get another job!" It was clear it was my turn now!

Comments were continually being made, which were obviously directed at me, by people who didn't really speak to me and weren't part of my friendship group. Many comments were made directed to me about my family, by people who didn't even know them. This became part of a pattern of bullying, both in school and outside of school. This was done deliberately to upset me, so that I would be distressed and would no longer be happy at work, so that I couldn't do my best at work. I now knew how Simon Coyles had felt! I now felt exactly the same as he'd felt before he left Firlane School! He too had felt afraid in school and afraid in case they bullied his family too! If it had happened to both of us, it was a pattern of bullying, harassment and unwanted behaviour! It didn't just happen to me!

I felt bullied, harassed and the victim of unwanted behaviour. It all started in Firlane School but continued afterwards outside of school! This form of bullying, harassment and unwanted behaviour is exceedingly difficult to prove, but I hadn't met it in this school before!

Even pupils were being bullied in school, then blamed for being bullied. This hadn't happened before either! I had taught two sisters, separately, in different classes, and both were happy and popular. However, one of these non-identical twins fell out with a group of pupils; she and a friend tried to keep out of the way of the group, to keep themselves out of trouble. Unfortunately, her mother told me, "Charlotte was blamed for isolating herself from others! Her sister, Jane, was distraught, but had her own set of friends, and was not in the same classes. Charlotte changed schools and was much happier." Their mother, Mrs Foster, continued, "The bullies still didn't leave Charlotte alone. They were always sitting on our garden wall, but I didn't report them to the police, because my other daughter still had to go to school with them." This bullying had happened to another teacher's daughter; this had now happened to four families, where one parent was a teacher. I found this to be part of a pattern too!

Who was next on the list? Who was Dawn's friend? Who had Dawn angered before she left Firlane School?

Others had left upset before me, so it was a pattern of management: Martin Smythe, Andrea Tweed, Simon Coyles, Jacqui Ayre, Dawn Simpson, Aidan Watt and Sharon Humphreys. The pattern was: identify a problem to management, management then blamed the person because they wouldn't blame themselves! It was a pattern of divide and conquer! It was the difference between heaven and hell! Situation irony! Dawn had told me, "They should pull the other one, it has bells on!" Wasn't she right?

It was about capitalism, not socialism: they didn't care about the employees. It was about capitalism: more profit, less costs, so people were too afraid to lose their jobs, so they didn't dare go on strike! Before she'd left Andrea Tweed told me, "I've just been to see Basil Wright and told him I was now very unhappy in this school and was considering even being a singer on a cruise ship! He told me and to leave, if that was what I wanted! I just wanted to cry when he said that! I've never been treated like this before!"

Before, we'd been valued; now, we were no longer valued, and it was a pattern of management! How convenient to force experienced and expensive staff to leave by creating an environment they couldn't work in, and then save large amounts of money by getting rid them! They knew what they were doing; it was a pattern of management! They made Ruthlessness look like a saint! It was a pattern of deceit, manipulation, fear and misery, the symptoms of bullying. How could they live with themselves, after causing so much grief and havoc? Pauline Laserton went on to bully all of our group, one by one.

Who was Dawn's friend? Who was next on the list?

I had a Commendation on my Teaching Practice and I had been President of the Students' Union when I was a student and I was also on the Disputes Committee as a student. I was one of the most able on my degree course. As a student, I had considered being a politician but loved being a teacher too. I was "best practice" by HMSI and I was identified as "... the type of teacher the government wanted to value" by HMSI too. I was also "excellent" in Sealand LEA inspections! My ability and qualifications were without question (an Honours Degree); the problem was that I had reported bullying to the new headteacher (change of headteacher) and I was then bullied out of my post. The third headteacher, Donald Tusk, made comments such as, "Your problem is that you've done so well before." This was made as he walked near me, not in a conversation. Others joined in, bullying me by making subtle, sly comments about me and my family! They were made by people who hadn't met my family and I hadn't confided in them! The same had happened to Simon Coyles, who had also felt distressed, unhappy and miserable at work! It was a pattern of bullying! The same thing had happened to Dawn!

I had reported incidents of the bullying of a family member to the relevant school, then, I was bullied at work. Victim Support and the police supported my family, but the management of this school didn't care. Wasn't that unprofessional of them, considering the police issued police cautions against the perpetrators? In contrast, the police told the victim of bullying, who was a pupil at another school and a family member, to ring them at any time, if they, the victim, ever felt frightened, the police would meet the victim wherever the victim was. If the victim was out and saw anyone, and felt afraid, the victim was told to go into a shop and to ring the police, and they would meet the victim at any time and any place and take the victim home. A change of school, a change of head of year and a change of headteacher stopped this bullying for the family member who was a pupil. This was the same pattern for a few children of teachers, who were bullied at school! Changing schools for the children of teachers, who were pupils at school, stopped the bullying, but no one stopped my bullying at school/work. It just got worse!

They changed my management role in the department, after I had been praised so much by HMSI and the LEA, without giving me Continued Professional Development for this change of role! Then, they organised for the new Literacy Inspector for Sealand to come into the school; they obviously did not ask the LEA Advisor who found me "excellent" at everything. The Literacy Inspector spoke to me and told me, "You're doing everything you should be, and you're doing everything I would do. They asked me to come in to check, so I will tell them you're doing everything you should be, and you're doing everything I would do too." I felt they'd tried to set me up. Again, there was no praise from anyone in the school; a feeling of their anger continued to overwhelm me; I had feelings of fear, misery and dread. I felt in danger but found it difficult to prove what they were doing. I would never treat anyone the way I had been treated; the people involved in this would not like to be treated like this either.

Pauline Laserton was playing mind games, to upset me. She was undermining me and made me feel afraid at work. Dawn told me, "Ignore it all and smile!" I had bought many things and had taken them into work, but they belonged to me (Dawn had done the same and the things she had bought had belonged to her). Staff kept coming into my classroom, looking at my things and kept making comments about them! This hadn't been happening over the years, but it had been done to Dawn! The implication was that the things belonged to the school, but they didn't! The comments were not made in a conversation, but the comments were upsetting and intimidating! This intrusion and invasion into a senior teacher's classroom had never happened to me before, but they had done something similar to Dawn and to Pauline Lane! It was a pattern of intimidation! It was appearance and reality. They appeared successful by worldly values but they were morally corrupt. I would never treat anyone the way I had been treated; the people involved in this would not like to be treated like this either.

I was terrified to go to work. I rang Dawn, but she wasn't in.

Richard told Dawn to contact me immediately, when she came in, because he knew how frightened I was! Dawn told me, "You must see your doctor and tell him what you've told me, as soon as possible. You should've confided in me earlier."

"I was just so very frightened of them, but I did tell my doctor."

"I was on the same path as you, but a long way behind where you are now. I can't abide injustice of any kind. There are obviously instances when your suffering was unknown to me. How you haven't had a nervous breakdown, I'll never know. I think they've done this to us all deliberately and have spread it well out, to minimise attracting attention to themselves. They had to keep up the pretence of normality."

"That's what they've done."

I had already told my doctor about how frightened I was, just to go to work. I went again and told him, "I have an environment I can't work in."

He replied," You do not have to go back. I will write out your sick note for you now."

I resigned immediately, citing my reason as their critical and unsupportive management. They didn't want to accept that the reason for my resignation was the emergence of the fear and misery they'd created. The management of Firlane School really had created fear and misery, where I felt too frightened to even go to work! It was the destruction of the team and teamwork! It was the lack of moral support, which caused stress that I had never felt there before a change of management.

I felt it was a set-up, as staff were not supporting me with disruptive pupils. I felt it was a vicious cycle because disruptive pupils felt empowered against the teacher! The teacher was the victim! This was happening to a teacher who had been praised by two HMIS inspections and Sealand LEA inspections! This is what had happened to Andrea Tweed, to Simon Coyles, to Jacqui Ayre, to Aidan Watt, to Sharon Humphreys and to Dawn Simpson!

Many others left upset after me! How strange! Many others had left upset before me too! Would this continue to happen to others?

All I found was that Martin Smythe was right. He'd told me he was leaving because there was a change in attitude by management. Wasn't he right? He told me that we would all see it.

The difference was in the lack of support from management, so we couldn't do our jobs! It was a pattern of behaviour, because they picked us off one at a time! The pattern was the same: feeling upset/ ill at the thought of going to work; going to see your GP; being told to leave and find another job, and to look after your reference! This was how the GPs saved our mental health! The difference was the lack of support by management. It changed from being happy and healthy at Firlane School, to a culture of fear and misery! Lilly Pegg left, Ellie Grainger left and other key staff in line management left; the line management who cared about the school, the staff and the pupils left! The caring headteacher left due to age, the head of department left and the head of year left! They all left! That was how we were later bullied out of our teaching posts.

Effective Continued Professional Development was only given to the favoured few, whereas previously, it had been given to everyone. They tried to blame each individual, but it was a pattern of the behaviour of their management! We were all supposed to be on the same team, but management destroyed the very thing that HMIS had praised Firlane School for! It was the change of management that was to blame for the demise of the school; they weren't going to blame themselves, were they? We'd all been valued members of a team, but that was all destroyed! We'd all been on the same side, but that was all destroyed. We'd all been happy and healthy at work, but that was all destroyed. That was how I knew it was all about power, status and money. They were totally ruthless! They didn't care about us! They didn't care about our families!

Strange how Roberta Oliver took textbooks out of my classroom, without even telling me. This was the same pattern! Percy Banks did the same thing to Dawn Simpson! Roberta Oliver was causing chaos but was supported by Pauline Laserton and Susan Stone. It wasn't just to me either! I wasn't the only teacher who reported bullying by the head of department! Disruptive pupils told me, " You think we're in trouble when you were send us to Mrs Laserton, but we' re not in any trouble at all!" This happened in class after class after class. I had seen Pauline Laserton do this to Simon Coyles! He had been totally undermined in front of disruptive pupils.

After the change of management, I reported many incidents

of bullying at work! I wasn't the only one! It didn't stop the bullying. They didn't support staff with disruptive pupils, yet for years, I had been valued and praised for my work with disruptive pupils! They then supported disruptive pupils against staff and manipulated the situation to defend themselves and blamed the individual. Everyone could feel the fear and misery, which are the symptoms of bullying. Bullies are just sad, weak people, who try to make themselves feel strong by hurting others. This was the immoral theft of jobs! They were telling lies! It was lying, deceitful and manipulative management; it was an invisible enemy. Our priorities changed, according to our circumstances! We are all affected by our life experiences. I'd been born to be happy and loved but had been upset by circumstances!

After I'd left, Molly Newsome, a friend, returned everything I had that belonged to the school. When I asked Molly to ask them to return my things to me, via her, they refused. Roberta Oliver told her, "I'm not doing that! No one in our department is either!" I regarded this as a form of theft! I had no doubt they would deny this, but I know the truth, and so do they!

7. Believed!

I felt that if I hadn't left Firlane School, I would have been driven to a nervous breakdown, at the very least; the general advice of fight or flight saved me and my mental health. Would they have cared? I left and saved myself! Simon, Andrea, Dawn, Pauline and Sharon had all felt exactly the same way!

Where was the happiness? Where was the effective Continued Professional Development? Where was the light? Where was the truth?

I was supported by Sealand Occupational Health, however, I did not act against Firlane School, for family reasons. Sealand Occupational Health told me, "The issues are your loss of wages and loss of pension. We'll support you against Firlane School because you've always done so well in the school and all through your career as a teacher."

"I just want to protect my family, so I don't think it's in their best interests for me to take them to court. I just want to protect my family from further distress. I'll just follow my GP's advice, of getting another job, as it's a quicker and easier solution."

Sealand Occupational Health informed me, "The issues are your loss of wages and loss of pension! We'll support you because you have been praised as "best practice" by HMSI and told by HMSI, "Part of our remit is to tell teachers like you that you are the type of teacher the government wants to know is valued by the government. Also, you have been "excellent" in all LEA inspections!"

This helped me to cope! The problem had been a change of management. Sealand Occupational Health understood why I was upset and why I'd left! It was the realisation of what the management of Firlane School had done, as witnessed by them, that saved my mental health! I knew why I'd been upset and why I'd left;

so did Sealand Occupational Health! Sealand Occupational Health had believed me! I told them I was just going to leave, to do supply, because it was a quick and easy solution, but I had no idea what would follow! Sealand Occupational Health rang me several times, after I'd left Firlane School, saying, "We know what they've done to you. We'll support you against Firlane School." Weren't they excellent?

"I'm much happier doing supply teaching and I want to protect my family from further stress. As I have children, who are all in education, my priority is protecting them." Would this solve the problem or would I live to regret this decision?

I simply followed my GP's advice, and accepted another post, and became a supply teacher. I couldn't work any longer in the bullying environment. I'd even applied for promotion which I didn't even want, just to get out! The problem was the lack of support by management with disruptive pupils! They were furious that I'd left for another post; in my resignation I told the headteacher I'd left because of their critical and unsupportive management. They were furious! I hadn't needed them for references, because I had written lesson observations, from the school and the LEA, which were all excellent. I also used letters of praise from line management and comments from HMSI, in their written reports, which were available for everyone to read. I had outmanoeuvred them, and they were livid. I left because I could no longer stand the way I was being treated. I had outsmarted them! Was that why they were so furious?

They'd been playing a blame game; they blamed everyone else, not themselves; they were trying to upset me, and then blame me for being upset! This was totally sadistic! I hadn't been making comments to upset them, so they couldn't do their jobs. They were upsetting me, and picked off a group of friends, one by one. We hadn't been picking on them; they were picking on us. We didn't make indirect comments about their families.

What possessed them to ruin a good school? What possessed them to ruin a good staff? What possessed them to ruin individuals? Bullies are usually sad people who try to eradicate themselves from their sadness by upsetting others!

I never made comments about Roberta Oliver's son being beaten by her husband for taking drugs. I never made comments about Roberta Oliver's son being nearly permanently excluded from school for his disgraceful behaviour, through taking drugs. I never made comments about the deputy headteacher of Firlane School being absent for a year, over the death of his son, because of drug abuse.

When I later reported more bullying to my teaching union, my teaching union told me, "If we'd known what Sealand Occupational Health had said, we would have supported you, with them."

"I just wanted to protect my family, as we'd already had the stress of a court case and we'd won. We didn't need any more stress! In the previous court case, the insurance company had employed private detectives to follow us. When they had to reveal their evidence to the courts, all they could say about me was, "It's fruitless following Mrs Lowry. All she does is to go to work and then she stays in every night. She never leaves the house after 9pm. Sitting in a car, every night, watching her and the house, is fruitless because she always stays in the house, after 9pm, every night." We had felt followed but hadn't been able to prove it. I believed it would have been an incredibly stressful court case with Firlane School; I didn't have any trust in their management at all!

It was a pattern of behaviour; even the office staff left! The underlying message seemed to be austerity: get rid of expensive, professionally qualified and experienced staff and save money! No wonder it was later reported in newspapers there would be a 50,000 shortage of teachers in five years' time. It was really about capitalism. It was about power, money and the distribution of wealth; the growing inequality was getting worse! It was about capitalism: making money for businesses, without distributing money fairly in society. Clearly, for the people at the bottom of society, there was something very wrong when their stress levels increased, due to the management of people in power! The people on the receiving end of this treatment were very upset when they worried about things they'd never worried about before, such as having a roof over their heads, food on the table for their families and money to pay bills. What a terrible change for people on the receiving end of this treatment, in one of the richest countries in the world!

Who would believe it?

Everyone had been highly motivated and had wanted to be

excellent teachers! As the staff was happy and highly motivated, everyone was happy to work above and beyond the call of duty, for pleasure. What had happened to this staff? How had their light been destroyed? Who would want to do this? They had destroyed a group of friends, colleagues and team members who had been praised by two HMSI reports and numerous Sealand LEA inspections. This was how they destroyed us; they destroyed our support group; they destroyed our light! How many years would it take us to recover from the stress, fear and misery they'd caused us and to work out what they'd done, how they'd done it and to believe they really had actually done it?

Clearly, this once happy staff had become miserable, afraid and terrified! Clearly, this unhappy staff could not work in this hostile, unfair and cruel environment. Clearly, this once happy staff was in danger of becoming ill! We were forced to leave, one by one. The problem was how upset we were; the problem was the unnecessary heartbreak; the problem was our shattered hopes, dreams and expectations.

Once I had identified the pattern of behaviour, it saved my mental health! It kept my marbles, which was the main thing! The problem with protecting your mental health is that the people who have upset you and others don't want to admit it; this has caused many court cases for many people, including world famous celebrities, throughout the years! Dawn and I supported each other over the years, which was how we coped, without being made ill! Who else would have believed it?

It was a pattern of behaviour everywhere! It wasn't just with teachers, it was with doctors, nurses, civil servants, supermarkets and even Amiable (an internet company)! Many people left work terribly upset at the way they'd been treated, even young university graduates in other occupations across the country.

I did what my doctor told me to do and found another job! All of that distress and upset over a job! I thought doing supply would be much less stressful, for my family. Trust your instincts and stay safe! Don't be fooled by others! The people who you are afraid of betray your trust and confidence and blame you! If in doubt, stay safe! Live to fight another day, or just live for another day! Win the war, if you can't win the individual battle. Staying alive and healthy is much better than living in fear and misery and being ill! Good management is about getting the best out of your staff, not the worst!

Sarah Hunt, an educational psychologist for Sealand Educational Department, and a neighbour, told me, "Derrick Tusk had been sent there to get rid of staff and your name was at the top of the list, because you've supported a family member, a pupil, at another school, and you've reported incidents to the police." Susan Stone also made many comments to the same effect. Roseanne Dunn also made a comment about my husband, who she had never met, "They're looking into him as well." I was very upset! Roseanne Dunn wasn't a friend of mine and didn't know anything at all about my husband. Why would she say something like this? What had been said to her, for her to say this? I didn't feel safe; I felt I was being bullied, behind the scenes! However, the headteacher, Mr O'Neary, of the school I had reported incidents to the police to was obviously who they were going to for information about us, as he made a comment of, "There isn't anything; I'll tell them." He was an older headteacher, short and very thin, with glasses.

I felt as though the headteachers were protecting themselves, but couldn't find problems between us, because my husband and I were united in protecting our family. Susan Stone also made similar comments, "Your children are in a good school," implying the problem was us! However, the police and the Crown Prosecution Service issued police cautions to protect our family over the bullying of our family member, a pupil, so we had been right to report incidents to the police! The headteacher, Mr Wright, and the head of year, Mrs Grace, of the new school had advised me to go to the police, so I did. In these circumstances, my employers should have supported me at work! Solicitors had protected our family over a road traffic accident previously, where we were the victims. I had no team of solicitors to protect me, daily, at work now!

My life changed for the better when we changed schools for the bullied family member, a pupil: the new head of year, Mrs Grace, and the new headteacher, Mr Wright, of the new school, advised me, " Go to the police about this bullying, because we have evidence of the bullying, by pupils from the previous school." The difference between the two schools was the difference in management of the schools: the second headteacher and head of year believed us and had proof that our family had been telling the truth. The issue had been about truth and lies. The second school told me to do this on two separate occasions. Police cautions were given, and the police were fully prepared to take the case to court, to protect the victim and our family. I gave all of the information, as requested, to the first school, who said they would support the police. Susan Stone didn't know this; she didn't know what she was talking about! She should have been supportive but chose to bully me instead! The problem of a pupil being bullied by other pupils was solved by the management of the second school; they were well organised and kept themselves in the light!

Why was Susan Stone involved at all? Was she a spy for others? It had nothing to do with her. She didn't even know what had happened. Individually, the many comments made in school seemed strange, but put together there was an unnecessary pattern of bullying. Bullying in schools affects families, so the police were involved to protect my family member; police cautions were given to the pupils from the school we had removed our family member from. The police told the pupils and their parents, "The Crown Prosecution Service will take this case to court if it continues."

The police told my family member, "No matter where you are, ring us if you ever feel frightened and the police will come immediately. If you feel afraid, go into a shop, so you are safe and then ring us. We will come and pick you up, wherever you are, and take you home, safely." The problem wasn't the police; the problem wasn't the second school; the problem was now the management of the school I worked in. Sealand Hospital told me, "It is your profession that is doing this to you."

I was always happy when I was younger, so someone or something had caused my distress now! Andrea, Simon and Dawn had all found exactly the same! We all felt that we'd been born to be happy and loved, so circumstances were causing our acute distress. I knew that they knew what they'd done to upset us all but would never admit anything at all! It was now clear that the problem was also proving what they'd done in court; they had known that and had known that most people don't go to work for such conflict! I know I didn't want the stress of taking employers to court, simply because I wanted to protect my family from more distress. With children in full time education, with crucial examinations in front of them, we didn't need the distress, distraction or anxiety.

Also, we'd been the innocent victims of a series of road traffic accidents, which was why our family had been protected and supported by solicitors. If I could take Firlane School to court now, I would, as my family are all older now! However, I have no doubt they were trying to find evidence against me and my family, to attack us, to defend themselves! It was really about appearance and reality! They could tell as many lies as they wished; they could manipulate the truth as much as they wished; they could lie to the courts, if they wished! They couldn't lie to God! They couldn't fool God! They couldn't trick my conscience!

The issues of my loss of wages and my loss of pension had already been identified by Sealand Occupational Health. It was really about truth and lies and appearance and reality; the truth had been that they wanted to employ newly qualified teachers, to save money! Would they ever admit that? They didn't want to pay high wages to successful, expensive and experienced teachers! How could they ignore the excellent exam results which I had achieved with my classes? For years, they were higher than the results for the same pupils in other subjects, including senior teachers in the school! Was that why they were upset when I saw the whole school's GCSE results?

I had contributed significantly to the exam results which boosted the good reputation of the school. Walking away from bullying was much better than being bullied! Concentrating on being happy and healthy is always far better than being bullied as well! They were only bothered about money and their own ruthless ambition. It made us all feel powerless and alone, because they did the same thing to each person, one at a time. No one wanted conflict because we'd all been happy at work. Each victim's doctor told each person to leave and to find another job. It was about having the wisdom to walk away from the things you couldn't change. Our doctors saved us all. The moral is: safety first and prevention is better than a cure! The doctors were right!

Clearly, it's better to change the things you can change and have the sense to walk away from the things you can't change. It was much better to follow the advice of flight or fight because none of us needed prescription drugs for depression, just another job! If you feel you can't work in that environment, find another job. Saving someone's health and life, with good advice, is much better than fear, misery and possible suicide! This is where I learned that money, wealth and power were not everything. This is where I learned not to be fooled by devious, ruthless and ambitious people. This is where I learned that people and health are more important than social status and worldly values. This was where I realised how Jesus and God had saved my mental health too! I had no trust or confidence in the management at Firlane School. I would never treat anyone the way I, and others, had been treated; the people involved in this wouldn't like to be treated like this either. They were trying to manipulate the truth; they were trying to make fools of us; they were trying to destroy the light.

They'd destroyed my trust and confidence in their management and everyone else's as well, which was why we were all so upset and why we couldn't work in that environment anymore. They'd crushed, destroyed and scattered our confidence. They should have been building on each person's strengths and developing each person further, through appropriate Continued Professional Development. Towards the end, we all received very few development course placements. They became an extreme rarity for us, but not for the favoured few! At one interview in Firlane School, Dawn was asked, "Why haven't you been on Professional Development Courses?"

She replied, "I don't know why. Perhaps you could explain it? My head of department is always allowed to go on such courses." At the end, we were all treated the same! They followed the same pattern to destroy our light.

Roberta Oliver and her friends went on Professional Development Courses but I was no longer chosen. How had it changed so much, since Keith Stephenson, the first headteacher when I had worked at Firlane School, told me, "Don't apply to work in another school and we'll look after you. We want to keep you in this school because we totally trust you and we can always rely on you to do your very best for the pupils and the school."

Percy Banks, Dawn's head of department made sure he went on every course that came up, and that was the pattern! The favoured few went on courses but the rest of us were never allowed! We were all left feeling unvalued, worthless and distressed. I left to avoid being ill; so did the others! I left so I wasn't driven to suicide, like so many others in life and a member of Firlane School! It was a dripping tap; it was a slow death by torture; it was a prison. We had been in chains. Spirits had been stifled in the staffroom, at meetings and in the classroom. One by one, we didn't smile anymore. One by one, we didn't laugh anymore. One by one, we couldn't stand it anymore.

Jim Catchpole also left. Jim was also a teacher at Firlane School, who we had worked with for years! He was small and very slim, with short, dark hair. He was always very funny and always made everyone laugh at staff meetings! When he met Dawn, years later, he talked about Derrick Tusk, the headteacher, saying, "What a horrible man he was!"

"He certainly was! I only met him at the end of term, before I left, but he was unfriendly, rude and intimidating."

"People left when he became head because he was such a horrible man!"

"I had a lucky escape because I left before he came."

"You did! I was just glad to get out alive!"

"I'm far happier now, just working at Dealey School. Mrs Cooper, my head of faculty, is always totally supportive. She asked me, "Why aren't you in permanent teaching?" I was so happy to be out of Firlane School that I used to sing Christmas carols on a morning, driving to school!"

I resolved to improve my life and to survive! I resolved to continue working, instead of being made ill! I resolved to succeed, by staying alive, enjoying life and appreciating every day! Dawn and I both had to dig deep, to cope, to withstand the situation and to maintain good health! Mary Evans had been right all along, when she'd advised me to never let them trick me into thinking they were everything in life! If I'd been happy before I worked at Firlane School and had been praised by two HMSI inspections and all LEA inspections, I could be happy again!

I decided to concentrate on the future, so I didn't take Sealand Occupational Health's offer of support against Firlane School, to protect my family against stress, distress and anxiety. Was this the quickest and easiest solution? Would this really solve all problems? Would the bullying really stop? Would my hopes, dreams and expectations come true? Or would I live to regret not taking them to an industrial tribunal?

8. A New Battle

I was happy teaching for a term at Essingland School, in Dinton. The headteacher, Peter McManus, told the whole staff at the end of term, "It's been a pleasure to have Mrs Lowry teaching in our school. Mrs Lowry has done a first-class job in this school as a teacher and we are one of the most challenging schools in the country! We wish her every success in her new school, which is one of the best in the country." Paul was small in height, in his 50s, with grey hair. Essingland School most certainly was in one of the most deprived areas in the country but it had an excellent behaviour management policy in place in the school, which made it a pleasure to teach in. Unsupportive comments were not made in this school at all! I thoroughly enjoyed working with the two assistant headteachers in the school, Patrice Lowe and Timothy Hall! They were totally supportive and were always full of praise. They were both in their 40s. Patrice was tall and slim with long, light brown hair. Timothy was small, thin and wore glasses. His hair was grey. On the day I left, as a treat, Timothy treated me, and the whole department, to lunch at the local hotel! Wasn't that kind of him? I still have the book they all bought me, as a leaving present. What a contrast to Firlane School!

My year 10 class, which was the lowest ability class in the year, had been an absolute pleasure to teach! When anyone walked in, they could have thought it was an "A" level class, in a private school! How did this happen? Graham, the most disruptive pupil in the school, was in this class and I was supported by management! Also, in conversation, Graham told me, "I live at Hail Rose, Philiptree but have to come to school at Essingland."

"My grandma lived near there, when I was young."

"No one can be naughty for you, if your grandma lived near where I live now."

No one was!

Graham was excellent in lessons and so was everyone else! Graham was probably the tallest in the year and the broadest! Graham treated me with respect, so all other pupils did too! He had light brown hair and no one argued with him! Linda Newton, assistant head of department, was also a pleasure to work with, as was the teacher next door, Linda Stephenson.

Timothy Hall, the assistant headteacher, was always popping into lessons asking, "Is everyone working Mrs Lowry?"

"Yes, Mr Hall, everyone is always working."

His job was to ensure the behaviour policy of the school was effective and it was! It was a pleasure to work in Essingland School!

I totally appreciated my cards, presents and meal out at The Half Sunset, when I left. I felt happy and valued when I left. The headteacher told me he would act as a referee for me. Laura Nelson's brother-in-law was a deputy headteacher, in one of the best schools in the country and he was looking for a teacher to cover someone who was extremely ill. Laura was second in the department and a pleasure to work with! She was tall with long, wavy, blonde hair. Laura was always working and was a pleasure to work with. I applied, supported by the agency, Essingland School and Laura (who was second in the department and the deputy headteacher's sister-in-law).

I had been supported by Essingland School. The headteacher, Peter McManus, the assistant headteachers and the head of department all told me, "I will support you for a permanent post. You can use me as a referee for any teaching post." I was lucky to be offered a supply post at Whiteland School, full time, while a teacher was absent with ill health.

Whiteland School also supported me for a permanent post and the headteacher saw me there as well! She was a pleasure to meet and a pleasure to work with. Dawn was supported by Dealey School, and was really pleased when Mrs Cooper repeatedly asked, "Why aren't you in permanent teaching?" The headteacher of the school also saw Dawn and praised her.

Dawn replied, "I'm happy here. I'm not being bullied in the school," to anyone who asked her questions.

Whiteland School was one of the best schools in the country, and was a pleasure to work in. Whiteland School was opposite the sea! It was a beautiful, calm and relaxing environment! I had never worked in such a picturesque school! When I parked my car on a morning, I felt relaxed, happy and calm, just watching the sea and the golden beach! What a privilege it was to work in an environment which appealed to the senses! The sea swished and rocked gently on the shore! I felt relaxed, happy and valued every day I worked in this school.

A family member did research in the school; my children went to church at Christmas, with me and the school. My husband and the dog had been to the interview with me, but had waited outside! We all felt welcomed by the school. Also, I was happy working in the school and contributed to some of the best results in the country for GCSEs. The school acted as a referee for me, as all of the senior management, the head of department and the head of year supported me for a permanent post. Unsupportive comments were not made in this school; I felt supported by the school. I loved working in this school; I loved going to department meetings: I loved going out with the department, on a lunchtime; I loved being invited to a colleague's house, after school with the department, and individually.

The school had a work ethic that I totally agreed with! It also used self-assessment and peer assessment in the same way that I did! I agreed with the expectations and ethos of the school and the headteacher was lovely! Patricia Whitman was always friendly, totally supportive and a pleasure to work with. At the interview, I was told, "We're employing you because of your degree and your Commendation on your Teaching Practice; this proves your ability and we want your best! Your ability is already proven so it's up to us to provide you with the right environment, so you can work to your maximum potential." I was incredibly happy in the school and felt valued, appreciated and respected.

Whiteland School had excellent Continued Professional Development (CPD) in the school, in the department and in the year group. They extended best practice across the department, the year group and the school! Everywhere I went, staff were kind, helpful and supportive. I was part of a team! I found they all thought the same as me, in essence, across the school! They were already doing what I thought, without me telling them! Comments were made in staff meetings such as, "You have to be good to work here.

We don't employ anyone who isn't." Continuous supportive comments were made, everywhere in the school.

However, an assistant headteacher, Christine Dickinson, who had previously worked with Derrick Tusk (the new headteacher at Firlane School) was often in the school. Christine was very tall, with short black hair. She never spoke to me directly but I still felt safe, as I trusted the headteacher, the senior leadership team and the staff. She never smiled but the staff in the school always smiled! She never looked happy with anything she saw but the headteacher, the head of department and the senior leadership team always looked happy. She turned up in lessons but was met with excellence in every classroom! The attitude of the pupils was, "Mrs Lowry, we showed her we're the best in the country, didn't we?"

"You certainly did! Everyone receives five merits for being outstanding all lesson!"

"Thank you very much! We'll all be outstanding if she comes back again!" the pupils agreed.

The only reason I left Whiteland School was because the person I was in the school for had been extremely ill, with cancer, and she recovered. I was then immediately offered another teacher's timetable, as I loved working in this school. This teacher, Alison Fairbanks, went on maternity leave but came back. Alison was young, small and had short, curly, auburn hair. When she returned from maternity leave she asked me to do her a favour, "Could you please keep away from my tutor group, such as in assembly, because they've all told me they loved having you as a tutor, and haven't wanted me back?" Other senior members of staff made similar comments, that the tutor group had loved me and missed me. I did as I was asked, but the tutor group came to the staffroom, at lunchtime, with the biggest bouquet of flowers in the world, for me, as a thank you. Wasn't that wonderful?

I also really appreciated the cards and presents from the department when I left, as I knew they were heartfelt and meant!

Whiteland School had identified the pattern of the teacher's daughter being bullied. I was told by Helen Acer, one of the senior management in the school, "The management of this school has identified the problem at Firlane School: you had a family member, a pupil, bullied at another school." On reflection, I realised they were correct! The same thing had happened to other teachers at Firlane

School! A parent (who was a teacher at Firlane School) who had a family member, a pupil, bullied at another school, was then bullied by the management at Firlane School; Dawn's daughter had been bullied at Firlane School and then Dawn had been bullied by the management as well! I then remembered Ross telling me that the management didn't like the children of staff at the school having any problems! He'd certainly been proven right, hadn't he? My family had not been the problem; we'd been the victims of actions by others!

Many comments were made regarding my family that had upset me at Firlane School, but it didn't happen at Whiteland School. Whiteland School made comments to me, directly, such as, "This school is supporting you, … wait until the GCSE results come out. If you ever have any problems, come to us!"

Firlane School had made me feel afraid and full of misery, for me and for my family! Dawn had felt the same, so had Simon! Andrea had also felt she could no longer work in such an unhappy environment, as did Jacqui, Aidan and many others! Was it also because we were all experienced and expensive teachers? We were all replaced by inexperienced and cheaper staff! Was this because a financial crash was coming?

I had felt happy, valued and appreciated at Whiteland School. When the GCSE results did come out, Janet Stubbs rang me up to tell me about them. She told me, "The GCSE results are some of the best in the country! The class we shared had the highest value added in the department!" Janet had been my colleague and friend in the department and went on to be the second in the department, on a temporary basis. She was small and slim with short, blonde hair. Janet had often invited me to her house and was a pleasure to work with. I was absolutely thrilled that our department had one of the best sets of GCSE results in the country. I had contributed to some of the best GCSE results in the country! Janet told me, "The class, which we shared, had the best value added (the class which had made the most progress) in the department; this was an outstanding achievement, particularly as this department's results are one of the best sets of GCSE results in the country!" The contrast was the way I was treated by the management of the school. The contrast was essentially the way I was treated by the management of Essingland School too! The problem at Firlane School had been the change of management!

I then went to Siperton School. Siperton School was in a remote area in Dinton. It was surrounded by some fields but kept the remnants of the mining community, which had been destroyed. They needed a full-time, temporary supply teacher and I had been recommended to them by the headteacher of Essingland School. Our class read a story about "Agatha and James". Agatha's father was James' employer; he sacked James because Agatha fell in love with him. The employer made sure James never worked again, so James died of starvation. Employers have the power to make lives happy or to cause extreme distress, because of the amount of power they have. I was incredibly happy here and this school repeatedly told me they would act as a referee for me too, as they didn't want me to leave this school either. It was a pleasure to work in Siperton School, but there was a pattern of comments made in this school too!

I had taught with Lilly Turner at Firlane School for years and now she was working at Siperton School! Lilly was slightly older than me and was very slim and tall, with short brown, curly hair. As soon as she saw me, on my first day at Siperton School, she ran over and gave me a huge cuddle, telling everyone, "We worked together for years, organising the exams at school. We always supported each other and enjoyed working together."

I was ever so glad to see Lilly, when at Sipton School; she kissed me and cuddled me every time I saw her! Lilly told me, "We all saw a pattern in the department you worked in. We could all see what was happening, because staff left in your department, one at a time. One left, then another one left, then another one left ..." I had worked with Lilly for years, and it had always been a pleasure to work with her. We organised the SATs together, for years!

"I'm glad you noticed what was happening as well!"

"I saw a change of management at Firlane School, then one teacher in the same department as you left, then another teacher in the same department as you left, then another person in the same department as you left. They all left, one at a time. I saw this go on for years!" Therefore, it was a pattern of behaviour by management, not one individual person! Lilly gave me lots of cuddles and that made me feel much better!

"I'm really pleased to see you Lily! You've made me feel

much better!"

"I'm sure you can easily see the difference in styles of management as well! They all say lovely things about you here!"

"This is a lovely school to work in."

"They've told me all about you working at Whiteland School, which is one of the best schools in the country, and you're now helping this school."

"I did! I'm glad to see you again!"

"I'm glad to see you as well! We've worked together for years, and we've always been happy working together."

"We certainly have!"

"Did you know Martin McVitie?"

"He lived near me at Essingland, many years ago. He was later a member of the clergy and went into the school my children were in, in Sealand."

"Did you know he'd committed suicide?"

"No!"

"There'd been a rumour that he'd committed a crime, which was never even reported to the police. It was made clear to him that his post as a member of the clergy was untenable! He was left in a bedsit in Newpalace."

"How could he then go to church, which was what he had done for years?" Were institutions defending themselves and blaming everyone but themselves? "I knew Martin as a polite, pleasant and well behaved young lad, who never hurt anyone." I couldn't believe, at first, he'd been driven to suicide.

"He was just left alone, without a job, in a bedsit, without friends."

"How awful! He always had friends when he lived at Essingland. It's very sad! His family would have been devastated."

"They were! They wouldn't allow anyone connected with what happened to attend his funeral."

"I don't blame them."

When the school needed a reliable supply teacher, I recommended Dawn who also found she enjoyed working at this school too! Lilly Turner obviously knew Dawn too! I had acted as a referee for Dawn, when they needed a Music teacher desperately. My friend, Veronica Goldsmith, was the Head of Music and needed a temporary member of staff in the Music department; I knew Dawn would be happy working in this school, with Veronica. Veronica was a young teacher, of average height and build and was slim, with shoulder length, black, curly hair. She was always smiling, pleasant and funny! This proved it was the ethos of the school/ headteacher, not us as individuals. The headteacher and heads of department supported both of us at Siperton School and we both felt part of a valued team.

However, although Chloe Crispin was always very friendly and supportive, I felt as though, at times, she was trying to trick me. Chloe was tall, with short, straight hair and she was very pretty. She kept making comments, such as, "I'll go with you to Whiteland School, and then once I'm in, you needn't go again and I'll go by myself!"

"I had no problems with Whiteland School, and I wouldn't need anyone to go with me! Why do you want to go to Whiteland School? Why do you think they'll let you into their school?" I asked. Also, I knew Whiteland School wouldn't be tricked by someone trying to go to their school to take their ideas and resources! The staff at Whiteland School hadn't been born yesterday! They didn't just let anyone into their school to look around! I also found it very strange that Chloe Crispin kept making critical comments about her husband and adopted children; I felt she was trying to trick me into saying something critical against my husband and my family, but I never did.

Chloe Crispin was often making comments which implied she was asking questions and making comments as part of a planned strategy. I felt as though she was trying to defend the school which had failed to protect my family member against bullying! The school failed to stop it but the police had had no problem stopping it! She probably didn't even know what had happened! I felt she was trying to trick me into saying something about my family, which they could use against me! My family was not the problem! I found this upsetting, so spent time with the retired deputy headteacher, David Wilson, who still taught some lessons in the school and often used the classroom I taught in.

David had retired from full time teaching but still did some supply teaching in the school, like many other retired teachers. He was an older teacher, tall, with short, grey hair. David was pleasant and polite every time I saw him, which was often, as he often taught the Sixth Form in my classroom. He actually knew my husband, so we didn't have any problems at all. He was a pleasure to work with. David also came from the mining community, so we had many shared values and expectations! You don't know what you've got until it's gone! We'd both been very happy, every day, in the mining community and had had many friends and good neighbours! We shared many common experiences.

Why was Chloe behaving like this? Was it because she had been a headteacher previously, in a school of the same faith as me? She'd worked in a faith school in Dinton, the LEA that I'd removed my children from, due to our family being the victims of a road traffic accident, that had not been our fault. I felt this was the game! They were trying to find some information against me, against my family, to use to defend themselves! This had not happened at Essingland School or at Whiteland School! Chloe had previously been a headteacher in a school of the same faith as me! Both Essingland School and Siperton School were in Dinton! Was this the connection? I no longer had a solicitor to protect me, as I did when I removed my children from that primary school! At the time, we had the best legal team in the area, to protect our family, as the result of a car accident! Wasn't it strange how no comments were made then? Was this the faith schools ganging up on me, to attack me, to defend themselves? I'd been told by the acting headteacher that the faith secondary school I was a parent at would support the police, who were supporting our family member, so why was this happening? Why was I being bullied and intimidated at work?

Was this type of strategy, of defending themselves, applied to Martin McVitie? Were institutions defending themselves and blaming everyone but themselves?

When I left Siperton School, I really appreciated the meals out with the school and the kind presents. As well as presents from children, the department and the year group, I received an expensive bottle of perfume from one of the assistant headteachers! Wasn't that lovely? The headteacher was a pleasure to work with. The headteacher, Peter Gilhead, told me, "It's really about the ethos of each school."

"I've thoroughly enjoyed working in this school. I totally agree with the work ethic of this school and I've thoroughly enjoyed making resources for the whole department, which the whole department really appreciated!"

"The whole department has benefitted from your expertise and you've made a valuable contribution to our school."

Siperton School also appreciated that I'd been working in one of the best schools in the country and we shared ideas, which was marvellous! Siperton School supported me!

I was happy at Whiteland School and Siperton School! I had been extremely successful: I had contributed to some of the best GCSE results in the country in both schools. The issue had been about mental health; another issue was the distribution of wealth and feeling valued. Clearly, a financial crash was building up, which explained why they'd behaved in the way they did! Dawn and I had turned into detectives and psychologists and this saved our lives and our health! It was all extremely logical!

As I was supporting a family member studying for a second degree, I applied for a post in another school, so I had a school to work in, when this post ended. The headteacher, Peter, asked me, "Can you stay at Siperton School?"

"I'd love to but is there a post for me in the school?"

"We don't have a post you could apply for, at this time, but we would all like you to stay in this school," Peter told me. "Southland School is well known for problems with disruptive pupils in the school. We wish you could stay here."

"I must pay for my daughter's second degree but I would love to stay here. I will apply if I see a post come up in this school."

"I just need to make sure I'm being fair to the next headteacher because we really want to keep you and will be recommending you for a post in any school," Peter advised me. I clearly didn't want to leave but decided to give the next school a fair chance; if the next school didn't really have the ethos and values of the best schools in the country, I knew I could apply back to this school or to another school. I now knew the issues had been the ethos of the headteacher, the management of each school and the distribution of wealth!

I then taught in Southland School. It was a war bunker! People went to work hoping for safety, but found it was easily destroyed! The only reason I went there was to pay for a degree course for a family member. Kerry Seasons, a previous pupil worked here and was a pleasure to work with. However, I felt there was a problem with support for disruptive pupils by management, so I soon left. I soon found out why this school had the dreadful reputation it had! Staff were not supported and felt unvalued, heartbroken and shot! The problem in the school was the ethos and values of the school, as I felt disruptive pupils ruled the school, not the teachers. I was in for a shock when I saw, and heard, a pupil swearing repeatedly at the headteacher! What a contrast from Whiteland School and Siperton School! Would this happen to other staff?

One teacher, Sheila Rothberry, told me, "I was coming out of school one lunchtime, in my car, when a pupil jumped onto the bonnet of my car. I couldn't see out of the window, so I had to stop! He laughed and smeared his cheese sandwich all over the window of my car! I was very upset. When I reported the incident to the school, I was blamed! I was asked why the pupil had done it to me, and not to another member of staff! I was off on the sick for months after that! The only reason I came back was because I was supported by my union."

"This is part of a pattern, isn't it? The disruptive pupil can harass a teacher, then the teacher is blamed! Just as well the union stepped in, to support you."

"I couldn't have come back if they hadn't!" Sheila added.

"They don't take that attitude if they swear at the headteacher, do they? That boy was suspended immediately."

"That's a common problem here."

Comments were continually being made in Southland School, which were obviously directed at me, also made by people who didn't really speak to me and who were not part of my friendship group. Many comments were made about my family, by people who didn't even know them. This became part of a pattern of bullying, both in school and outside of school. It was done deliberately to upset me, so that I would be upset and would no longer be happy at work, so that I couldn't do my best at work. I felt bullied, harassed and the victim of unwanted behaviour. The same assistant headteacher, Christine Dickinson, who had previously worked with Derrick Tusk (at Firlane School), was always in this school as well.

I felt there were problems of management not supporting staff, and that the problems were in the school well before I'd arrived! Jack Forrest, the headteacher at Southland School, supported himself but not his staff. He was in his late 40s, was of medium height and build, with short brown hair. HMSI (Her Majesty's School Inspectors) were in the school, but they were not the problem! Everyone worked well when HMSI were in school, and the school was a much better to work in, when HMSI were in the school. Without HMSI, I didn't feel safe in the school, and it was noticeably clear to me why so many staff had left, with ill health problems.

The teaching assistant in the tutor group, Jane Scott, told me, "I'm not joining in the comments and asking you questions, to report back to them! They did ask me but I said I enjoyed working with you and I wouldn't feel right joining in with this! The others are lining up to ingratiate themselves with them, which is why they're doing it! I don't want to be involved in how they're treating you because I think it's bullying." Jane was in her late 30s, was small but well built, with short blonde hair. She was honest, truthful and trustworthy! Jane told me, "I'm really upset to be asked to ask you questions and I'm terribly upset that others are making comments about you, in your presence, and asking you questions, to report the answers back to management!"

My instincts had been right, when I had felt I was the victim of a form of bullying, harassment and unwanted behaviour! I knew this was what had been happening in Firlane School, and Siperton School with Chloe Crispin. The pattern was the same in each school: comments were made about me, in my presence, questions were asked and reported back to management! It was appearance and reality. They appeared successful by worldly values but they were morally corrupt. I was clearly the victim of bullying, harassment and unwanted behaviour!

I left Southland School, to go to Dinton School. The pattern of continuous upsetting comments continued to be made, not directly to me, but when passing near me. The headteacher made comments too, for example, "It's your schools who're doing this to you." I felt this was a reference to the faith schools I'd sent my children to! Although this headteacher was successful in worldly values, she was bullying me! I felt powerless, distressed and afraid! This seemed to be a reference to religious schools ganging up to attack me, to defend themselves! My children were no longer in

Dinton schools! Bullying in schools affects families, the police had been involved, and police cautions had been given, and those families bullying my family member were told the Crown Prosecution Service would take them to court if it continued. The police had told our family member, a pupil, to ring them immediately if the victim was ever frightened, and the police would go immediately. The pattern of bullying, harassment and unwanted behaviour continued; it was clear schools were trying to defend themselves and blame me! How dare they? I felt afraid, powerless and worried! What could I do? How could I cope? Who could protect me? The bullying, harassment and unwanted behaviour was carried out in such a way that it was difficult to prove; they hid in the shadows, destroying the light, with their bullying, harassment and unwanted behaviour.

The sly, subtle comments made about me and my family went on in this school too. It was a pattern of deceit and manipulation, which caused fear and misery, the symptoms of bullying. The comments were never made as part of a conversation. I had no doubt that this was a form of bullying, harassment and unwanted behaviour, as this school was in the same LEA as the primary school where I had reported problems, at a time when we were using a solicitor. I later found that many teachers had problems with primary schools, over them giving them spelling tests which were too difficult for the children! The school concerned had had nothing at all to say to our solicitor! We had moved house because we were victims of a road traffic accident that was not our fault! We didn't have this problem in the next primary school! Was this why they treated me like this? Were they trying to attack me, to defend themselves? Is this how they treated Martin McVitie, which drove him to suicide?

It was clearly a pattern of bullying, harassment and unwanted behaviour! Why did they hide in the shadows, destroying the light, instead of being open and honest, in the light? It was also a religious school and the pupils who were given police cautions were in another religious school, in Sealand. Were these headteachers worried about being taken to court? If I'd been rich and powerful, I'm sure none of it would have happened! I was in a weak position and I had no power against this form of bullying, harassment and unwanted behaviour.

I met Carole Renwick again, at Dinton School. I had worked with Carole at Firlane School; she took Andrea Tweed's place in the department when Andrea left! Carole was tall, extremely well built and physically powerful; she had gone to judo classes for years! Carole was much younger than I was but had a large family of five children. Carole Renwick showed me the letter she had written to Derrick Tusk, headteacher of Firlane School, or I would never have believed her story! They had done the same to her! I knew she was telling the truth! Carole told me, "They made my life a misery too. I've been on the sick for almost a year and I thought I'd never work again." Carole had been driven out of Firlane School too. I also met Jack Bevan again, in the staff room at Dinton School (he'd given his girlfriend a lift to work). Jack had also taught at Firlane School for years! He was of small stature and thin, with short black hair. Jack was approximately my age. I was then 50. He told me, "Firlane School had become a corrupt place. The problem for you was the ambition of the headteacher and the head of department."

I worked with Carole Renwick at Dinton School. Many staff were a pleasure to work with, and again, I contributed to some of the best results in the country, for GCSE. Rob Brewer, the deputy headteacher, was always friendly, supportive and a total pleasure to work with; Rob was tall and slim with short, dark brown hair. He was always pleasant, smiled and talked easily to me. He also wore glasses, just like me! Laura Holmes, who was the Advanced Skills Teacher, was also a pleasure to work with. Both were tall and slim, with dark hair; both were very clever. Laura appreciated my work ethic, as I shared a classroom with her. She used some of my ideas and resources when she showed newly qualified teachers examples of good practice. The head of department, Paul Hunt, was not as supportive as others! I did not agree with Paul Hunt: I didn't think he was as good as the deputy headteacher Rob Brewer, who had been the previous head of department, who I did agree with. Although Paul Hunt was tall, slim and handsome, he was not as honest, reliable and trustworthy as Laura and Rob.

I found a complete contrast between the two! Whenever the head of department (Paul Hunt) was around, comments were made continuously about my family! I felt terribly upset! I rang Dinton Town Hall, to tell them, as my mother was ill, and comments were made about her. The social worker I spoke to told me, "This shouldn't have got back to you." Clearly, some form of process was going on, about my family. Comments were then made about other members of my family. This type of thing had happened at Southland School, and Jane, a member of staff, had told me that management was behind it all! This obviously applied here too! It was sly, murky and in the shadows! Why didn't they say things to our solicitor, when we were victims of a car crash? They had nothing to say to our solicitor then! Why did the headteacher of the secondary faith school tell me the school would support the police, who were supporting our family member? Why was I in a cloak and dagger situation?

Comments were continually being made, which were obviously directed at me, by people who didn't really speak to me and were not part of my friendship group. Many comments were made directed about my family, by people who didn't even know them. This became part of a pattern of bullying, both in school and outside of school. It was done deliberately to upset me, so that I would be upset and would no longer be happy at work, so that I couldn't do my best at work. I felt bullied, harassed and the victim of unwanted behaviour. This happened in Dinton School and this continued outside of this school too! The headteacher was of the same faith as me, so that was the connection. She was defending the faith schools too! That was the only explanation! No one had anything to say to our solicitor, when we were the victims of a car crash and the secondary faith school had told me they were supporting the police, who had given police cautions to pupils from their school! This form of bullying is exceedingly difficult to prove, but it was a continued pattern of bullying, harassment and unwanted behaviour. No wonder I felt so upset, anxious and worried! Was this how Martin McVitie had been treated, before he was driven to suicide?

It was not me that was making comments to deliberately upset others. However, the deputy headteacher, Rob Brewer, was always friendly and a pleasure to work with: he didn't join in with this. He was always totally supportive, and a pleasure to work with. He worked in the same department too. He began to make supportive comments in front of the department, which made me much happier. Carole Renwick always made comments, which implied line management was using her to upset me! I had found this to be a common pattern in schools! She had done this at Firlane School, to Dawn too, and Dawn had been very upset by her! At one point I told her, "I have read "Macbeth" and the motive was ambition".

Her reply was, "You really do know what's going on!" It was appearance and reality. They appeared successful by worldly values but they were morally corrupt. However, Carole also left Dinton School when I left; she was obviously too expensive too! Newly Qualified Teachers were employed. This was part of a pattern in schools: drive older, expensive and experienced teachers out of schools and replace them with younger, cheaper teachers, if the older, expensive teachers weren't part of the power clique.

The continued comments were part of a common pattern. It was also a reference to problems the schools had, but they were trying to defend themselves and blame me! The schools never said anything to our solicitor when we had moved house because our family had been the victims of a road traffic accident! Therefore, it was part of a pattern of bullying, harassment and unwanted behaviour. This continued in many schools! I was too afraid to tell anyone because I was so frightened. Dawn later told me, "You've suffered at the hands of colleagues who were totally jealous of you. You were showing them up and they certainly didn't like it. The staff were jealous of you."

The truth was that they wanted to employ newly qualified teachers to save money! They didn't want to pay high wages for older, expensive and experienced teachers! Walking away from bullying is much better than being bullied! Concentrating on being happy and healthy is far better than being bullied as well! Dinton School was in the same LEA as a particular primary school which had left a lot to be desired, regarding my children. This school didn't have anything to say to our solicitor at all! Why did this school throw away this opportunity, when we were the victims of a car accident that wasn't our fault? They had an opportunity to help but they declined! Fortunately, the next primary school was excellent!

After I'd left Dinton School, Laura Holmes told me, "Your class had the highest grades the school has ever seen for GCSE!" This was similar to what Janet Stubbs had told me at Whiteland. Laura also told me, "The GCSE results for your other class, which we shared, were also the highest the school has ever seen for that set. They were much higher than Claire's class, which was a similar set. Also, we didn't have the behaviour problems in our class that she had. We all tried to help her with the behaviour, but the others didn't have to help us with our class." Claire was a permanent member of staff at Dinton School, while I was only there for the year.

Laura Holmes also told me, "Rob Brewer, the deputy head, and others in the department have looked at the files and work of your classes, after the GCSE results came in. Your classes' files were also better than similar classes." Laura Holmes then added, "Paul Hunt, the head of department has now left, because of what he did to you, so I'm head of department now."

"Congratulations Laura! That's a well-deserved promotion! You really do deserve it! You were always an absolute pleasure to work with."

"So were you."

What a different life I would have had at Dinton School if Laura Holmes had been head of department when I was there, because she really was kind, professional and a pleasure to work with.

I was extremely glad Laura Holmes kept in touch after I'd left, when I was at Forth School, so I sent her a large bouquet of flowers, for her continued kindness and support, after I'd left.

Then, Firlane School did the same thing to Percy Banks! He hadn't expected that, had he? They knew what they were doing! No one wanted such conflict. Percy Banks was upset and was extremely glad to see Dawn after he'd left too! Percy was tall, of average build, with short, light brown hair. Percy was then in his late 40s. He gave Dawn a big cuddle when he saw her! Dawn was flabbergasted, after all those years of bullying. Dawn cringed. Dawn was with Richard when this happened; he'd known what had happened to Dawn too. Richard wasn't fooled by Percy Banks at all! Percy certainly knew what they'd done when the management of Firlane School did the same to him. Dawn told me, "I was so glad that Richard was with me that day. I called Percy's performance an Oscar winning performance! He didn't fool Richard at all. What is good to give should be good to receive! I bet he was totally shocked by what the management did to him. I felt totally in the right for refusing to mark and assess his GCSE class' work. I knew that legally they couldn't make me."

9. More Threats

At Forth School, the same pattern of bullying continued. Forth School was a small, cheap building with no air conditioning! The wind could easily blow it to the ground, if it wanted to! The pupils didn't all wear their school uniform correctly! What a contrast to Dinton School, Siperton School and Whiteland School! It seemed to be more like Southland School, where disruptive pupils ruled! Forth School had previously been forced to close by HMSI and had reopened under the name of Forth School; as I knew Angela Rivers from Firlane School and she'd been very glad of my friendship then, I expected her to be pleased to see me. However, was I right to think of her in such a positive light? Were my friends at Firlane School right about her, when they told me she was cunning, sly and manipulative?

Comments were continually made at Forth School, which were obviously directed at me. Many comments were made about my family, by people who didn't even know them. This became part of a pattern of bullying, harassment and unwanted behaviour, both in school and outside of school. It was done deliberately to upset me, so that I would be upset and would no longer be happy at work, so that I couldn't do my best at work. I felt bullied, harassed and the victim of unwanted behaviour. It all continued in Forth School and outside of Forth School! This form of bullying is exceedingly difficult to prove. My family was not the problem; the problem was that I felt afraid for them; we were all being victimised! I would never treat anyone the way I'd been treated; the people involved in this wouldn't like to be treated like this either. The web of deceit and bullying was far wider than I had ever imagined! Who could have expected this? Forth School was also in Dinton! I had two management points in this school. The wind howled as I entered the building and the lights flickered!

It was a common pattern. Also, there was a constant reference to problems in schools, but they were trying to defend themselves and blame me! The school in Dinton had never said anything to our solicitor, at the time! Therefore, it was part of a pattern of bullying, harassment and unwanted behaviour in the shadows, away from the light. This continued in many schools! I had been too afraid to tell anyone because I was so frightened. I was even too afraid to report everything to the union, about what they were really doing, in the beginning, because this form of bullying, harassment and unwanted behaviour is so difficult to prove. However, the results for GCSE went up in the previous schools I'd worked in, so I knew they were the problem, not me! I was becoming terrified to go to work. They clearly wanted my knowledge and expertise; Angela Rivers had worked with me at Firlane School and had wanted my friendship then! She also knew I had "best practice", as identified by HMSI and that I was "excellent", as identified by Sealand LEA. I couldn't believe the change in her when she was in a position of power! I found that my group of friends at Firlane School had been right about her! She was deceitful, manipulative and a bully!

The truth had been that they wanted to take my knowledge and expertise and then get rid of me and employ newly qualified teachers, to save money! It was because they didn't want to pay high wages to experienced teachers! Walking away from bullying is much better than being bullied! Concentrating on being happy and healthy was far better than being bullied as well! This was in Dinton LEA, where a school had left a lot to be desired with my children, but we had moved house because of a road traffic accident, which was not our fault! They didn't have anything to say to our solicitor at all! The comments were never made as part of a conversation. I had no doubt that this was a form of bullying, harassment and unwanted behaviour, as this school was in the same LEA as the primary school where I had reported problems, at a time when we were using a solicitor. The school concerned had nothing at all to say to our solicitor! This was their revenge!

As I left Forth School one day, someone waved and approached the car. It was Judith Gentle, who I'd worked with at Firlane School. Judith was tall, slim and very pretty! She looked like a model! She told me, "Everyone has been leaving Firlane School, because the new headteacher, Derrick Tusk, has bullied them all out of the school! I tried to continue to work in the school, but I left because I couldn't stand it any longer. That's why everyone else left as well!" She was also terribly upset about it all! What a contrast to the many lunchtimes where we'd all met in the staffroom and laughed! Judith added, "I left to do part-time supply, because that was all I could get at the time."

"That's why I left too, and everyone else! It wasn't just me and it wasn't just you! They were doing it to older staff, to save money!"

"That's exactly what happened! They did it to everyone in our department. I was lucky to get some supply!" Judith added.

It was plainly obvious that the headteacher and the senior leadership team had made Judith's life a misery too, with bullying, harassment and unwanted behaviour. It had all been done deliberately by the headteacher, supported by his senior management team. It had not been about one individual at all. They had done it to a group of friends! Poor Judith! I was in good company with Judith.

I was frightened of Angela Rivers, not HMSI, in the school. Angela Rivers shouted at me, in front of two permanent members of staff, as she was a tyrant! "Don't tell them anything about me, the staff or the pupils in this school!" she screamed! I hadn't done anything at all! I hadn't even spoken to HMSI! This was the same Angela Rivers who'd been glad of my friendship at Firlane School, when not many people had liked her! She was short, of medium build with long brown hair; she was also in her 50s now. She was married, with a daughter. In this school, she had portrayed herself as a happily married woman, who didn't say anything about her two divorces, so I didn't either! I wonder why they left her? She'd always blamed them and defended herself but I certainly saw another side to her in Forth School! I tended to believe her husbands had been her victims! This was the same Angela Rivers who probably knew I had been identified as "best practice" by HMSI and the "type of teacher the government wanted to value!" Why was she now a dictator? Why did she feel the need to silence the staff? Why didn't she allow free speech?

HMSI were in school and Angela Rivers intimidated all members of staff, "No one says anything against me or anything against this school to HMSI if they want to continue working in this school!" She was protecting herself, not the staff and not the school! All I found was that the previous teacher, who had held my post, was right about the bullying in the school. When I went to meet her during the school holidays, Laura Hedley had told me, "Don't be fooled by any of them! Angela Rivers is a bully and so is Jack Ashton. They all work together! I'm leaving because I don't trust the management in this school and feel undermined, intimated and bullied. If they do the same thing to you, just remember what I've said! I've seen them drive others out of this school too! They're horrible bullies." Why was the caretaker standing outside of the door, listening? Laura was slightly younger than me, was very pretty, with long, blonde, straight hair. She looked very upset!

It was the difference between appearance and reality. Angela Rivers appeared successful by worldly values but she was morally corrupt. Was this how Martin McVitie had been treated, before he committed suicide? I decided to turn to God for strength, to cope with it and to ignore it all. Prayers helped! I was no longer alone! All I had to do was to concentrate on doing the right thing; I could always walk away, and go back to supply teaching. I also remembered what a lecturer told us, when I was a student, " Bullying is the intention to hurt: look the other way, turn back and smile. If you're not hurt, they haven't won."

Jack Ashton told me, "They always work together, to do this to staff. Sometimes one is the good cop and the other one is the bad cop; then they take turns." He was referring to Angela Rivers, the headteacher, and to her deputy headteacher, Philip Duncan. What a contrast this deputy headteacher was to the previous deputy headteacher! Philip Duncan was of average build, with short, grey hair and untrustworthy. What a contrast Angela Rivers was, as a headteacher, to when I worked with her at Firlane School and she had arguments with Pauline Laserton and others! Then, she had needed my friendship; now she didn't!

Jack Ashton was small, thin and wore glasses. He had short auburn hair and glasses; he was in his late 30s. The teacher, Laura Hedley, who I met when I came into the school during the school holidays had told me, "Jack Ashton is a bully, as is the headteacher and the deputy headteacher. I'm leaving because I'm so miserable here and I can't stand working in this department one second longer." Laura was small, pretty and friendly; she came across as honest, believable and trustworthy. I found it strange that the caretaker was always hovering near us, listening in on our conversation. Was he a spy? I decided to hope for the best. Would it turn out well? I wondered ...

Angela Rivers never allowed me to see this particular HMSI report; I saw it years later, on the internet, and I had been praised as a new member of staff. The school had been strengthened, with the addition of me, "an experienced member of staff with complimentary expertise". The pattern was: identify a problem to management, management then blamed the person because they wouldn't blame themselves! The comments continued in Forth School, which were made regarding schools I had removed my children from! It was a common pattern. However, no comments were ever made to our solicitor, following a road traffic accident, which was not our fault! Fortunately, at that time, we were well supported by a highly reputable legal team, which prepared, and won, a court case! Why didn't any school have anything to say to our solicitors? Also, we'd moved house because of a road traffic accident, which was not our fault! Why were the comments made later, in different schools, where the headteachers were friendly with the religious group of headteachers? Why were the comments made slyly, in the darkness, away from the light, when I had no power?

Why weren't they made openly to our solicitors, at the time? Why did the religious school, where the police gave police cautions to pupils in that school and threatened prosecution through the courts if the bullying continued, say that school would support the family member who had been bullied by the children in their school, but other schools didn't? Was this because they simply didn't know the truth? The same had happened with the good headteacher at Firlane School; he had been prepared to give evidence in court, to protect our family. When he left, so did my protection. Was this because no one else knew the truth? He had been supporting me, with the truth.

Clearly, these schools were using this method to defend themselves and to blame me! They never made any comments at all to our solicitor! If I could have afforded to employ a private solicitor against them, I would have. I simply couldn't keep going to work with such conflict if I wanted good health! Therefore, it was part of a pattern of bullying, harassment and unwanted behaviour. This continued in many schools! I was too afraid to tell anyone because I was so frightened. What right did they have to make such comments via second-hand information? I understood why Martin McVitie had committed suicide. I rang the agency I used to work for, "I'm very unhappy here, in this school."

Theresa Oak answered, "You don't have anything to worry about! We know all about the schools you're unhappy in and other teachers say the same things about the same schools! The schools you've been happy in have happy and valued teachers. You aren't the problem! We have excellent references for you so you needn't stay in that school at all. Just stay for the year, or as long as you can manage it; you still have your job here, with us, when you want it."

However, the bullying continued in Forth School for me, as Angela Rivers was friends with, and had worked with, Derrick Tusk before (who later worked at Firlane School after Angela had left)! Comments were made continually about my family, and the school where I had taken my children out of the school, after a family member had been upset over spellings! This school was in Dinton LEA, so it was the same pattern of bullying, harassment and unwanted behaviour as at Siperton School by Chloe Crispin, who had also been a headteacher, previously, in the religious group of schools, in Dinton LEA.

This form of bullying, harassment and unwanted behaviour had continued in other schools and it continued at Forth School. Angela Rivers and others were always making snide comments, showing others were being manipulated by her and I had no voice. I felt too frightened to tell anyone about what was really happening! It was done deliberately to upset me, so that I would be upset and would no longer be happy at work, so that I couldn't do my best at work. I felt bullied, harassed and the victim of unwanted behaviour. It all started in school but continued outside of this school too! This form of bullying was exceedingly difficult to prove.

Threats!

Jack Ashton, in Forth School, made continuous, sly comments about my family; this was obviously a reference to schools I had removed my children from! It was a common pattern. Also, he continually made references to problems the schools had, but were trying to defend themselves and blame me! The problem for him was that we had moved house because of a road traffic accident that was not our fault! After we'd moved house, we were all happier!

Unfortunately, the person who'd had this post before me, Laura Hedley, was correct about him! She was right! He was a bully, a liar and deceitful! The schools Jack Ashton kept referring to had never said anything to our solicitor! Therefore, it was part of a pattern of bullying, harassment and unwanted behaviour. I was still too afraid to tell anyone, because I was so frightened. Years after we'd moved house, bullying began for one family member! Again, our family was the victim, not the perpetrators! Bullying in schools affects families, so the police were involved, and police cautions were given, and those families were told the Crown Prosecution Service would take them to court if it continued. The police told the victim to ring them immediately if the victim was ever frightened, and the police would go immediately. Also, Victim Support came to our house to support the victim and our family. I couldn't understand how any teacher or school could justify this form of bullying to me and to my family, because no one would want to be treated like this! Why wasn't the family, the victims of road traffic accidents and bullying, being supported by schools and teachers? Why were they doing the bullying? Why were they lurking in the shadows, so afraid of truth and justice? Could they really escape God's justice? Is this what had happened to Martin McVitie? Is this why he took his own life? Is this happening to others too?

Jack Ashton threatened our whole family. In anger, he raised his voice when I had a year 9 class and he asked to speak to me outside of the classroom, where the children could listen, shouting, "It's them! It's your whole family," in anger. This was shouted clearly, and directly, to me. When I reported it to Angela Rivers, he denied it! He was a total liar! I couldn't believe he would dare to lie about this, but he did! I knew there was no justice or fairness in this school; it was a place of bullying and injustice! The teacher, Laura Hedley, who had the post before me, had been correct! I found everything Laura had warned me about, namely the management of this school, was true! Naively, I had given them the chance to show me they were trustworthy, but all they showed me was that they weren't! The previous teacher, Laura, had been telling the truth about them! She told me Jack Ashton and the senior management were bullies, manipulative and barefaced liars! It was a pattern of deceit and manipulation and fear and misery, the symptoms of bullying. Jack Ashton was a liar and so was Angela Rivers.

The previous person, Laura Hedley, who had my post in Forth School previously, told me, "The head of department, Jack Ashton, plus the senior leadership team and headteacher, bullied me out of my post. I was frozen out until I just couldn't stand working in this environment any longer." I found exactly the same! The same pattern of events happened to me that had happened to her! Laura had kept telling me, "Jack Ashton is the problem, along with the management of the school." I often heard Jack Ashton make comments to turn staff against me, such as, "It is against us. We are using you against her!"

This implied the strategy was to divide me from other colleagues and to manipulate other colleagues against me! This was the same pattern that Simon Coyles endured from management at Firlane School. A number of parents at Forth School told me, "We're supporting you, but we all know they're not." The comments of the parents showed they knew the same as me! Even the pupils made comments of, "We know they're bullying you! They ask the disruptive pupils to tell them of any problems they have and listen to them. They never listen to us because we defend you … If we did that to another pupil, the way they've treated you, we all know we'd be done for bullying."

Disruptive pupils felt supported by management and felt they didn't have to follow instructions by all teachers . (Years later, when I watched films involving court cases, where one side was attacking the other side, I could see their strategy. They were bullying me, yet were defending themselves, and kept attacking me. This was clearly not a working environment!) I hadn't been making comments about anyone else's family at all! They didn't even know my family, who were all enjoying education and work, and were thriving, happy and healthy!

Dinton Occupational Health later told me, "Jack Ashton has made a threat against your whole family and that would upset anyone at work!"

"At the time I was so frightened at school, that as soon as I could, I rang my husband and my children, to make sure they were alright, because I was so frightened. I didn't tell my friend Dawn, because I was too frightened. Jack Ashton lied, saying, "I didn't say it! He denied saying it when I told the deputy headteacher and the headteacher of Forth School. I was very frightened because I didn't trust the headteacher either!"

When I told Dinton Occupational Health, the doctor replied, "You've already won against Firlane School with Whiteland School! Your whole family should not have been threatened in Forth School at all! You have the right to work in a safe environment; you're not the only one who's reported incidents like this at Forth School."

"I was previously supported by Sealand Occupational Health; however, I didn't take action against Firlane School to protect my family, as we had children in education, and we didn't need the stress! Sealand Occupational Health had told me, "The issues are your loss of wages and loss of pension." Sealand Occupational Health was right to say they would support me against Firlane School, but I couldn't take them to court, because of family reasons at the time! I chose to protect my family from further distress.

"At the time, I thought I should just follow my GP's advice, of getting another job, which was a quicker and easier solution. Sealand Occupational Health had told me, "We will support you because you were awarded a Commendation on your Teaching practice, you have been praised as "best practice" by HMIS and told by HMIS, "You are the type of teacher the government wants to know is valued by the government. This has been extremely high praise by HMSI and you have had an exemplary career!" Sealand Occupational Health knew what was really going on! Also, Sealand Occupational Health knew the value of the grading "excellent" in all Sealand LEA inspections! Sealand Occupational Health had known the problem had been the change of management at Firlane School. I walked away from that conflict, to protect my family and I know I would protect my family again! Walking away from bullying seemed an easier solution!"

Dinton Occupational Health told me, "You have already won against Firlane School and the problem had been a change of management." Dinton Occupational Health continued, "Jack Ashton has threatened your whole family, and I can understand why you feel frightened in the school." I was too frightened to tell anyone everything that Dinton Occupational Health had told me. I would never treat anyone the way I'd been treated; the people involved in this wouldn't like to be treated like this either.

Beatrice Milton, a friend who was also a teacher and worked in Dinton LEA, had also previously made a threat to me: "They'll be on the other side of every problem against you." However, this threat was very real and it did happen! Beatrice had never spoken to me like this before. Why was she doing it then? We had been friends for years but she suddenly changed towards me, after I had left Firlane School. Beatrice was very slim, with short, curly hair and had been in my classes in secondary school. We had gone to school together and had taken our dogs for walks, for years! How could she change so quickly? What had been said to her? She later denied ever saying anything to upset me at all! The lies were part of the same pattern. No wonder Beatrice didn't want to admit what she'd been involved in! She would have to tell the truth, under oath, before God, in court!

When I told Dinton Occupational Health what Beatrice Milton had told me, the doctor explained, "She has threatened you as well! Both you and your family have been threatened! No teacher should have been threatening you in school or out of school! I don't blame you for not wanting to tell anyone at this school anything about your family, as your whole family has been threatened in Forth School. You're not the problem and your family is not the problem! You're saying the same thing about working in Forth School as other teachers, who've also found that bullying goes on in this school, since Angela Rivers became the headteacher. Other teachers have also reported bullying, in this school, by the management of this school, to us."

The pattern was: identify a problem to management, management then blamed the person because they wouldn't blame themselves! This was the pattern of the bullying, finding an area the victim was upset about. It was a pattern of divide and conquer! It was the difference between heaven and hell! It was a pattern of deceit and manipulation and fear and misery, the symptoms of bullying. Making the victim afraid, for fear of someone hurting their loved ones, was also what criminals had been doing throughout the ages! It was a common strategy, creating fear and misery, which were the symptoms of bullying! Had this happened to Martin McVitie?

Was that why he committed suicide? Fear, misery and suicide are the symptoms of bullying! They weren't worth my life! I had a family to protect and they were important; I had learned safety first and prevention was better than a cure in the mining community! Would that philosophy keep me safe now?

Wasn't it strange how Beatrice Milton never made comments about the pupil who'd committed suicide in the school she worked in? When she'd been upset, over another pupil dying, and the parent sought legal action against the school, I didn't make comments to upset her. Not only did that pupil die, it was reported in the newspapers, a pupil had committed suicide, over bullying in their school. She told me, "Percy Mullaney," (her headteacher at Benedick School), "is behind it all, because he's sticking up for Ruperton School." I found that strange as the acting headteacher of Ruperton School had told me, "This school is supporting the police and the police are supporting your family. We will be seeing the parents of the children the police have given police cautions to, but we don't have the powers of the police! Police cautions have been issued to pupils from this school for bullying and we will support the police!"

Beatrice Milton later denied saying anything, which was a blatant lie! Beatrice Milton had also told me, "They've won now, with you, because you're upset."

I didn't contact Beatrice Milton again! Clearly, bullying is the intention to hurt. I continued to put my faith in God and left all problems in Forth School and Dinton LEA with God! I couldn't stop this wave of bullying, but I could continue to be honest, reliable and ethical! If I trusted in God, I didn't need to worry about what I couldn't change! If I concentrated on being a good person and on doing the right thing, I could cope! If I stayed until I couldn't stand it any longer, I still had a job to go to, with Theresa Oak! I had never encountered such bullying when I was a pupil at faith schools; the problem was the bullying management in each school; it wasn't religion and it wasn't God! I kept praying to God, for the strength to cope and for happiness! I felt I wasn't alone and could concentrate on being ethical, moral and a good person.

I had always been happy when I went to faith schools, when I'd lived in the mining community, therefore, bullying was the problem, not faith schools! It just showed me that living in the mining community was happy; everyone knew everyone and our fathers all had to work together, to prevent danger at work! This forged a safe, happy and secure environment, which was something that couldn't be bought! I'd learned that it was safety first and prevention was better than a cure, after a mining disaster that happened before I was even born. The Memorial Gardens had a tree planted for every death and everyone knew that such a disaster must never be allowed to happen again! I had learned an important lesson about safety in the mining community and my happy memories, every day, from when I was younger, flooded back every night! I knew the problem was the way I, and others, had been treated!

Clearly, bullying is the intention to hurt! They had accomplished what they had intended to do, because I was upset! That was why I never contacted Beatrice Milton again. Her daughter rang our house, "Hi Ellie, my mam asked me to ring you. Here she is, because she wants to talk to you."

Her daughter, Susan, then gave the phone to her mother. Beatrice Milton immediately told me, " I haven't said anything to you." She'd lied again!

I replied, "I won't be contacting you again." This was because she'd threatened me, denied it and then tried to make a fool out of me! This was the pattern of mind games! I was much better off out of this form of bullying, harassment and unwanted behaviour, although I was incredibly sad and upset about this, as we'd been friends for years. For years we'd enjoyed doing our homework together and taking our dogs for walks, when we were much younger. This was an enormous upset and betrayal for me. She had lived across the road from me, when we were younger and I'd always valued her, in the past. She had now changed and was no longer the person she used to be! My heart was heavy, sad and broken by her betrayal!

However, the reality was, I felt, that she'd been tricked and manipulated by her headteacher, Percy Mullaney. I was sure her ambition would be rewarded! I had thought she was much better than that but I felt sure Percy Mullaney would be laughing at the distress he'd caused me! I didn't ever think she would be tricked by worldly values! However, I put my trust in God because I didn't have the power to deal with the lies, the bullying and the betrayal. I had no doubt Beatrice Milton was tricked by the management at her school. These people professed to believe in God, but, as I had no power on earth, I chose to leave the truth of this with God. I knew the truth; they knew the truth; God knew the truth. They might be able to fool people on earth, but they couldn't fool God; you can fool some of the people some of the time, but not all of the people all of the time.

The many comments and threats had made me feel frightened! My family was not the problem at all; the problem was the threats and comments which made me feel we were all being victimised. There was nothing wrong with my family other than the fear and misery for their safety that they'd created! How strange! This had been exactly the same for Simon Coyles, as he'd told me how he'd felt when he was in Firlane School. I could still remember Pauline Laserton making spiteful comments about single parents in the staff room, when they were not there! "Dawn doesn't have the family I have! She's just alone over Christmas, with Jane. She doesn't have anyone else. I do." On reflection, I also remembered other comments Pauline Laserton had made about other teachers, who were my friends, calling them names in the staff room, when they weren't around! Yet I had found all of them kind, friendly and supportive! Who was right? Had she been unprofessional?

On reflection, it was the management of each individual school! My family was happy and healthy and the sleepwalking of one family member over worry about spelling tests at primary school, many years ago, was long gone! All of this fuss over my family was over the primary faith school in Dinton failing to protect a family member who'd been worried about the spelling tests, every week, because the teacher refused to listen and to care, when the spellings were too difficult and bullying by pupils, in a faith secondary school in Sealand, who had been given one or two police cautions (depending on the actions of the perpetrator) for bullying/ harassment/ unwanted behaviour! It was not me who was causing this worry for a primary school pupil! What a contrast to Essingland School and Whiteland School! In Essingland School, Leanne Newton had told us all, at break, "I've received a letter from my son's primary school saying that Tim needs to revise for his weekly spelling test more!"

Kerry Marsey replied, "It's the primary schools! They're putting too much pressure on children to achieve more, so they look good!"

"That's what it is! I was very upset because Tim learns his spellings every night and can't do anymore! He's only seven!" Leanne had replied.

I hadn't thought anything of it at the time, but after Siperton School, Dinton School and Forth School, I could see the pattern of bullying by management! It would be very difficult to prove but I trusted in my own instincts, to keep myself safe! Safety first and prevention was better than a cure was something that I'd learned in the mining community! Were the faith schools using every means possible to destroy me, to defend themselves? Was this what had happened to Martin McVitie, who had committed suicide? Was this how others were driven to suicide, by bullying?

I hadn't been making comments about anyone's family at all!

My possessions were taken out of my bag, which I used for school at Forth School! My own DVD of "A Christmas Carol" was taken, even though it belonged to me and I was using it with a class. The pupils were annoyed and told me, "Mrs Lowry, we know your DVD has been taken, because when you went to get it, out of your bag, it wasn't there! We can hear the other class, next door, watching your DVD. You had it last lesson and they didn't! They'd wanted to watch it, but their teacher hadn't bought a DVD of "A Christmas Carol" but we know you bought one for us to watch! We think yours has been stolen because we know you had one and now you haven't got one, but the class next door has!" It had been taken and the teacher next door had not had a copy the previous lesson! Guess what? My DVD had been taken out of my bag, without my permission, and this teacher's class was watching this film the following lesson, even though they couldn't earlier in the week! I regarded taking something out of my bag, without my permission, as a form of theft! This happened with a number of my personal items! I knew what they were doing! They were liars and would deny it, then they would blame me! In addition to this, comments about pens kept being made near me, then a packet of school pens went missing from my desk.

I knew what they were doing! They were trying to frame me! I asked the newly qualified teacher, Lois Pickford, about the pens. She replied, "Jack Ashton, the head of department, asked me to give them to another teacher, so I did." I reported this to the deputy headteacher, who did nothing! He was nothing like the deputy headteacher at Dinton School! That was also part of the problem! It was lying, deceitful and manipulative management; it was an invisible enemy. I believed the head of department was behind it, fully supported by Angela Rivers. I had no doubt they were trying to present me as ill, because Jack Ashton had been making these types of comments to the admin staff! It was a malicious form of bullying, harassment and unwanted behaviour and I felt they were trying to frame me, to present me as mad! I wasn't!

Fortunately, my prayers saved me, along with my happy memories which came flooding back to me every night, when I went to sleep! I believed in God and I had always been happy in the mining community! The mining community hadn't been fooled by management either! In the depths of my distress, this saved me! I had lived through many years of strikes, due to industrial action, when the miners felt there was an injustice! I knew better than to be tricked by liars, deceit and manipulation! I believed in God, so I gave my worries to God, and felt protected by truth, honesty and kindness! I just had to do the right thing and to trust my own instincts!

The pattern was: identify a problem to management, management then blamed the person because they wouldn't blame themselves! It was a pattern of divide and conquer! It was the difference between heaven and hell! It was about capitalism, not socialism: they didn't care about the employees. Thank goodness for the Occupational Health employees, who weren't fooled by them either! They also knew that I thought the problem was a change of management, so they had information about me as well! I trusted the doctors, Sealand Occupational Health and Dinton Occupational Health. My GP was right: find another job; that's what all of our GPs told us! My health and happiness were more important than worldly values of money, status and worldly success!

Months later, after I'd left Forth School, my missing DVD was sent to my home, with a note saying I'd left it at school! That was another lie! This was the real problem! I was the victim of bullying, harassment and unwanted behaviour. Some of my things were returned in the post, at home, months later, but they wouldn't have admitted that they'd taken them out of my bag, would they?

Dinton Occupational Health found that other teachers had

been saying exactly the same as me! I was told by Dinton Occupational Health, "It is her," when talking about Angela Rivers, and was told, "It is them," when referring to the management of the school. I felt ever so much better because they knew the truth as well! I felt I was right to feel I shouldn't be tricked by others! I felt a simple solution was to trust my own instincts and to stay safe! I felt it was much better not to believe their lies. I felt I should believe in myself, tell the truth and do the right thing. Then, if it came to it, I could tell the truth in court. I was too afraid to tell anyone what had been discussed, in case it caused more trouble at work!

Dawn was happy at Dealey School; a former pupil of Dawn's was on the staff; he supported her and the people in school believed him. Dawn's doctor had previously told her, "You show all the symptoms of being bullied!" Dawn had stayed as long as she could stand it at Firlane School, but then left, when she couldn't stand it any longer. Percy Banks took books out of her classroom at Firlane School, while she had a large class in front of her, and laughed, referring to the books, "If you don't use them, you'll lose them." This didn't happen to Dawn at Dealey School.

This was part of a pattern; during school half term, my textbooks went missing from my classroom at Firlane School; the head of department, Roberta Oliver, took them, without asking, which caused problems for me! She told a smiling Pauline Laserton, "I can do what I want because I'm head of department," at a department meeting. How strange, because a similar thing happened at Forth School, where Angela Rivers was headteacher. Pupils' files were removed from my classroom and were lost! The head of department, Jack Ashton, merely smirked, "I was trying to help, but I don't know who's taken them, after I moved them!" How strange! How could he get away with hiding/ throwing out pupils' GCSE coursework and folders of work for so many of my classes? How could Angela Rivers ignore his actions? I knew I was being bullied by him and by her, because he threatened my whole family and then denied it! The management in these schools all seemed to follow a pattern of bullying, harassment and unwanted behaviour. I had no trust or confidence in the leadership of the school! I knew they would support the lying, deceitful and manipulative Jack Ashton!

The common problem was that each person wasn't treated the way other people would like to be treated themselves. Each person should have been treated as a professional, and treated with respect and valued, with effective Continued Professional Development. Each person should have had an environment where each person could reach their maximum potential. Distress, fear and misery plagued me, which are the symptoms of bullying; the loss of wages and the loss of pension were the consequences of the bullying for me and for my family! Distress, fear and misery plagued Dawn, which are the symptoms of bullying; the loss of wages and the loss of pension were the consequences of the bullying for her and for her family! Distress, fear and misery plagued other teachers, which are the symptoms of bullying; the loss of wages and the loss of pension were the consequences of the bullying for others and for their families! Privatisation was allowing this to happen; who was supporting this system? Why?

Chloe Crispin, who I had worked with at Siperton School, later, made the same comments the same as Beatrice Milton, "It's Percy Mullaney who's behind this process you are involved in, but no one was supposed to tell you! She's told you because you asked her so many questions! She didn't intend to tell you and I didn't either!" It was Percy Mullaney, the headteacher of Benedick School, who was behind the bullying, harassment and unwanted behaviour. Chloe Crispin, Beatrice Milton and Percy Mullaney all worked in Dinton LEA, in the same LEA where I had removed family members from a primary school, because of a road traffic accident and we were all much happier after the move! Chloe Crispin told me, "If you ever tell anyone who the person is behind all of this, the headteacher of the secondary school she works at, they'll make sure you never work again! They're protecting their friends, the faith schools. Percy Mullaney is behind it all, because he's sticking up for Ruperton School. He's defending Ruperton School (which is a faith school) against you! He's their friend! They've told him what you've done to them!" This was clearly deliberate bullying, harassment and unwanted behaviour because I had reported the bullying of a family member, by pupils from Ruperton School, to the police! The police had given police cautions to pupils who attended Ruperton School!

Chloe Crispin threatened me, by saying, "If you ever tell anyone that Percy Mullaney is behind all this, you'll never work again!" Chloe Crispin had threatened me as well! I didn't tell anyone at the time, because I was so afraid, shocked and frightened, in case

I never worked again! It was all cloak and dagger because I knew neither of them would ever admit the threats and intimidation! However, I knew that this was a part of a pattern, because Simon Coyles told me he'd been threatened by Basil Wright, then headteacher at Firlane School, who told him, "If you ever go to the newspapers about what's happened here, you'll never work again!" The pattern was: identify a problem to management, management then blamed the person because they wouldn't blame themselves!

Previously, Chloe had been a friend, but was obviously approached by someone, and then she changed! This was part of a pattern of behaviour! It was a pattern of divide and conquer! It was the difference between heaven and hell! It was a pattern of deceit and manipulation and fear and misery, the symptoms of bullying. How strange that Chloe Crispin told me, "Percy Mullaney is behind it all, because he's sticking up for Ruperton School." How strange because the acting headteacher for Ruperton School told me he was supporting the police; the police were supporting our family, and police cautions were issued to pupils from Ruperton School!

Chloe Crispin had used exactly the same words as Beatrice Milton! Chloe was another person who professed to believe in God! These people all professed to believe in God, but, as I had no power on earth, I chose to leave the truth of this with God. I knew the truth; they knew the truth; God knew the truth. They might be able to trick people on earth, but they couldn't fool God. Why weren't they supporting the victims of crime? Why weren't they supporting the police? Why weren't they doing the right thing? All I had been doing was protecting my family, by following the advice of the headteacher and the head of year at the family member's new school! Child protection is an issue for everyone! If I hadn't done this, they would've blamed me for that as well!

I hadn't been making comments about anyone's family at all!

Angela Rivers: evidence of her deceit and manipulation had been found by Dinton Occupational Health! Angela Rivers was the headteacher and had asked me, "Can you sign this piece of paper please?"

I thought it was strange but as she was the headteacher and I was afraid of her, I signed it!

Dinton Occupational Health asked me, "Is this your signature and do you agree with what Angela Rivers has written on this piece of paper?"

"It is my signature but all I did was to sign a blank sheet of paper! There was no writing on it when I signed it!" As I read through it, I answered, "I don't agree with a single thing she's written! It's lies!"

She'd later written on the paper, which made it look as though I'd signed what she'd written! I had never seen it before! Dinton Occupational Health told me, "Others have reported exactly the same problems as you, so we know she's the problem, not you!"

The pattern was: identify a problem to management, management then blamed the person because they wouldn't blame themselves! It was a pattern of divide and conquer! It was the difference between heaven and hell! It was a pattern of deceit and manipulation and fear and misery, the symptoms of bullying. The common problem was that each person was not treated the way other people would like to be treated themselves. Each person should have been treated as a professional and treated with respect and valued, with effective Continued Professional Development; each person should've had an environment where each person could reach their maximum potential.

I felt if I hadn't left, I would have been driven to suicide: the general advice of fight or flight saved me and my mental health. Walking away from bullying was easier than staying to be bullied, when I had no power to prove the bullying in court! All I was doing was going to work; I didn't need the stress of a court case! Would they have cared if they'd driven me to suicide? Is this what had happened to Martin McVitie?

I left and saved myself! The common advice to walk away from bullying saved my life! My GP's advice to find another job had saved my life! Sealand and Dinton Occupational Health had both saved my mental health! I agreed with the Senior Crown Prosecutor who told the court, "Angela Rivers is deceitful, manipulative and a liar!" I was relieved when she was sent to jail for eight years! The issue was truth and lies! The issue was appearance and reality. The issue was bullying and harassment. The solution was to trust my own instincts and not to be fooled by anyone else! Stay safe, stay alive; live to see another day! The values of the mining community of safety first and prevention is better than a cure had saved my life and my mental health! All I had to do was to walk away and find another job! I might have lost the battle but I won the war! I was alive, to tell the truth!

I hadn't been making comments about anyone's family at all!

I was always happy when I was younger, so someone or something had caused this distress! I also knew that they knew what they'd done to upset me and others, but they would never admit it all! It was clear now that the problem was proving what they'd done in court; they would've known that and would've known that most people don't go to work for such conflict! I didn't follow that route, simply because I wanted to protect my family from further distress. My children were in full-time education, with crucial examinations in front of them, and they didn't need the distress. I prayed to God for the strength to cope, and he filled me with light.

I just needed to be an honest and truthful person; worldly values were not as important as being honest and truthful! Sealand Occupational Health was right when they clarified the issues of loss of wages and loss of pension. Dinton Occupational Health had told me I'd already won against Firlane School, with Whiteland School. They clarified that I'd been threatened by two people; the two people were Jack Ashton and Beatrice Miller! I'd forgotten to mention the threats by Chloe Crispin to Dinton Occupational Health. Dinton Occupational Health told me that other teachers had had the same problem with Angela Rivers. Dinton Occupational Health told me, "It is them!" My GP, Sealand Occupational Health and Dinton Occupational Health had all saved my mental health, as did Dawn, as they all knew the truth!

Someone else knew the truth too! I wasn't alone with this! It was poetic justice when Angela Rivers was sentenced to jail! The way we, and many others, had been treated had really been the makings of a court case, but no one really wanted the conflict with employers! The Crown Prosecution Service clearly showed Angela Rivers was a liar, a manipulator and a criminal, in court! The Crown Prosecution Service had not been frightened of Angela Rivers! The judge had not been frightened either! It was poetic justice! Although she had had a meteoric rise, reality came crashing down and smashed her dreams! Did she really think she'd get away with the continued abuse, by lying? Did she really think she'd get away with contempt of court? Did she really think everyone would be fooled by her deceit and manipulation?

I felt relieved and vindicated when she was later sentenced to jail for eight years. The police would have had access to all information associated with her, so the irony of it was, she had been unexpectedly caught out! She'd thought she was invincible, because power corrupts, and she was the headteacher. I was too frightened to tell anyone at the time! At the time, I'd felt absolutely terrified.

The truth had been that they wanted to employ newly qualified teachers to save money! They didn't want to pay higher wages to experienced and expensive teachers! They'd obviously employed me for my expertise, ideas and resources but once they had the resources I'd created, using my expertise, they could use them again; I'd also shared my best practice, so they didn't need me! Walking away from bullying is much better than being bullied! Concentrating on being happy and healthy is far better than being bullied as well! Forth School was in Dinton LEA, the same LEA where a primary school had left a lot to be desired with a family member, who had been sleep walking over weekly spelling tests! They didn't have anything to say to our solicitor at all, when we were victims of a road traffic accident! How ironic that all of this happened near the financial crash of 2008! How could they live with themselves for what they'd done? Had they no consciences as they put worldly values, and ambition, before people?

Eight years in jail was a long time for Angela Rivers to reflect on her actions; all I had to do was to move forward, enjoy every day and protect my family.

Sandra Summers, a friend I had met doing supply told me, "I'm heartbroken! I'm an experienced teacher, at the top of my payscale, and every interview I go to the post is given to an NQT. If an experienced teacher does get the job, we are all forced out of the post, as they make our lives a misery, so we can't work there any longer. If I do work in a school for over 12 weeks, and they do end up paying me to scale, it's only for a few weeks because they then employ an NQT." Sandra was younger than me and was married, with a young family. She had long, blonde, curly hair and wore glasses. She was very friendly, honest and totally trustworthy.

"I find the same. Everyone I know, who does supply, says the same thing! Christine Hall, who is also at the top of her payscale, has accepted a much lower payscale, to find work."

"It's disgraceful! Agencies pay us less than our payscale and if we want to work in the same school, many experienced teachers have to accept a lower pay scale, even if they're paid by the school, or they'll give the job to NQTs."

"It's terrible! When I first did supply, there wasn't this problem! I was always paid according to my payscale. This problem is only happening in England, not in Scotland, Wales and Northern Ireland."

"It's exploitation of the workforce!"

"It is! It must be terrible for people who earn the minimum wage; no wonder there's so much poverty in England now. I never saw such homelessness when I was little! Homeless, dirty and starving people are now a common sight in 21st century England, but I never saw such sights when I was young."

"They don't care! So long as the rich get richer, they don't care about the homeless, the starving and the destitute."

"If we keep concentrating on being good people and aren't tricked by worldly values, we can cope. We just have to appreciate all the good things we do have in life. You can't buy a family."

"No, you can't! I'm just annoyed at the injustice of it all!"

"We can try to change things but we need to protect our health first."

"I feel much better now; you make it all sound simple."

"That's what friends are for!"

The internet was full of stories on the news, and in the newspapers, and they all told the same story! Also, the many studies and reports on the internet showed how many teachers had left the profession because of stress. Ceiling News had many examples of teachers suffering from stress, caused by bullying headteachers and senior leaders in school! Ceiling News reported, "There is a problem about what employees say about former employers, which is causing anxiety and depression. As a result of this problem, many people, mainly teachers, are unable to find another job, and this had led to many suicides!" Suicides were mentioned briefly, but the teaching profession was mentioned and no other occupation! Clearly, it was a pattern of management. The problem was to save people's mental health! It was appearance and reality. They appeared successful by worldly values but they were morally corrupt, driving employees to mental illness, depression and suicide!

After I left Forth School, I went back to work for my old

agency and Theresa Oak. When I taught at Whickton School, I found Laura Nelson was head of department! Whickton School was a local school. I had worked with Laura at Essingland School. Laura came up to me and told me, "I'd wanted it to be you, when I saw your name on the list! I asked for you and was lucky to get you before another school did!"

"I'm really pleased to work with you again Laura, as I was always happy working with you at Essingland School and there weren't ever any problems!"

"You're just what this department needs."

"It's my pleasure to work here."

Laura was now married with a stepdaughter. Laura was tall and well built, with long, blonde, curly hair and was really pleased to see me! What a pleasure it was to work with a previous colleague!

However, I couldn't believe what another teacher told me! Malcolm Newson had been a student teacher at Southland School and told me a terrible story about Sheila Rothberry! He was always charming, friendly and trustworthy. Malcolm was tall and slim, with short brown hair and extremely handsome. I couldn't believe it when he told me, "Sheila Rothberry was beaten up in a classroom and no one went to help her!" Sheila Rothbury was about my age, short and extremely well built, with short, light brown, curly hair.

"I know Sheila! She's lovely and she's a pleasure to work with! How could that happen in a school?"

"Sheila had reported problems with a number of disruptive pupils in the class but felt unsupported by management! One day she went into the classroom and told a pupil to move seats. The pupil refused and asked, "What're you going to do about it?" As the girl got up out of her seat, Sheila thought she was going to move. The girl approached Sheila and thumped her, hard, in the face! Sheila told her to sit down but the whole class was then out of control and cheered the disruptive pupil on! She continued to thump Sheila, as hard as she could, and the whole class was shouting, cheering and laughing, saying things like, "Let her have it! … Give her one from me!" Everyone must have been able to hear the noise but no one went to stop it. Sheila was left with two black eyes and bruises all over her body, where she had been hit and kicked on the floor."

"That's absolutely disgraceful! I bet she never went back,

after that!"

"No, she didn't! The school tried to blame her, by asking, "Why did it happen to you? This hasn't happened to anyone else in the school?"

"Well, I had a lucky escape when I left that school, didn't I? I worked there very briefly, after Siperton School, before I worked at Dinton School. How awful! That shouldn't happen to anyone!"

"Everyone else just got on with their jobs, afraid of being dragged into trouble and conflict."

"How awful! I bet people felt afraid!"

When I was in a lesson at Whickton School, a year 8 pupil, Johnny Sykes told me, "Mrs Lowry, I'm not very good at writing things down but I can answer questions."

"Can you carry heavy books?"

"Yes!"

"Well, I once hurt my arm carrying heavy books, so I can help you with writing but I might appreciate it if you sometimes offer to help me to carry books."

"I'm good at carrying heavy books! I'll help you."

"Thank you because that would be a good help to me and then I can help you with writing."

"We can help each other!"

"Of course we can!"

After that, Johnny always helped me to carry any exercise books or text books and he was always a pleasure to teach. However, in the tutor group I shared with another teacher, Chris Booth asked me, "Have you heard about Johnny Sykes?"

"Why? He's in my year 8 class. I haven't seen him today."

"At morning break today, he hit Jack Ainsley!"

"The assistant headteacher?"

"Yes! How do you find Johnny?"

"He's a pleasure to teach."

"That can't be right! He's one of the biggest trouble makers in the school! Jack only got the job because he gets on well with the kids."

"What happened?"

"Jack told him to move but Johnny refused so he thumped Jack! He was excluded immediately!"

The headteacher, Martin O'Neary, in Whickton School

always spoke to me and was always friendly. I was happy every day in the school and was totally supported by Laura, the senior management and the headteacher! Every day was a pleasure to go to work! Martin stopped me in the corridor one day, "Have you seen our advertisement, in the newspapers? We're advertising for our own supply teachers and we would like you to apply for a post in our school."

"I did see the advertisement in the newspaper, but wanted to see if I was happy in the school before I applied. I am and I love working here."

"That's why we want you to apply. You'll also be paid more by the school than through an agency."

I did and I was successful at the interview! I thought my dreams had come true! However, would I be paid to my payscale? I knew I would be paid much more than I was from the agencies, but the advert did not show it would pay to a teacher's full pay scale, but I was paid to payscale years ago, when I did supply, in every school!

Unfortunately, the teaching agency complained and gave the school a large bill! Theresa told me, "We put you in that school, so you shouldn't have applied to work in the school!"

"I told you I wanted to work in schools and would apply to work in schools."

"The school should not have asked you to apply."

"I did see the advertisement in the paper, before I went to work in the school."

"If you ever do anything like this again, you'll never work for us again."

I decided to apply for other agencies and the school backed up my story, when I was truthful at the interviews! "We would never stop a teacher from applying for a permanent post in any school we placed them in," Stephen Potts, the director of my new agency, told me.

The school promised to give me an excellent reference for a post in any school! Over the summer holidays, I received the equivalent of one month's wages, without paying tax or national insurance; the money was paid straight into my bank account, from Sealand LEA (Local Education Authority), without working for it! I was sad to leave Whickton School. I hadn't done anything wrong at all and I'd been very happy there! I had told Theresa Oak, at the agency, that I was looking for a permanent post and I had actually seen the advertisement for this school in the newspaper! I had applied and I went to the interview! I had found out the harsh, brutal and ruthless reality of earning a living! I was lucky to have the support of Whickton School!

Ruthlessness wasn't the only employer who could have been kinder to employees, was he? There were also many Martin McVities in the world.

10. Who Had the Power to Stop Them?

Later, while doing supply teaching, still in Sealand LEA, HMSI (Her Majesty's School Inspectors), while I was at Granterland School, were totally supportive. The Chief Inspector told me, "You are doing the same job as us, and you are saying what you think of the schools as well! You are judging schools yourself!" He was certainly right there! As so many schools were making comments near me, I now reported any problems to my teaching union and this worked! Granterland School was also in Sealand LEA and had previously been a private school! It had to change into a state school, due to a lack of funding! It still had its beautiful buildings, which were far superior to the state school buildings! It still had its impressive football fields, playing fields and recreational fields. It still had the aura of a private school.

As well as HMSI, I was praised by the vice principal, Alan Dunn, "Thank you very much for all of the excellent work you've done for us, while HMSI have been in the school!"

The Chief HMI from HMSI, inspecting that school told me, "We are the same team inspecting all of the schools in the area. We are the same team that inspected Batheland School, where you were last week. If we did this to schools, what we have done to you, inspecting them within a couple of weeks, there would be an uproar." This HMSI had seen me twice, in two schools within two weeks, and the Chief HMI was extremely clear that schools would complain if schools were inspected by HMSI within two weeks, without any notice, in this way!

The lead inspector was totally supportive, and told me, "This team is now going back into every school you have ever left, to see the real reason why you left. We are the people who know you and we will go to every single school you've been in, to see the real reason why you've left!"

Thank goodness for this HMSI team and this lead inspector! I couldn't believe his kindness, support and friendliness! Granterland School was in Sealand LEA, so I felt much better, because someone else knew the truth too! I felt this team would have known that the first time I was in a school during an HMSI inspection in Sealand LEA, was when I worked in Firlane School, where the HMSI told me I was "best practice" as a teacher; in the second inspection they told me I was the "type of teacher the government wants to know is valued by the government". HMSI knew the truth! HMSI had seen me in two schools within the last two weeks, and they had the power to deal with this. This Chief HMI from HMSI knew the truth! I felt relieved, happy and safe! I was not the only one who knew the truth! HMSI did too!

After this, most of the schools which had been making comments about me and near me, to upset me, and had been unsupportive with disruptive pupils, went into special measures: Firlane School, Forth School, Undercastle City School, Queensmeadow School and Southland School. The headteacher (Derrick Tusk) had moved from Firlane School, Sealand LEA, to another school in Dinton LEA, but he lost his post at this next school, after HMSI inspected this particular school. When I went to the school, on supply, the staff were incredibly supportive and made comments of, "It was him. He's not here now but you are." Justice had been served. Revenge is a dish best served cold! I had been vindicated; I could sleep easily; God knew the truth and so did HMSI!

Angela Rivers was also severely criticised as a headteacher, after the HMSI inspector was so kind to me. HMSI told me, "This team is now going back into every school you have ever left, to see the real reason why you left." I felt relieved! This HMSI team knew the truth too! Firlane School later went into special measures and was closed. It was then taken over by new management, and the name of the school was changed! Forth School also went into special measures; Undercastle City School also went into special measures as well. Turnerlane School also went into special measures (comments were later made when I went there on supply as well!) Southland School was closed altogether! Southland School had been closed by HMSI, who agreed with me about the school, and no one else would take the school over because it had been so dreadful!

Other people now knew the truth too! Thank goodness for that! I was no longer alone with the knowledge of how I had been treated!

The headteacher, Angela Rivers had been sentenced to jail for eight years in prison! The Crown Prosecution Service told the court, "Angela Rivers is a liar, manipulative and deceitful!" The Crown Prosecution Service knew the truth too! In essence, they agreed with me and with Dinton Occupational Health Service. Most people who had regarded her as a liar, untrustworthy and manipulative were proved right. I had given her the benefit of the doubt and later found out for myself, to my cost, that Angela Rivers was a liar, deceitful and manipulative. I had treated her in the way I would like to be treated, but she certainly didn't treat me in the way she would like to be treated. I was incredibly sad to find this truth out! I had hoped for the best with her, but found the worst was true! However, the police proved she was a liar, untrustworthy and manipulative, in court. When Angela Rivers went to jail it was poetic justice! She went to jail, but she thought she could get away with it all, but she didn't! Poetic justice! I totally agreed with the Crown Prosecution Service, but I had given her every chance to redeem herself, but she had chosen power, ambition and worldly values! How empty were these values when she was in jail?

At Dinton School, the headteacher (from when I worked at the school) was no longer at this school and left, after HMSI had spoken to me. The deputy headteacher, Rob Brewer, sent me a message through an agency. Stephen Potts told me, "Dinton School would be very happy to welcome you back! The problem when you were in the school was the headteacher and the new headteacher and deputy headteacher both know you and would welcome you back to the school, on a long-term contract, with a high wage. They want you and aren't bothered about how much they pay to have you back."

How lovely! I greatly appreciated this, but I was then doing supply, so the many bullying, harassing and unwanted comments which were made continuously in schools, were more manageable. I knew I couldn't cope with the build-up of the bullying, harassing and unwanted comments, which was why I did daily supply. I replied, "Thank you very much! I would have gone back straight away, as the new headteacher and the deputy head are both lovely and a pleasure to work with. Unfortunately, I now feel too old and too tired to work in schools on a long-term basis, which is now why I do day to day supply; day to day supply also allows me flexibility with my family. I am very grateful for their offer."

I had learned that my health and safety were more important than worldly values of status, money and wealth. I had a change of family circumstances, so supply suited my new family circumstances; I also wondered if I would really end up with the wage I really should have had, because I was an awfully expensive teacher, as I was at the top of the teaching pay scale!

Money had been the real problem behind all of this! However, if I had been younger, and had the family circumstances I had previously had, I would've loved to have gone back, if I could have been sure that the comments, which were a form of bullying, harassment and unwanted behaviour, would not continue. Laura Holmes was a friend, a colleague and a pleasure to work with, so was the deputy headteacher. The new headteacher had also been a pleasure to work with, so I totally agreed the real problem had been the headteacher, who had now left! I would've been happy to go back on a day to day supply basis first, to check how I was being treated at first, and then to build up, to see if I would be happy. Unfortunately, they really needed someone there immediately, on a long-term basis. I was thrilled that the deputy headteacher had been so kind as to ask me back to the school, because I really did value him, the new headteacher and the new head of department!

I really had valued the staff who were now in charge of Dinton School, when I had worked there! I really did value them then and now! However, I was growing older and was happier doing supply teaching, around my family, rather than working on a full-time basis.

"What is the knock-on effect on the pupils who didn't get their expected GCSE results, because good schools and "best practice" staff were destroyed by ruthless, selfish ambition? What is the knock-on effect on the pupils who didn't get the expected GCSE results, because expensive, experienced staff were replaced by newly qualified teachers? What is the knock-on effect on the staff who were destroyed by ruthless, selfish ambition?" Dawn asked.

"I often wonder about this as well".

Years later, I found the 2000 HMSI report for Firlane School, which proved everything about my success before the change in management! I also found the 2009 HMSI report for Forth School and I also found the 2014 HMSI report for Forth School, when Angela Rivers was in jail, and the school was placed in special measures! This confirmed everything that I'd already known! The HMSI reports at Forth School confirmed what I had thought: there were serious weaknesses with management, and they had supported middle management when they shouldn't have! That is what had happened to me! I knew middle management had made sure they were doing what the headteacher had told them to do! The HMSI Report also highlighted the fact that I had been a good appointment for the school as I had "complimentary expertise"!

I had been right all along! The people who had regarded Angela Rivers as a liar, untrustworthy and manipulative were right; I had given her the benefit of the doubt, and had found out the hard way, that she was a bully, a liar and deceitful. I had treated her in the way I would like to be treated, but she certainly hadn't treated me in the way she would like to be treated. The Senior Crown Prosecutor had proved she was a liar, untrustworthy and manipulative, in court. I had learned the truth the hard way, but, even so, she had hurt others far more than she had hurt me! She had totally destroyed lives, in a way that even I hadn't imagined! She was far worse to others than she had been to me! I found the crimes she was convicted of as disgraceful, disgusting and criminal! I had no doubt it was all true!

I then remembered the personal stories that she had told about herself at Firlane School, that others hadn't believed when I'd given her the benefit of the doubt! There was no doubt now, about the type of person Angela Rivers really was! I'd found out the hard way, for myself, that she really was a liar, deceitful and manipulative! Dawn had been proved correct! Mary had been proved correct! Pauline had been proved correct! Andrea had been proved correct! Janette had been proved correct! The Crown Prosecution Service proved Angela Rivers to be a lying, deceitful and manipulative character in court! The Crown Prosecution Service was not tricked by Angela Rivers! The Crown Prosecution Service did not believe Angela Rivers' lies! The Crown Prosecution Service believed in itself; the Crown Prosecution Service told the truth; the Crown Prosecution Service did the right thing. The Crown Prosecution Service told the truth in court. Justice had been served.

All of our group had been targeted in the same way, so we were prevented from moving forward! It was a pattern of divide and conquer! It was the difference between heaven and hell! We, individually, felt sad, persecuted and disillusioned! None of us would ever treat anyone the way we'd been treated; the perpetrators involved in this wouldn't like to be treated like this either.

The consequences of leaving Forth School were the social and emotional consequences of bullying at work and leaving a well-paid job. I then did supply again, and was praised by Whickton School who asked me to apply for a permanent supply position which was advertised, but Theresa Oak, the senior manager of the agency I was with, was furious! This meant I left Theresa Oak and Whickton School, to avoid an industrial dispute! I was too frightened to tell anyone! Whickton School did tell the truth when others asked, and did support me, so I could continue to teach. Sealand LEA later sent me an unexpected sum of money, which was extremely kind of them.

In schools, it really had been about ethos: the schools that I had strongly agreed with had been the best schools in the country, such as Whiteland School, Heartland School and Emmerland School. I knew it was really about the ethos and expectations of these schools too. How ironic! HMSI agreed with me about these schools too! Who would have thought it?

11. The Destruction

Had it been a pattern of management over the years?

Many years ago, my family members knew the power of employers! Lies were told by management; the Coal Board had promised to pay Graham Lumsden; the work was done but the employer refused to pay! When this young man, Graham Lumsden, told them, "I haven't been paid the money you promised but I've done everything you asked me to do!"

The management replied, "We've got the work done now so we're not going to pay you!"

This resulted in an argument; tempers were lost; the manager refused to pay the money. Graham hit the manager; Graham lost his job! Everyone in Graham's family was shocked, because they knew Graham shouldn't have hit anyone, but they also knew the manager had refused to pay him, even though he'd agreed to. They knew it would not have happened if the manager had just paid him, as agreed. They all knew it meant serious consequences.

Graham came from a large family of five boys; they all had a similar build; they were all well over six foot, broad and strong! They all worked at the same mine ("the pit").

However, many years ago, management didn't just take revenge on an individual! The whole family lost their jobs, even uncles! At the time, Graham was lucky to get another job, and so was his family! Graham and his whole family (any relation) were blacklisted, this included every member of his family, including uncles! This family was lucky, because each family member received a note, pushed under their door, that there was a job for each family member, but it was miles away! Every family member had to move miles away for work! Terry, one of the young cousins, no longer went to school with the Earl of Perth! All cousins had to move away and were forced to change schools too, all because an employer had promised money to someone, then refused to pay it!

Years later, the youngest son, Jim, committed suicide, because of the bullying management at the family's next place of work, at this particular branch of the Coal Board! Jim had been a witness to an accident at work, so the management threatened him with the loss of his job, if he said anything about this accident. This had not been Jim's fault; the accident had been caused by a fault, with a machine, at work. He was frightened to go to work; he had no power against this management; he was frightened he'd lose his job! His manager had threatened him: it would not just be his job that would be lost, but the jobs of all his relatives. Jim and his brother had the same build as his father, Graham; they were both well over six foot, broad and strong! His sister, Martha, was also tall and strong; she was acknowledged by everyone to be the prettiest girl in Essingland! Jim was a well-loved brother, son and uncle! He had two nephews and a niece, he loved and doted on them all, as well as a safe, secure family.

Jim knew his father was an old man now and he'd never be able to keep the house he lived in! He felt frightened and intimidated, because he knew the power of management, and it would not just be his job that was lost, but the jobs of all his relatives! Jim hadn't done anything wrong at all! He just happened to be there, as a witness, when a machine caught another man's arm! Jim had tried to stop the machine but had been unable to. Jim heard his friend's screams but had had to run for help, to stop the machine.

Jim's family knew he had been driven to suicide, and so did others, but many were too afraid to say anything, in case they lost their jobs too! At the inquest, the family knew that bullying management had been behind it all, but management wasn't named on his death certificate! They made Jim sign pieces of paper: if he didn't sign, he couldn't work! His family and friends were afraid of dying in poverty and disgrace, and were also afraid of losing their jobs! The reality was power, money and appearance! The management had the power and the money and appeared respectable but didn't admit to the threats, bullying and intimidation at work!

How terrible that Jim, a young man, lost his life over something that wasn't his fault. The management tried to blame Jim!

They alleged, "He committed suicide because he didn't have friends."

Jim's brother, Terence, told the inquest, "I was always Jim's friend, throughout life, and I would never have abandoned him." The management had made false allegations, to try to defend themselves and to attack Jim! What a disgrace, but I could see the pattern of lies, deceit and manipulation! It was about appearance and reality. They appeared respectable, but the truth was that they were liars and manipulative.

At a similar time, a similar thing had happened to Dawn's father, at The Star Cokeworks, near Sealand. A man's arm was trapped in a belt and Dawn's father was the first on the scene, so he cut the belt, to save the man's arm. The management tried to criticise him for cutting the belt! Dawn's father stood up to the management and told them, "A man's arm can't be replaced, but a machine can be replaced. I am prepared to say this in court." Needless to say, Dawn's father lost his job shortly afterwards. Luckily, he found another post in a glove factory, shortly afterwards.

Dawn's father was eventually made redundant, through no fault of his own. The Unemployment Benefit Office made a bureaucratic mistake in calculating his money. One week he was only given half a crown (two shillings and sixpence) in old money, to feed a family of five for a week. He threw the money back at them and it hit the wall, behind the assistant at the counter, saying, "We'd rather starve." Later, a senior officer came to his house to resolve the problem.

Years later, Jim's nephew, Ben, worked in one of the offices for the Coal Board. The manager approached the window, banged on it loudly and shouted at Ben! The manager had the area manager with him. The manager was totally shocked when the area manager spoke to Ben, saying, "Hello Ben. How's your dad?"

Ben replied, "He's fine, Mr Connor."

Mr Connor replied, "You don't need to call me Mr Connor, just because we're at work! Dave will do!" Showing it's not what you know but who you know, the manager was then much more polite to Ben, and he never shouted at him at work again, and he never banged on the window at him again either!

As Ben knew Dave Connor, he knew many important pieces of information that the general public never found out! In 1971, Ben was told that the local coal mines (the "pits") would be closed in 1993; the local "pits" were Essingland and Horton.

At Essingland coal mine (the "pit") someone kept writing poems, about the destruction of the mining industry, which could easily be seen by management! The manager was furious and told everyone, "Keep a lookout for whoever's writing these poems; when I find him, he'll be sacked." Although some people knew who'd been writing the poems, no one told the manager!

The strike of 1984-1985 was to save jobs.

The miners were on strike for a year, to try to save their jobs; because there hadn't been a ballot, some of the miners in some areas didn't go on strike. This caused the destruction of the mining industry. At the end of the strike the miners went back to work, without any guarantee that their jobs would be saved.

They destroyed the mining communities!

The first poem was:

From coal's white heat the cannon came.
Napoleon's defeat was Britain's gain.
We were needed then.

While on Flanders' Field they fell,
'Midst mud and gore and shot and shell,
Beneath Britain's vales so green,
They gave their lives, in some dark coal seam.
We were needed then.

Now Coal was King, in 39,
And helped build the ships of the navy.
Our boys, on foreign fields, did fall,
To save this world, for one and all.
We were needed then.

So here we are in '93.
What is there left for you and me?
Our glory's gone, into History's past,
But we fought for jobs, to the last.
But a final shot came from their side,

Which caused my people's genocide?
They don't need us now.

The second poem was:

The white hare was seen on the village green,
What omen of doom had been foreseen?

Down at the colliery,
Pulley wheels are still,
Cold winds blow o'er Beaton Hill.
They have taken our jobs.

With foreign coal,
They put the workforce on the dole.
And now they've bought,
The miners' souls!

(Obviously, no one told anyone who had written the poems, so that person did not lose his/ her job! This was done to protect not only the person, but this person's family!)

The mine at Horton was closed. My brother, Oliver Mitchell, who had worked there, transferred to Essingland coal mine. He worked with Robert Hall, his friend from when he was younger, who had lived across the road from us, at Essingland. My brother Oliver was very popular and had a pleasant word for everyone! He'd lived at Essingland all of his life, so knew everyone when he worked at Essingland mine.

The government destroyed the jobs in the mining communities!

Our Uncle Oliver had been the first soldier to die from Essingland, during the second world war. Then, the message to the country had been "Your country needs you!" Oliver's Uncle Oliver was KIA WW2, Western Desert Battalion, 3rd/ 4th September, 1942. The Royal West Kent Regiment had been transferred from the Devonshire Regiment. 750 plus were killed, wounded or missing, out of the 2,000, who took part in a night attack, which the Germans knew was going to happen. Our Uncle James was a sergeant in the RAF.

What had happened? What happened to the new world,

which was going to create a land for heroes, after two world wars?

There was mass unemployment in the 1980s! Why was that? What had happened? Why were so many unemployed?

The Steel Works, the Coal Board and other industries as well, including the Cokeworks, all complained about management. Ben had worked in an office for the Coal Board, and he took redundancy at 48. Having had polio as a baby, Ben never worked again; Oliver, never worked again, age 38. It was a pattern of divide and conquer! It was the difference between heaven and hell! It was about capitalism, not socialism: they didn't care about the employees. It was about capitalism: more profit, less costs, so people were afraid to lose their jobs, their food and their homes, so they dared not go on strike! Also, the fear of losing jobs happened in other industries too! In newspapers and on the news: one in three doctors were suffering from stress or feeling undervalued.

However, at the time, the coal mines (the "pits") were closed unnecessarily, and many years later they didn't deny the government had really closed the pits because of the years of strikes at the pits, across the country, for years! The pits were not uneconomical; they were not making a loss; they were not making a profit. Why had they stopped making a profit? Why did the employers offer overtime every weekend, with high bonuses? Why did they destroy all of the surrounding industries, which made money when the miners spent their wages? Why did they cause destruction and poverty in the mining communities? Was it really a civil war?

The closure of the coal mines (the "pits") hadn't been because they were uneconomical! Years later, the propaganda bragged, "We know how to deal with the unions! We stopped the strikes and industrial action!" No one had admitted that at the time. It had all been done deliberately because the pits were not making a loss. They deliberately gave the miners lots of overtime, with big bonuses, then announced the pits were not making a profit! The pits were closed, jobs were lost, lives were destroyed and communities perished. They paid the police a fortune and paid them overtime! Dawn's husband (now ex-husband) earned a fortune, working as a policeman! How could they justify this now, when, at the time, they claimed they closed the pits because they were uneconomical?

The local coal mines ("the pits") were closed in 1993, including Essingland. Horton had been closed years earlier. It really had been planned years earlier, as Ben knew, because his father was friends with Dave Connor!

Even worse, they destroyed happy, supportive mining communities and the shops and businesses that relied on the trade from the miners were destroyed too. This had all been done deliberately. Cheap coal was imported from abroad. The miners were initially only going to receive small redundancies, but some older members of the government would not allow this and insisted on higher redundancy packages for the miners. However, this money came from the Mineworkers' Pension Scheme.

To add insult to injury, they brought people from the probation service, ex- convicts, into the mining communities, so many mining families moved away, because the happy community life was destroyed. I never saw a policeman when I was younger in a mining community, because people knew each other, so no one could "get away" with anything! Everyone's father worked at the "pit", so it was safe. Everyone was expected to help others, because of the element of danger, of working in a mine. The government destroyed this! Years later, it was the same story across the country. Jobs were lost, communities were destroyed, and a criminal element had been brought in! There was an unprecedented rise in the number of homeless people! Yet, the truth was, it had all been planned in 1971! They didn't admit that, did they? Ben knew the truth because his father had been friends with Dave Connor!

Years later, Clive Baker, a young teacher at Heartland School, told me, "I was in Hatton School before I came here and the problem in the school now is the number of children in school waiting for their next heroin fix!"

"I worked in that school years ago, and that problem hadn't been there then."

"It's the same story everywhere, in the mining communities now!"

"At Essingland, many houses that had previously belonged to the mining community were destroyed or burnt, by the criminal elements that had been brought into the area by the Probation Service. An old mining building, which was being renovated, was also destroyed. Children put concrete through the new roof, and the police found the children responsible! It had stood for over 100 years, without any criminal damage, until they destroyed the mining community and brought ex- convicts into the area. In a neighbouring area, criminals broke into the house of an elderly man, living alone, to rob him! Neighbours heard his screams, alerted the police and shouted a message to the man, as he screamed in pain and agony, as they broke his bones! Sharon, his neighbour, had shouted, "Ted! The police are on their way! I heard you! I've rang the police. I telephoned 999." Immediately, the thugs ran out of the back door!

"As a result of cutbacks, the police didn't arrive for 20 minutes! Sharon's quick thinking saved the elderly man's life! All that was really outside of the house were the neighbours, two concerned pensioners, both with health problems."

"That's disgraceful, but that's what's happening in all of the ex-mining communities; no wonder everyone's moved away!"

"This didn't happen years ago."

"Of course not! They've destroyed the safety of the mining communities! By closing the pits, the government has destroyed the safety of the mining communities! By bringing the ex-convicts into the mining communities, the Probation Service has destroyed the safety of the mining communities! By attacking the ex-miner, the thugs destroyed the safety of the mining communities!"

"At least we both know the truth and can see the pattern!"

"They've made these schools a nightmare to work in as well!"

"When I went to school, everyone was well-behaved because no one would have allowed any bad behaviour then!"

"They've destroyed the good behaviour in the mining areas, by bringing the criminal element in."

"No wonder everyone's moved away."

My husband, Paul Lowry did find other employment. However, Paul retired from this second job when they gave him more work for less money; after he'd been treated like this, he couldn't face working again. This became a common pattern, so it was a pattern of management! Alex came in from work, all of the time, saying people were leaving his industry constantly! When we met his colleagues at the shops, they all said the same, "They make us work ten hours a day, without proper breaks, give us too much work, cause too much stress and don't share the work out fairly. No wonder everyone leaves, because they're worn out and can't stand going to work anymore!"

Also, it was the same for many senior police officers! Gary Vaughan, a decent, hardworking, polite detective inspector told Paul, "I was forced out of my job, which I was very happy in, by the management! I took my pension early and left!" He'd always been a kind, friendly and helpful person; amazing how the same thing had happened to him too! Gary Vaughan was originally from the mining community too. These employers made Ruthlessness look like a saint. There are many Martin McVities in the world. Have they watched the news on TV? Do they know many people really do commit suicide because of the way they've been treated by management?

Many never worked again! It led to dreadful social and emotional consequences for many. There was widespread homelessness and poverty! What a contrast to the strong, happy mining communities, who supported each other through thick and thin. It was a time when people knew their neighbours. It was a time when shop workers knew the community. It was a time when all household doors were left open, if you went to the shops, up the street. All of this was destroyed. The government destroyed the jobs. The government destroyed the communities. The government destroyed a way of life! They created homelessness. By closing the pits, the government created poverty. By closing the pits and bringing ex-convicts into the mining communities, the government had created crime in the mining communities. Homelessness, poverty and crime hadn't been in the mining communities before. Then, the government blamed everyone but themselves! Why didn't they have jobs? Why were they on unemployment benefit? Why were they scroungers?

This pattern of management led to increased homelessness across the country. Who cared? What chance did they have? What could the poor and less fortunate do? Life and daily living were becoming harder and more difficult for many, by the day. The rich became richer and the poor became poorer. The inequality and unfairness were becoming more acute. Some people had luxurious lives, while others didn't have enough money to live on, and they had much less status than others. Compared to many others, we were lucky, but we were still upset. How much more must others have been upset? How much more must others have suffered? How much more pain was ignored? Many must have been devastated, lonely and sad, beyond belief.

The unfairness and inequality in society was acute. It was everywhere, right across the country, in every town, city and village. The homeless were everywhere, something I had never seen before! Dawn had never seen anything like this before either. My family had never seen anything like it before either! No one cared! Pupils at school regarded homelessness as normal! The problem was the distribution of wealth, in one of the richest countries in the world; the plight of many was ignored and the people who were in distress were blamed! They denied the UN report and recommendations! How could they do this? How could they deny the food banks? How could they deny the homeless? How could they ignore the inequality? It was appearance and reality. They appeared successful by worldly values but they were morally corrupt. My father had been right: "The rich get richer, and the poor get poorer."

There were also social and emotional consequences of bullying at work and not having a well-paid job.

"The Talk Shop" programme showed the level of crime in a once peaceful, happy mining community: the pattern was drugs, theft and assault! The light of Essingland Community had certainly been destroyed! What a contrast to years before, when people didn't lock their doors when they went out! What a contrast to years before, when people helped each other. What a contrast to years before, when people felt happy and safe in their homes!

They didn't need the police then, but they did now!

I knew what they'd done! People used to have jobs for life, but following the strikes and threat of strikes, they made having a job a luxury, that could be taken off individuals. It was a pattern of divide and conquer.

Strikes!

<u>Miners:</u> they had their jobs destroyed and then had their mining communities destroyed. <u>Teachers:</u> went on strike. Years later, many older, well-paid teachers felt bullied, unsupported and harassed. <u>Civil Servants:</u> considered strikes, then were threatened with tests every 18 months, to prove they could still do their jobs. No strikes!

Politics reflects how people have been treated. Resentment gradually built up, as the government had been dismantling the welfare state by their brutal cuts, which implied a dismantling of the welfare state. "The Liberals started the Welfare State, but it was a Labour government that made the Welfare State greater," Ben told me. "There are homeless families in Dublin! After World War 1 and World War 11, an increase in social/ council housing was a priority, creating homes fit for heroes. Our country needed people to win the war; is this the vision that people expected after the war? Why is it there's an increase in homelessness in 2019/ 2020, that the country has never seen, since the end of World War 11? After two world wars, did they expect to see an increase in homelessness, poverty, drugs and knife crime?"

"Surely, one of the richest countries in the world can do better?"

"The government has shown all they care about is power, money and capitalism."

"Even the 19th century had workhouses, to stop homelessness. The UK was made rich by the use of child labour and low wages in the 19th century."

" The orphans worked in the mines, the mills and the workhouses; they were given food and somewhere to sleep and to work."

"They made England rich, but at least they weren't homeless or dead! 21st century Britain leaves much to be desired."

"The reality is that the 21st century has homelessness and poverty; the UK has many homeless people dying in the streets."

"Who cares? The World Bank has found the UK's income inequality to be worse than Mongolia and Pakistan!"

"The 19th century had workhouses, so they weren't homeless and didn't die so easily. The UK, in the 21st century, has left many of the poor and homeless to die! The 21st century UK has homelessness!"

"I'd never seen this before in my life! We all saw people picking things out of bins! Dawn and I saw a gaunt man in Dinton town centre, holding his trousers up; he was dirty and was keeping his trousers up with a piece of string! He was a walking skeleton."

"The moral is: people are more important than profit. Why do we need food banks in the 21st century?"

"On the news, it reported there's a 40% increase in the deaths of homeless people."

"It's really about power and what you believe! Life's all about how you really treat people!"

"You don't have to be clever to know that everyone needs money in the 21st century, and basic necessities, to live. The UK was one of the world's richest countries in the world, but the reality was the UN did write a report citing the homelessness and poverty that they saw in the UK!"

"This should never have happened, and the problem is the distribution of wealth. The people in power deny it!"

"Shame on them! Why don't they care about the living standards of ordinary people?"

"The real issues are power, money and politics! There has been an increase in homelessness. The UN report showed the UK was the fifth, (then the sixth, then the fifth again) richest country in the world; the issue is the distribution of wealth in the UK!"

"This is the cycle of despair! Why and how is this happening in this country? Surely, if years ago, the homeless were allowed to sleep in bed and breakfast accommodation and were given money to live on, something better could be done now, rather than allowing them to die, on the streets, in the 21st century?"

When I informed the police about homeless people in Newpalace, they told me, "We'll see them, and individual support will be offered to them. However, many of the homeless have drug problems, so we advise people not to give them money directly but to donate to organisations, so they're offered appropriate support. Some homeless people want to be on the streets, because the public give them thousands, some earning over £40,000 a year, with nothing to show for it all, at the end of it."

In London, I had felt frightened when we were approached by the homeless. "Have you any money?" one rough, tough young man growled.

I did what was advised on the television reports about homelessness, "If you're in difficulty, you can go to the Job Centre Plus, as they can make emergency payments."

Why did he swear? Why were my kind thoughts met with verbal aggression? Why didn't he ask them for money? I actually did care and had worked at the Job Centre, years ago, and knew they handed out emergency payments, over the counter. I knew this was the organisation which could give financial support. I actually had wanted to help. I actually did still want to help the homeless.

Nevertheless, Ceiling News reported, "There has been a decrease of 80% in spending on social housing, which has contributed to the increase in homelessness!" Therefore, it was a common problem, and not just for the people on drugs! The whole situation seemed to have been about capitalism: more profit for employers and less money for the workers. What about the Michael McVities of the world? Did anyone care if people were driven to suicide? Did anyone care if employers made employees' lives a misery, instead of treating them with respect and developing their workers to their maximum potential? What about the poor? The problem was also about mental health; it was also about the distribution of wealth and feeling valued. Did ANYONE care?

The financial crash of 2008! On the news, a chart was displayed, showing the problems of government finances from 2006! That explained what they'd done and why they'd done it! They'd destroyed the careers of many experienced and expensive teachers, to save money! The government later suffered the consequences because they couldn't meet their targets; they knew too many teachers had been leaving the profession, but they still needed teachers in classrooms! A new approach by the government was made: to offer new teachers £30,000 a year and a higher pension, saying they would now be supported with disruptive pupils! What a change!

This was exactly what I and others, were saying the issues were many years ago: money and poor pupil behaviour and a lack of support with disruptive pupils! The problem had been the ethos of management behind the problems faced by many experienced and expensive teachers. They'd been trying to save money by forcing expensive and experienced teachers to leave their permanent posts. Poetic justice! The government now found they did need experienced teachers in schools. There were now at least 750 applicants for every job going, across the country, for any job of any description! People needed money to live.

Unfortunately, capitalism continued. My life would have been much better if management had wanted to value staff and to develop staff to their maximum potential. Many other teachers' lives would have been much better if management had wanted to value staff and to develop staff to their maximum potential. Many doctors' (and nurses') lives would have been much better if management had wanted to value staff and to develop staff to their maximum potential. Why did they destroy happy schools, where there were clear expectations, which had been praised by HMSI and LEA inspections? Why did they do the same to many in the NHS?

The problem was a set of circumstances that had upset so many people; the problem had not been mental illness, when so many staff had left work because of stress. Too many people were working longer hours, for less money. Fantastic for the privileged few, but soul destroying for many! It also made life exceedingly difficult for people who were 60+, without an occupational pension! Did anyone care?

During the years of austerity, by the government, there was rising homelessness, rising poverty and many lost their jobs, or rather felt bullied out of them. The richest 1,000 people were £50 billion a year better off than the previous year, because they didn't have to pay corporation taxes! All of this had happened in the fifth richest country in the world. When the UN wrote a report about homelessness and poverty in the UK, the government denied the level of homelessness and poverty in the UK, but I knew the UN was right! Everyone, even children in schools, saw the common sight of homelessness, which had not happened before on such a large scale, in the past 60 years. I had never seen anything like it before in my life and neither had my family, friends and colleagues!

I had witnessed the ever-growing problem of homelessness in the UK. Pupils in school had witnessed the ever-growing problem of homelessness in the UK. My family and others had witnessed the ever-growing problem of homelessness in the UK. Years ago, homeless people had access to bed and breakfast accommodation; personal issue money had been paid over the counter at Job Centres, so why did they stop doing that and make people homeless? The police told me, "The problem is often drugs," so why not solve that problem and destroy the drug lords instead?

Poverty is a vicious cycle of despair! If people don't have enough to live on, how can they escape their poverty, without others helping them? No one would want to live in such circumstances, which creates a breeding ground for criminals and drug dealers! Many people were dying every month because of appalling conditions and lack of food! How could this happen, in one of the richest countries in the world? How could it happen that many schoolchildren, in receipt of free school meals, were hungry during the school holidays? How could it happen that many mining communities were now less well-off than 60 years ago? Did anyone care? The headlines on the news were, "There are fears by teachers over potential violence in schools, and a strike could be considered by the teaching profession!"

I then became an expert in GCSE exam marking, in this country and around the world. I found this extremely therapeutic. However, comments continued to be made towards me, in schools and out of schools, which suggested the form of bullying, harassment and unwanted behaviour, in the shadows, continued! It was the same pattern of comments! They were made indirectly, but the pattern was the same! They eventually stopped and I worked for the departments that were not making the comments, so I was much happier. The comments that were made to me directly were that I was a valued member of the team in schools and I was a valued member of the country's expert team for GCSE exam marking. The GCSE marking was therapeutic, marking at home, because I felt safer.

Brian Jones, told us all, "The answer to the country's problems is capitalism and the free market." What about the feelings of ordinary people? David Raine lectured, "We know what it is: namely, hire, fire and retrain." What about the emotional and social consequences for people who were treated like this? The report showed 50% of workers were up to breaking point, with stress. Was anyone surprised? Was there too much capitalism and not enough socialism? It was appearance and reality. They appeared successful by worldly values but did they really care about the feelings and lives of the people who were ruthlessly disregarded by people in power?

12. Truth is Stranger Than Fiction

Who would believe it? Truth is stranger than fiction. You couldn't make this up! What doesn't kill you makes you stronger.

Who would have thought the years of strikes and industrial action (when I was younger, living in the mining community) would've prepared me for this? My parents, neighbours and community were right! The problem was the way employees had been treated by management. In the past, people had taken their own lives because of bullying by management at work. (It didn't just happen at work!) Often, it had been a battle of power, where management had picked off teachers/ employees one by one: the strategy had been to divide and conquer. It was incredibly sad to find this was the reality and the effects on individuals were fear, misery and poverty.

Moral support costs nothing but saved my health! I decided to build a new life and to solve problems, instead of crying over them and being crushed! I decided to trust my instincts; I wasn't going to be fooled by others! This worked! Concentrating on my health, happiness and well-being meant I felt stronger, so I could then support others in life, such as my family, friends, neighbours and colleagues. Kindness and moral support costs nothing, yet empowers the receiver; the best things in life are free.

The problem had been the recruitment and retention of staff, not only in teaching but also in the NHS, the Police and the Civil Service. The government seemed to be doing it to prevent future strikes and/ or industrial action! It seemed to be about power and control. All I learned was: don't be tricked by others and trust your instincts. No wonder teachers were leaving the teaching profession in droves! A pattern had been created: the creation of badly behaved pupils, where teachers weren't supported, so teachers left the profession! Why not create an environment, which has traditionally been in schools, where everyone has the right to teach and everyone has the right to learn? The disruptive pupils weren't in control of schools years ago, so why should they be now? At least with supply teaching you aren't trapped in an unfair situation forever, and you have the freedom to work in different schools!

Everyone should have financial security and emotional security, to live and to be happy. Everyone should have good mental health. Everyone should have access to the same opportunities in life. If everyone was valued and allowed to develop to their maximum potential, everyone would feel happier and could contribute more to the country and that would make the whole country safer, more productive and richer too.

At Dinton High School the deputy headteacher and the assistant headteacher told me, "We'll give you a reference for any school, for any post!" Dinton High School was a private school and the pupils followed the rules in the school and were allowed in classrooms at break, lunchtimes and after school, in a way that would not be allowed in state schools! However, while I was there, comments were constantly made by others but were clearly directed at me, which upset me! They were constantly being made about my family. How did this school know so much about my family? It was a culture of mental torture! I knew management was behind it all! I could see the pattern of management using the victim's family to hurt the victim! This had been the pattern in the other schools too; it happened in school and outside of school. The problem wasn't my family, it was the fear and misery these sly comments, made in the shadows, created. I reported all comments to my union, as evidence.

This empowered me, so I had the strength to ignore the comments. I now knew the comments were being made to upset me! In the end, management was kind to me and they did stop making the upsetting comments. Unexpectedly, the deputy headteacher came up to one member of staff, David Raine, who was making the most comments near me and told him, "You enjoy working in this school, don't you?" After that, David Raine never made any more upsetting comments near me again. However, I had no doubt he'd been set up too! David Raine was a member of a different church to me, and was much older. He was short and thin, with short grey hair. The continuous comments were a pattern of bullying, harassment and unwanted behaviour; they created negative feelings, which created negative thoughts which could have created negative behaviour! So I could ignored them: I reported them to my union, so I could maintain positive thoughts and therefore, positive behaviour! This worked! That was how I survived the bullying, harassment and unwanted behaviour!

Comments were continually being made while I was at Dinton High School, which were obviously directed at me. Many comments were made which were obviously directed at my family, by people who didn't even know them! This was the same pattern of bullying, harassment and unwanted behaviour, both in school and outside of school. It was done deliberately to upset me, so that I would be upset and would no longer be happy at work, so that I couldn't do my best at work. I really did feel trapped: I was a victim in the never ending prison of bullying, harassment and unwanted behaviour. How could I escape? How could I cope, without committing suicide? How could I prove this form of bullying? At night, my prayers saved me and the advice from my lecturer, when I was a student many years ago, came flooding into my dreams and memories! I clutched at these straws, as I lay drowning! All I could do was to ignore it all, and to report it all to the union. Unexpectedly, I found this worked! Was it God? Was it the advice from my lecturer? Was it my parents, saving me, in my despair? The memory of the priest, at my father's funeral, telling everyone he "met Jesus, Our Lord" when he met my father was with me every night, when I closed my eyes.

While I was studying for my degree, many years ago, Tim Hall, our lecturer, who was also a psychologist, had told us all, "The best way to deal with bullying is to ignore it. Look the other way, then smile at the bully! This will annoy the bully because bullying is the intention to hurt! If you look the other way and then smile, you're showing that the bully hasn't upset you, so the bully hasn't won." In practice, I found this very difficult but it did work!

It was a common pattern: references were made to the schools I had removed my children from; the management of each school was trying to defend themselves and blame me! The primary school in Dinton LEA had never said anything to our solicitor! By not talking to our solicitor, and pursuing this form of bullying, harassment and unwanted behaviour, the primary school and each school who pursued this behaviour had now implicated itself in corrupt practices. Therefore, it was part of a pattern of bullying, harassment and unwanted behaviour which continued in many schools! I was too afraid to tell anyone because I was so frightened. How could I escape this pattern of behaviour? Was Tim Hall really right?

Was this really the best way to treat an innocent family, that had been the victim of a road traffic accident? The independent psychologist, used by our solicitors, had told me at the time that I needed more support at work than others, because of the trauma of the road traffic accident on our family. They weren't doing that, were they?

However, ignoring them, and reporting them, in a written form later to my teaching union, worked for me! It removed the stress and anxiety because I had reported this form of bullying, harassment and unwanted behaviour. When it was written in black and white, it was clearly a form of bullying, harassment and unwanted behaviour. Clearly, they had done it in this form so they could deny it! I had no doubt they wouldn't want to admit any of this in court! I felt it was a hidden court case. I felt I was the victim of their power, their intention to hurt and their ruthless ambition. I felt afraid and intimidated. It wouldn't have happened if I'd been wealthy enough to employ expensive solicitors in court! It did help when I reported everything to the teaching union, because then I had written evidence in front of me. Unexpectedly, writing everything down saved my mental health! I hadn't expected that! Writing everything down helped me to remove my emotional distress! Writing everything down helped me to sleep at night.

The truth was that they wanted to employ newly qualified and cheaper teachers to save money! They didn't want to pay high wages to experienced teachers! Walking away from bullying is always much better than being bullied! Concentrating on being happy and healthy is far better than being bullied as well! This was in the same LEA, Dinton LEA, where a school had left a lot to be desired regarding my children. They didn't have anything to say to our solicitor at all! The comments were never made as part of a conversation. I had no doubt that this was a form of bullying, harassment and unwanted behaviour, as this school was in the same LEA (Dinton) as the primary school where I had reported problems, at a time when we were using a solicitor. The school concerned had nothing at all to say to our solicitor!

When I left Dinton High School, the head of department, who was also an assistant headteacher, told me, directly and to my face, "Thank you for everything you have done in this school. We will recommend you for any post you wish to apply for, in any school."

The deputy headteacher, Molly Summers, told me, "You've done everything, brilliantly, and you've been a model example of how to do everything. We will support you for any post, in any school, you wish to apply for." Obviously, they were covering themselves so that they could defend their actions if this ever went to court! Molly was short, pretty and slim. Molly always smiled and was always friendly when she spoke to me directly.

I didn't apply for permanent posts, because I was growing older and I just couldn't have put up with the continual comments, which were a form of bullying, harassment and unwanted behaviour, every day, over a long period of time. The continued comments in each school, usually regarding my family, were mental torture! They ruled by creating fear and misery. The only way to cope was to totally ignore it all, to take the moral high ground and to report it to my teaching union. At least by doing supply teaching I could leave and keep my health! I was doing the same job as a permanent teacher, but worked in different schools, so I could ignore the comments, which were clearly being made deliberately, to upset me, which was why I only worked in schools for a short space of time.

They won't be able to fool God and they didn't fool me either! However, while I was in schools, comments were constantly made, near me and clearly directed at me, which upset me! They were constantly being made about my family. It was mental torture! I knew management was behind it all! I could see the pattern of management using the victim's family to hurt the victim! Wasn't this the same strategy as the mafia and other criminals? However, my family wasn't the problem, they were!

This had been the same pattern in other schools too; it happened in school and outside of school. I reported all comments to my union, as evidence. I knew this had happened to my family in the past, by management, where they attacked not only the person, but the whole family. Isn't that what criminals do too, to intimidate people?

Later, I met an older man at Heartland School in the foyer, in the school. This older person (about the same age as me!) smiled continuously and then asked, "Are you Mrs Lowry?" Who was he and how did he know my name?

"I am," I smiled.

"You haven't changed at all, over the years."

"I wish that was true!"

"I would recognise you anywhere."

I now knew he was charming but was economical with the truth! How did he know me? "I'm sorry, but I don't know your name?"

"I haven't weathered as well as you. Can't you recognise me at all?"

Who was he?

"Have we worked together before?"

"We have."

"Where?"

"At Firlane School. Do you know who I am yet?"

"I'm sorry, but you'll have to give me another clue."

"I'm Simon Grant."

"It's lovely to see you again." Simon approached me and gave me an enormous hug!

"I left Firlane School and felt terribly upset and ill! I just couldn't face going into school anymore! I felt too frightened to go to school! I wasn't being supported with disruptive pupils and I felt ill every day! I was off work for months, with stress, so I left. I'm now working, taking bibles into schools. My mam was friends with the mam of the headteacher of Heartland School, Keith Gibbon, which is why I'm here now. We always went on holiday together, all our lives, when we were younger."

"He must know the truth about Firlane School as well!"

"Keith does! He knows it was the management as well!"

"We all know the truth then." I had worked with Simon at Firlane School for years, without any problems and we were always good friends. I knew he was telling the truth! Simon was now in his 50s; he was tall and slim, with grey hair. Years ago, he was tall and slim with brown hair. Simon had always been happy, smiling and funny! Simon had always spoken to me and was always kind and friendly, to me and to my group of friends. "The problem isn't you!

It's all about money because we're older and experienced teachers."

"I know the problem at Firlane School is the lack of support for disruptive pupils; Keith Gibbon, the headteacher of Heartland School, also knows it as well."

"I'm glad he knows the truth then. It definitely wasn't you because it's been a pattern of behaviour!"

"I wondered why you left and why everyone else left! Now I know!"

"They're not important! We're important and our health's important!"

"I'm glad to see you and I'm really glad you know the same as me!"

"You're not ill! It's been the effect of the way they've treated you! The symptoms of bullying are fear and misery."

"So you're saying it's been bullying as well."

"Bullying is the intention to hurt! I was best practice by HMSI and excellent in all LEA inspections, as well as having a commendation on my teaching practice! I was then told by HMSI that I was the type of teacher it was part of their remit to tell was valued by the government!"

"And they upset you as well?"

"They did! We're better off leaving than being ill."

"So you know it was them upsetting us and making us feel ill?"

"Sealand Occupational Health was going to support me against them, but I left to do supply, to protect my family from stress."

"We're just going to work to look after our families, we don't want the amount of stress of a court case!"

"Dinton Occupational Health told me I'd already won against them, with Whiteland School."

"You look marvellous! You look just the same as you always did! I would've recognised you anywhere!"

"The problem is the mirror never lies!" I laughed. "Pupils asked me ages ago if I had phones when I was young, and they were the good pupils!"

"I think you look the same as always."

"We were young once, weren't we?"

We both laughed.

I also met Christine, a teacher at Heartland School! She recognised me straight away. She approached me, smiling, and asked, "Are you Mrs Lowry?"

"I am." I didn't recognise her either! Who was she?

"Did you work at Whiteland School?"

"I did."

"I was in your tutor group. I'm Christine." As she turned to me, with her open smile and wide eyes, I could remember her clearly. She gave me a big cuddle, and I remembered and laughed, "Christine and James." I certainly remembered them, because, initially, they'd been friends, then had fallen out; they'd then divided the tutor group, because everyone had taken a side! Eventually, this was all resolved and they were friends again! Christine laughed and said, "You do remember." We both laughed, as we remembered things about the tutor group.

"Thank you for the beautiful bouquet of flowers you all gave me."

"Everyone in the tutor group contributed to your flowers and we were all very pleased and proud to give them to you."

"The flowers were beautiful and I was surprised when you all came to the staffroom to give them to me."

"We were all pleased to do it! We'd wanted to keep you as our tutor and none of us wanted our previous tutor back! We were all happy when you were our tutor and we all enjoyed our PSHE lessons."

"I did as well! We all laughed a lot and learned a lot as well."

"We all loved doing the role play!"

Christine told everyone in the department, "I can vouch for Mrs Lowry because my whole tutor group loved her as our tutor!"

"If anyone wants a reference about me, ask Christine." We had both had a fantastic time in the tutor group, and so had the whole tutor group. I knew I could rely on Christine to tell the truth about me. 12 years later, Christine had changed, as she'd grown up!

My classes at Heartland School were a pleasure to teach and all had excellent behaviour. The expectations were the same as in the private schools and at Whiteland School, which I totally agreed with! This was not in a privileged area; this was not in a desired area; this was not in an affluent area. However, the expectations and work ethic were the same as mine; the expectations and work ethic were the same as in schools years ago; the expectations and work ethic were the same as in the private schools. The pupils worked harder, the pupils were happier and the pupils achieved more in this school! I taught a small year 7 class, which had the same ability as many pupils in special schools, which followed the same expectations! This year 7 class was also a pleasure to teach and one of the best behaved classes in the school! No wonder HMSI thought the same about this school as me!

This small year 7 class had a much better chance of success in this school and in life after school, than in a special school. In discussions about relationships in school and in life generally, the pupils and I worked out how to cope with bullying. In discussions, we worked out it was better not to react to the people who were deliberately trying to hurt us and not to react if anyone tried to upset us, because then they would blame us if they possibly could! Together, we understood that the idea behind bullying was to hurt us and to trick us into doing something we shouldn't! We thought the best solution was to take control of how we reacted, so they couldn't have anything to use against us.

This class was well behaved. This class was a pleasure to teach This class achieved much more than similar pupils in other schools. They achieved much more than similar pupils in special schools. No wonder this was one of the best schools in the country! This small class also thought it was more important to be a good person and to do the right thing, than to follow worldly values which may lead to riches and a life of crime! We all decided to do the right thing! We all thought it was better to do without things we didn't need, than to follow a life of crime! We all wanted to do the right thing in life. It was a privilege and a pleasure to teach this class of children. I found this class a complete contrast to similar classes in other schools and in the special schools! This class had the same ability as classes in other schools and the special educational needs schools but their attitude was different!

When I left the school, I received a beautiful bouquet of flowers and a card from the department. Diana Dobson, the head of department, was very complimentary and had appreciated my hard work and so did the rest of the department, which was lovely. However, due to family reasons, I couldn't commit to being available for the following term.

This showed that the problem was not me, as the pupils in this school were a pleasure to teach and this school was just in an ordinary, working class area. The overall situation really was about the ethos of the school and the management of the school. Clearly, if anyone feels members of a school staff, or any staff, are not truthful, trustworthy and honest then you must protect yourself and stay safe. Don't be tricked by others, if you feel they're not honest, trustworthy and truthful. Good management is really about getting the best from your staff. Constructive dismissal is creating an environment where staff can't work, where staff can't do their best and where they feel bullied; this is when you must leave, when your doctor advises you to. Don't expect people who do this to you to tell the truth in court, because these people are not going to tell the truth willingly!

If a situation doesn't feel right, keep yourself safe and trust your instincts. Prevention is better than a cure, so recognise what people have done over the years; learn from events in history and recognise who has created the fear and misery in your life; think and understand why you've felt so upset. Appreciate the people who make you feel happy and keep as far away as possible from the people who make you feel fear and misery. Walking away is one solution; the other solution is to take them to court. Going to court is extremely stressful and you need enough evidence to win. Now that my family are older, I would take them all to court, if I had enough evidence to win! At the time, I protected my family, because our children didn't need the stress, so I put them first! We'd already been followed by private detectives, over a road traffic accident which was not our fault! Inadvertently, all they'd done was prove we were telling the truth!

I fully understood how right Sealand Occupational Health had been; I fully understood how right Dinton Occupational Health had been; I fully understood what the management of schools had really done to me, to my colleagues and to others, over the years. My colleagues, others and I had left schools because management had chosen to be unsupportive but had saved themselves money by not paying high wages and our pensions! I'd been doing the same job as a teacher in a permanent post but had suffered a loss of pension and a loss of earnings! This hadn't happened years ago, when I'd done supply teaching, but it had happened after I'd left Firlane School.

Years ago, when I was employed by the school or the LEA, either on a full-time contract or as a supply teacher, I was paid according to my teaching payscale and my pension was paid too. Why wasn't it now? Who had done this to teachers who were now doing supply teaching? Why were agencies making money out of supply teachers, when years ago supply teachers were paid according to their payscale by the LEA?

The problem was when I was employed as a supply teacher through an agency; Sealand Occupational Health and Dinton Occupational Health had both been correct! Fortunately, I wasn't ill; I didn't live in poverty; I wasn't homeless! The reality was that was what could have happened! It was noticeably clear, from the comments in Firlane School and Forth School, they would've blamed me, and others, for any illness too! Luckily, I wasn't fooled by them, neither were Sealand Occupational Health and Dinton Occupational Health! I appreciated everything I had in life, and I concentrated on being happy and healthy, with my friends and family. That's how I survived! I protected my mental health; I felt I hadn't been tricked by them; they weren't worth the distress they'd caused! The problems were proving it in court, and consequently, unnecessary stress for my family. I felt that health and happiness were more important; I had both met Fear and Misery, the symptoms of bullying.

Dawn told me, "I've had nightmares and bad dreams for years, but now realise I've had a lucky escape. My recurring nightmares are from my most unhappy memories, from my worst days at work at Firlane School. My recurring nightmares became a regular occurrence and I have been diagnosed as having post-traumatic stress disorder."

"At least you're alive, to tell the tale, unlike Martin McVie and many others, who've been driven to suicide."

"Who's he? It's terrible when you put it like that!"

"Someone I knew from Easington; he committed suicide years later, after a problem at work. He was forced to leave his job. We have to concentrate on being happy and healthy every day; they're not worth the distress they've caused."

"That's tragic! They don't care about the consequences on people. Being praised by the headteacher at Dealey school (who came into my classroom in person), and by the head of department,

Mrs Cooper, at Dealey School, saved my mental health. I was singing Christmas carols in the term leading up to the first Christmas I'd left Firlane School, while driving to work at Dealey School!"

"Dealey School was marvellous for you! What a contrast to Firlane School!"

"A past pupil worked there and made me cups of coffee! The headteacher came into my classroom, unannounced, one day and was totally supportive; she praised how I was approaching the work I'd been given to do and how I approached working with difficult pupils."

"You also thoroughly enjoyed doing private tuition, as well as working with university students!"

"I did! I taught (and still teach) the children of doctors and university lecturers, who were delighted when their children were years ahead of everyone else at school. My youngest pupil is approximately three years ahead of others in her year group at school. Another pupil I taught, in year 10, has already passed her GCSE and is halfway through work done by the average year 12 pupil (a sixth former) in school. I've found these pupils an absolute pleasure to teach."

"You've thoroughly enjoyed private tuition and working with university students, including composing music and performing this music, for films made by the students."

"I felt very proud when one of my former pupils was awaiting the result of completing a four-year B. Mus. Degree, at London Glidehall School of Music and Drama. Needless to say, when the results came, he passed!"

"Now we knew why you've suffered such awful nightmares, even years later!"

"I'd suffered mental torture! I knew management had been behind it all!"

"I can see the pattern of management hurting the victim! This has been the pattern for others too. All we can do is to appreciate everything we have in life and to be very glad we've escaped!"

"I saw Susan Stone at the shops: she spoke to me, which was something she didn't do at school! Susan Stone looked tired and years older. I was amazed, because she'd never bothered to speak to me at Firlane School!"

"You look years younger now than when you worked at Firlane School because you've thoroughly enjoyed doing supply, private tuition and working with university students! It's kept you young and it's helped you to keep your marbles, and even earned you money!"

"You're right! Away from the bullying, work's become an absolute pleasure."

Dawn and I met Laura Harper separately! Laura gave us both big cuddles and was genuinely pleased to see us!

I met other teachers from Firlane School over the years: Sharon Humphries at Essingland School and Denise Marsey at Oxen School. At first, I didn't recognise Denise, when Denise kissed me and cuddled me, and she mentioned, "You left Firlane School."

When she made this comment, I knew who she was! Denise Marsey had been appointed as second in the department, to Roberta Oliver, and had fawned on her every word! I then explained, "I left Firlane School because I was "best practice" by an HMSI Inspection and "valued by the government" in HMSI's second inspection and part of their job was to tell teachers like me that I was valued by the government. I left because I'd been "excellent" in Sealand LEA inspections and an environment had been created that I could no longer work in. Like many others, I just left." I bet Denise loved me!

"We thought best practice was in the department because of us! We didn't know it was already in the department!"

"Why did you leave then?"

"It was just time to go!" Of course it was! They must have forced her out as well!

"Others left as well!"

"I've seen the others."

"Carole Renwick left to go to Dinton School."

"I was working with Carole at Dinton School, so I know the real reason why she left."

"Did she tell you?"

"I know all about it. Carole left for the same reason as me; she felt bullied and couldn't stand it any longer either."

"I didn't know she'd told you what happened!"

Denise didn't know what to say because I knew the truth! She had joined the department and joined in with the bullying but was now pretending to be my best friend! No wonder she loved me!

"What happened after you left?"

"I worked at Essingland School and the assistant headteachers, Patricia Long and Thomas Hall, were totally supportive. I was praised by both and was happy working with them."

"I found that when I worked at Essingland School."

"It was a pleasure to work there and Essingland is one of the most deprived areas in the country."

"That's right, it is. The assistant headteachers were always supportive with the disruptive pupils."

"They were. Also, at Whiteland School, I contributed to some of the best results in the country and the class I shared with my colleague had the best value added in the department! At Dinton School, they'd never had such high grades as I achieved with my classes! My results at Dinton School were higher than other teachers' results in the school!" I was sure Denise totally loved me now!

Denise had obviously left Firlane School feeling unhappy there too, as had Sharon, Simon, Carole and many others, but she obviously didn't want to admit the whole truth about why she'd left, did she?

When doing supply, I sometimes enjoyed working less hours and less days. This gave me more time for long walks and more holidays; this gave me more time to think and to relax. Every cloud has a silver lining! I coped by turning everything into a positive! More holidays make you happier. Many others were not so fortunate but enjoying walks and nature helped me to keep life in perspective!

Our home was now practically paid for, therefore we had less bills and no rent to pay! I was acutely aware that others were not so lucky! Renting small rooms at Newpalace was £100 a week! Renting houses at Essingland was £390 a month (one of the most deprived areas in England)! However upset I'd been, others had been much more upset in life than I had! How terrible! Owning our home helped us, because we didn't have to pay enormous rents! Our occupational pensions saved the day! We were lucky compared to others! We had a home and enough money for food, bills and holidays, while others didn't. We all saw the hardship of others; we all witnessed the homelessness; we all felt upset about it all! No one had ever seen such hardship as in 2019! The amount of homeless people in the UK was dreadful and none of us had ever seen anything like it in 60 years!

Doing supply teaching for agencies meant we were paid less wages, and no Teacher's Pension, unless schools decided to pay according to our payscale and Teacher's Pension, depending on the individual school. However, it didn't matter if you were doing supply or not, we were all still doing the same job, as we were still teachers! Agencies took a cut of our wages. Schools also saved a fortune! I knew this was a form of social injustice, because I'd been paid to scale before doing supply by Sealand LEA and had recently been paid to scale by an individual school (and paid my Teacher's Pension)! It was all a con, to save money! They often offered work at the same school but offered less pay with different agencies! It was happening to others too, and in other jobs! What a contrast to the beginning! They knew what they were doing, and so did I! Many others found exactly the same! They must think we were all too stupid to see what they were really doing! In the beginning, when I first did supply teaching, I was paid to my payscale, and didn't lose any money or pension.

Schools, which employ me directly, must pay me according to my payscale! Working for agencies now means I'm receiving less money and less pension, unless the individual school decides to pay it! This is what Sealand Occupational Health told me at the very beginning! If so (and if I've already won against Firlane School, with Whiteland School as identified by Dinton Occupational Health)) I should be paid compensation, for loss of wages and loss of pension, because Sealand Occupational Health was correct! If they'd wanted to save money, why didn't the senior leadership just leave, because they earned the highest wages? I should not have received less wages; the agencies were making a fortune! It was the schools, not protecting their staff, that had been the problem. Sealand Occupational Health had been correct; Dinton Occupational Health had been correct too! Fortunately, the teaching unions knew the truth too! However, all they were told was that it was privatisation!

If a supply teacher asked the agency to ensure the AWR (Agency Workers' Regulations) were adhered to, requesting being paid to payscale after 12 weeks (which was legally their right), they soon found out it was their problem! The teaching unions didn't always support them and it was a lonely, isolated path to walk down alone, as many teachers told me, at online meetings. This was why so many supply teachers and permanent teachers accepted a lower payscale, to avoid unemployment, poverty and stress. It was the fear and misery associated with taking employers to court, and having to prove constructive dismissal!

One member of staff in school in Barnwell School told me, "I felt forced to leave the school I worked in because I was so unhappy and I couldn't stand it anymore! I cope by not worrying about money, by buying less and I feel much happier; it's less stressful and I've saved money."

"At Heartland School, that's one of the things Buddha talked about, and my year 7 class discussed this topic. That was a wise response, if you can't change things, make the best of them! A simple life is better than worrying about things you don't need!"

"That's what I found as well! They're not worth the distress they cause. My friends keep buying lots of things and then worry about paying for them! I just buy what we need and I'm much happier."

"That's an excellent way of looking at things!"

"It works for me!"

"It works for me as well."

It was a common pattern, for older, more expensive teachers/ staff in schools; isn't that constructive dismissal, deliberately making employees' lives a misery, so they feel forced to leave, to save their mental health? Sealand Occupational Health had been correct, when they'd told me the issues were loss of wages and loss of pension! They'd known the truth as well! I'd walked away to protect my family, from further distress! We'd already had the stress of one court case (which we'd won) and didn't need the stress of another one!

Bullying in schools, for a family member, was stopped when the police were involved and police cautions were given, and those families were told by the police that the Crown Prosecution Service would take the perpetrators to court if it continued. The police told the victim to ring them immediately if the victim ever felt frightened, and the police would go immediately. Surely, if the police and the Crown Prosecution Service were stopping the bullying in schools, the employers of the family should have been supportive too? What a disgrace! They thought they were protecting their school's reputation, but don't they look silly now, for not supporting this particular family? Was this why the schools were defending themselves and bullying me? Was this because they didn't want to be blamed for their lack of support and skills over the bullying? Was this really because the police stopped the bullying and they didn't?

Late 2019 and post-traumatic stress disorder continued for Dawn, as nightmares about Firlane School continued, including one of the worst Dawn had ever had. "My nightmares are a collection of injustices, with one scene after another; the hospital knows the truth, and it's post-traumatic stress disorder, and that helps!"

"We know it was them that upset us but they'd just defend themselves and blame us."

"And that's why I've felt so upset."

"That's why I've felt so upset as well and everyone else who felt forced to leave because of their bullying management. I met Jeff Bainbridge and he told me my problem was their ambition! He said they furthered their own ambition at my expense and the expense of everyone else."

"He's right there. I've found Sealand Hospital helped. They told me, "You haven't lost your marbles and they have upset you, no matter how much they try to deny it." I now know the truth and so do Sealand Hospital."

"They created stress at work and made life a living nightmare. Even after leaving it was difficult to relax because they'd created fear and misery, which are the symptoms of bullying!"

"My nightmares show what it was like, working in torturous conditions! It was acute anxiety and stress!"

"I was saved by my GP, Sealand Occupational Health, Durham Occupational Health and Sealand Hospital, who all knew the truth."

"We both know the truth now, as does Sealand Hospital!"

"The problem's really been about power, status and money! The moral is: if you're feeling very upset, trust your instincts, so you don't become ill! Management know what they're doing and will blame the person, who's the victim, because they won't blame themselves! If they do this deliberately, to save money, is this really constructive dismissal and a court case?"

"We know how stressful that would be as well!"

"They'd be ruthless!"

"We're just better off without them."

We still both felt powerless and extremely upset but knowing HMSI had been supportive did help me. Also, the fact that Angela Rivers had gone to jail helped because that had been poetic justice! Justice had been served! I wasn't the only one who found her a liar, deceitful and manipulative. Many people found the same, including the Crown Prosecution Service and a jury! Having a family and a friend, who was also a witness, kept me sane. People are important, not the pursuit of power, wealth and status. Dawn and I still missed the laughter at work; Dawn and I still missed our happy jobs, which the change of management had destroyed at work. I appreciated what I did have. I appreciated my family, friends and good neighbours. I appreciated financial security, because although I'd lost wages and pension, I was still more comfortable than many!

Many supply teachers felt the same! "I should be paid on Upper Pay Spine, but the school won't pay that much, so I'm now employed by the school but I'm still not paid according to my payscale," Christine Hall told me. Christine was much younger then me, with a teenage family. She was tall and beautiful, with long, black, straight shoulder length hair. Christine was always smiling and very friendly.

"Why aren't they paying you what they should be?"

"I either accept this rate of pay or find another job! The school says it can't afford to pay me more, so it's this or nothing! I'm still paid more than when I did casual supply, but not what I'm worth."

"That's terrible! It's the injustice and exploitation that's the problem."

"At least it's a regular wage, which is better than nothing."

"Schools should be paying all teachers according to their qualifications, experience and payscale."

"They should be, but they're not."

"It's the principle of social justice that I believe in."

"So do I, but this wage helps my family, so I'm pleased to have a reliable income."

"I hope it all works out for you."

"So do I."

"The problem is the exploitation of the workforce."

"We all need money to live, which is how they get away with it."

"Sharon Surtees is now being paid to scale, but the school isn't keeping her on. They've employed an NQT instead."

"That's what my headteacher told me as well! If I don't accept this payscale, they'll give the job to someone who will. I'm now employed permanently by the school, but at a lower payscale; if I don't accept it I know I won't have a permanent income at all! I'm working on the basis that a good, permanent wage is better than none."

"But you should still be paid according to your payscale."

"I should be. If I don't accept a lower pay rate, I'll not have a permanent wage."

I still believed in doing the right thing. This belief saved my mental health! I concentrated on me, my conscience and being a moral person, rather than following worldly values. My parents' goodness helped me to cope with everything! When my father died, the priest told everyone at church, "When I met Michael, I met Jesus our Lord, at the same time." Wasn't that lovely? At my mother's funeral, the priest told everyone in church, "Margaret was blessed, and her reward will be in heaven."

My parents were kind and they helped other people; they didn't look down on others; they practised what they preached! I soon found out that everyone else in life was not as truthful, honest and reliable! Thank goodness I had decent parents, who were excellent role models. I didn't need to be tricked by liars, manipulators and bullies. Dawn didn't need to be tricked by liars, manipulators and bullies either. Others didn't need to be tricked by liars, manipulators and bullies. I simply tried to follow my parents, who were certainly not tricked by power and wealth; they were kind and helpful people, who always cared about others and would always help someone in need. What a contrast to the people I had met in life, particularly at Firlane school and Forth School! Thank goodness for my GP, Sealand Occupational Health, Dinton Occupational Health and HMSI, who all knew the truth too, as
well as Sealand Hospital!

13. Light at the End of the Tunnel

I'd been right all along: the problem in different schools had been the management and their ruthless ambition! Others had been right all along too: the problem in different schools had been the management and their ruthless ambition!

Also, I had the opportunity to work in leading private schools: Deighton Alana School, Dinton High School and Altea School. Comments were made at these schools, but they were not on the scale of many other schools. However, I found that both staff and pupils shared my expectations and work ethic, in the best schools in the country! They all agreed with me, about expectations, work ethic and ethos! The expectations and work ethic were also the same at the best state schools in the area: Whiteland School, Heartland School and Emmerland School! I'd found what I had in common with the best schools in the country: expectations, work ethic and ethos!

Emmerland School was now the best school in the North East; they didn't put up with disrespectful or bad behaviour; what a marvellous, refreshing change! I enjoyed the company of the head of department and the staff at Emmerland School! The whole situation had been about ethos and expectations because I totally agreed with Emmerland School's ethos and expectations. Theirs were the same as mine! The ethos and expectations had been the same at Heartland School and at Whiteland School! My conclusion: the problem at Firlane School and at Firlane School was with management because I should have been supported with disruptive pupils, consistently. Conclusion: the problem was management because Dawn should have been supported with disruptive pupils consistently. I knew it was the same problem for the other experienced, expensive and successful teachers who felt forced out, because of the bullying, harassment and unsupportive management.

Dawn's conclusion: the problem was with management because Dawn should have been supported with disruptive pupils consistently. Dawn's evidence was that Dealey School had loved Dawn and the management had supported her, wholeheartedly, there. The headteacher continually congratulated Dawn on her personal work ethic and classroom management. What a contrast! Dawn was more than happy to work in a school which supported her.

I returned to Heartland School where comments were made in this school too, everywhere I went, which was very upsetting, as they implied a hidden court case was going on, where I had no right of reply. I coped by reporting all comments to my teaching union. I later worked at Heartland School again, as it was one of the best schools in the country and I totally agreed with their ethos in school, regarding expectations for pupils. I wasn't surprised they were such a successful school, because I agreed with their ethos and expectations for pupils! However, comments were still made near me in this school; the pattern of bullying, harassment and unwanted behaviour was the same in this school as well! I did exactly the same: I ignored it all and I reported it to the union, in a written form.

I was surprised when the headteacher walked into my classroom, one morning, before lessons. I was told by the headteacher of the school, Keith Gibbon, "You are the expert in the department for one of the GCSE exam papers, because of the exam marking you do. Our weakness is in this area, where you are the expert. Will you work with us, to improve our GCSE grades?" Keith was tall and well-built, with short blonde hair. He was very friendly.

"I would love to." I also had certificates from the exam board to show I was an expert in this area.

"I knew you were in our school last year. You think the same as us, which is different from many other schools, which is also why we want you to work in our school," Keith added.

"Yes, because other schools seem to have lost the plot! We both expect pupils to work in lessons and to allow everyone else to work too! Years ago, when I went to school, it was exactly the same expectations. Everyone was expected to work at school and no one was allowed to disrupt anyone else's education."

"We have a high number of children with special educational needs in this school too," Keith continued.

"I taught those last year as well! The class I had was probably one of the best in the school! They have the same expectations as us!"

"We're always praised by HMSI for the way we look after them," Keith informed me.

"HMSI are right! The other schools do not expect the same, so they don't get the same! You must keep them here and if there are any problems, keep them in the unit, but don't send them to special schools, because they're not as good as here!"

"That's similar to what HMSI tell us, but we don't really know what's going on in other schools."

"They should see what's going on here, so they do the same as this school. This is better than all of the special schools I've been in."

"Thank you for letting me know, because I didn't know what was really happening in other schools."

When I returned to Heartland School, the headteacher, Keith Gibbon, had come into my classroom to talk to me!

"I knew you were in the school last time but I thought I should meet you. We're very pleased with everything you're doing for this school."

"I saw Simon Grant in this school last year, who I worked with years ago!"

"He did tell me he'd seen you in this school, that's why I'm here. I know you know him. Our mothers were friends and we always went on holiday together, when we were young. That's how I know Simon."

"We worked together for years, at Firlane School, and we never had any problems at all. We both used to be happy there."

"I know the problem in Firlane School is behaviour! I know Simon left with stress."

"I had always done very well in Firlane School. The good headteacher, Keith Stephenson, also helped my family to win our court case, following a serious road traffic accident. He told me to tell our solicitor to tell the other side to contact him, and he'd be happy to answer any questions about me. That ended the court case, and the other side, the defendants, agreed to pay our family member compensation, as a victim of a road traffic accident."

"I bet they didn't want to pay out."

"No, they didn't. When the evidence came out, to present to the court, they showed they'd hired private detectives to follow us! The private detective, who followed me, reported it was fruitless following me because I stayed in the house, every night, and never went out of the house after 9pm."

"So they paid a fortune to prove you're a responsible adult!"

"They did!"

"They wouldn't have liked that!"

"I left Firlane School because of a change in management; I felt bullied and I couldn't work in that environment.

"That's why Simon was upset and why he left as well."

I knew he knew how upset Simon Grant had been when he'd left Firlane School too, because Simon had already told me!

"We also know Sandra Surtees, who you worked with at Emmerland School; we all know her, because Sandra used to work here too."

"I did work with Sandra at Emmerland School, which is now the best school in the whole of the North East."

Heartland School had also contacted Whiteland School, which was also one of the best schools in the country, so they knew I had contributed to some of the best GCSE results in the country.

"We appreciate your awards from Ofqual for exam marking."

Although I had now retired as a permanent teacher and manager, I still did supply teaching and exam marking. "You're regarded as the expert in this department. Tell your classes you're in this school because you've been invited into this school by me, the headteacher, and I'm a personal friend of yours. Tell all pupils that I expect them to behave for you in exactly the same way as they would behave for me. If they don't, tell them to come and see me, because I want to see them, so they can explain to me why they don't behave for you in exactly the same way they would for me."

"I don't think they'll be queuing up to knock on your door."

"No, I don't think they will either."

The staff and management were then totally supportive! They constantly told me, "We're pleased to have you working in this school … You're more than a cover/ supply teacher," and they then made positive comments, which were the same as Whiteland School "You're a teacher and many teachers do not have your level of expertise." I knew this was true! The evidence of my contribution to Whiteland School was that I had contributed to some of the best GCSE results in the country, and the class I'd shared with my colleague had the best value added in the department (that is the class we shared had made the most improvement from the beginning of the year compared to the end of the year, based on the results). I had done exactly the same at Dinton School!

Diane Dobson, the head of department was a pleasure to work with, every day, after Keith Gibbon came to see me.

What a difference it made, working in one of the best schools in the country and being supported by the headteacher! I worked with a lovely head of department, who had listened to me when I reported problems with the marking in the school last year. I was relieved when she acknowledged I was the expert in the department and realised I could contribute to improving the school's GCSE results, as I knew what skills the exam board was looking for. If she hadn't listened, and had ignored my concerns, I wouldn't have felt able to work in the school again and I would not have returned! I was relieved to find she agreed with me, and she wanted to improve the school's exam results too! The head of department wanted to work with me, so we were a team, working together, to improve the school's GCSE results. What a change! Wasn't she marvellous? The school was not in a posh area, but the behaviour of pupils was much better than other schools. The head of department was now a friend, a colleague and an excellent head of department to work with! Good management made a difference! I thoroughly enjoyed working with well-behaved pupils (even though they were from ordinary backgrounds, like me).

After this, the comments around Heartland School stopped.

Dawn later told me, "Roberta Oliver would be extremely jealous of you now, if she knew where you were working! She took your good classes off you and swapped them for disruptive classes! That's what Percy Banks did to me too! He took my good classes off me and gave me all disruptive classes!"

"That was how we were all victims of bullying at Firlane School; the management victimised us all, one by one, in this way. Previously, everyone had a mixture of good classes and disruptive classes, but that all changed with a change of management."

By chance, I had known one of the parents (for over 40

years) at Heartland School! My friend and parent at Heartland School, Gail Simpson, told me, "A friend of mine had been deputy head and had been incredibly happy at another school with the old head, but was ill with depression within a year, because of the new headteacher." Gail was short and slim, with short brown hair, with highlights. She was always happy and content with life.

It was a common story! Our neighbour, Carole Fenwick, told us similar stories, "A deputy headteacher rang a friend up and asked him to go to his school to work, but he couldn't, because he'd already agreed to work in another school. Our friend, the deputy headteacher, soon left with depression too!" A similar pattern?

The Head of School and the Senior Leadership Team were often popping into lessons at Heartland School, unannounced, and were totally supportive, so all pupils shared my expectations, and their expectations too! There were not any behaviour problems! It was a pleasure to see the senior leadership team pop into lessons, as they were always supportive. This was the same strategy as at Essingland School, where pupils were well behaved in one of the most deprived areas in the country!

Ellingland Junior School had a headteacher who was lovely and a pleasure to work with, when I went there one day (as well as working part-time at Heartland School)! Again, comments were made by pupils and staff, but they were all supportive comments! The headteacher at Ellingland Junior School was young, tall, slim and handsome. He was very friendly, polite and pleasant to all staff. Ellingland Junior School was near Heartland School; it was in a remote area but was very small and friendly.

However, comments were continually being made when I was at Sealand School, which were obviously directed against me, by people who didn't really speak to me (I still did other supply teaching in other schools, as well as working part-time at Heartland School). Sealand School was obviously in Sealand LEA; the LEA wasn't the problem! I was still working part-time, in Heartland School. Many comments were made directed about my family, by people who didn't even know them. This became part of a pattern of bullying, both in school and outside of school. It was done deliberately to upset me, so that I would be upset and would no longer be happy at work, so that I couldn't do my best at work. I felt bullied, harassed and the victim of unwanted behaviour. It all started in school but continued after this, outside of this school, at church and at the shops! Was this because I had taken my children out of a faith primary school, because the schools had left a lot to be desired, when we had been victims of a road traffic accident? Was this because pupils in a faith secondary school were given police cautions for bullying a member of my family? This form of bullying is exceedingly difficult to prove. All comments were reported to my teaching union.

Sealand School's headteacher then came to see me in lessons. He was tall, slim and called a spade a spade! I agreed with his ethos of allowing all pupils in the class to work and that no pupil was allowed to disrupt the learning of others! He showed himself to be an effective and supportive headteacher; he kept coming into lessons and asked me about the behaviour of the classes, in front of whole classes. He told all classes, "This is my colleague and I have asked Mrs Lowry to come to into this school. I expect every pupil to be as well behaved for her, my colleague, as you would be for me. Let me make this crystal clear: anyone who misbehaves for my colleague, Mrs Lowry, is responsible to me. You will meet me if anyone fails to follow this teacher's instructions." Suffice to say: everyone chose to be excellent and a pleasure to teach; no one chose to see this headteacher! Conclusion: the problem was management in different schools because I should have been supported with disruptive pupils consistently, in each school. Dawn found the same, when she was supported by management in other schools too! Andrea found the same as did others! What a surprise!

After the above support was given by the headteacher in Sealand School, comments were still made around the school, but they were all supportive. I reported all comments to the union. I could now see why the comments were being made inside of school and outside of school. They were deliberately trying to provoke me, to upset me, and then to blame me for being upset! This was the pattern of the bullying, harassment and unwanted behaviour. However, all unsupportive comments stopped in Sealand School, after the headteacher kept popping into my lessons! On every occasion he was totally supportive; I found the behaviour of the pupils reflected his attitude. When he was totally supportive, the pupils were totally supportive too.

14. What Really Happened?

Firlane School went into special measure and was then closed after HMSI saw me again in Sealand LEA. GCSE Music had long been forgotten on the timetable too! Dawn found this out, quite by accident, from a pupil who had wanted to do GCSE Music, but had not been allowed to, in Firlane School. What a disgrace! The pupil went to Dawn for private lessons, after making enquiries about music teachers.

Forth School also went into special measures and the headteacher was sentenced to jail in Crown Court! The two deputy headteachers at Forth School were also suspended for a year. HMSI had found out the truth, as seen in their HMSI reports. They knew the head of department and the senior leadership team had not been supporting teachers with disruptive pupils! They had been found out! Forth School went into special measures and was also later closed, and that headteacher (Angela Rivers) was sent to jail for years!

At Dinton School, the head of department was made to leave after I'd left the school. After I spoke to the HMSI team, the headteacher of Dinton School left too. Whickton School, Undercastle City School, Granterland School, Altea School and Stonehill School had all asked me to apply for a full-time teaching post. I did apply for a supply teaching post at Whickton School but this caused problems with the agency, as the agency thought the school should pay the agency if I then worked in Whickton School! The manager of the agency, Theresa Oak, had then told me, "They've done this because they know you're a good teacher. We know you're a good teacher, but you'll never work for us again if you apply to schools for posts directly!" Whickton School didn't pay the agency the money but did give me money after I'd left.

Undercastle City School was unsupportive with disruptive

pupils, but the HMSI team I'd met at Granterland School told me they were going back to all of the schools I'd left, to find out the real reason why I'd left each school. Undercastle City School then went into special measures, which I totally agreed with. I felt that this HMSI team was right. At Altea School, the chair of the governors at the school had offered me a permanent post at the school. I had had no idea that was going to happen. The management of Altea School was annoyed that I didn't take their job offer, offered to me by the school governor, so they didn't offer me any more supply teaching after that! HMSI then went back to Altea School, and Altea School also went into special measures. I thought that this HMSI team was correct, because again, the problem had been the lack of support by management. Altea School didn't ask me back to their school again, after I didn't accept the permanent post at the school; they also went into special measures after I'd spoken to the HMSI, after the same Chief Inspector had seen me in two schools, within two weeks! I would have been happy to continue working at Altea School on supply, because I felt safe doing supply teaching.

Stonehill School was also awful to me when I didn't apply for a teaching post in the school! Granterland School later went into special measures; again, the reason was the lack of support by management for staff with disruptive pupils, and I totally agreed with HMSI. Stonehill School's attitude towards me also changed. They were lovely and bought me cards and presents before I left the first time I was there. However, when I still didn't apply for a permanent post at the school when I returned for a second time, to do supply teaching, their attitude changed! They then became unsupportive with one class, with some disruptive pupils in it! The other classes were lovely, and were really pleased to see me, when I went back to the school a second time.

I really was glad I hadn't been tricked into applying for a permanent post in this school. I was so shocked, because the assistant headteacher had given me a kiss and a cuddle when I first went back! It was the new head of department and the cover manager, who were unsupportive over some disruptive pupils from one class! No wonder this school went into special measures and closed after I'd left! I felt HMSI were right to close Stonehill School!

Turnerlane School, where I originally worked years ago, also made many upsetting comments when I returned to the school to do supply teaching, which should not have happened, because I'd left this school for family reasons. Patricia Best also worked there years ago and was still there when I went back. She told me, "The senior leadership is furious because your family has done so well and better than my family and all of their families!" I stopped doing supply at Turnerlane School because I just couldn't stand the many comments that were constantly being made! I found this was a common problem! No one wanted to hear how marvellous my family really was! The head of department had been a pleasure to work with, but they made her ill too, and she left! Tim Hopkins, a friendly male member of staff told me, "I'm terrified of the senior leadership team; I'm afraid because they're on the warpath and want to know who's been telling you they're afraid of them!" He'd been very friendly and supportive towards me, which was why he felt afraid! The senior leadership team was wanting to find out who had been kind to me because they were angry with them! When the HMSI team went back to Turnerlane School they placed the school in special measures, then closed it. I agreed with HMSI, because the problem had been the bullying, harassment and unwanted behaviour of the management.

One by one, each school that had been unsupportive with disruptive pupils (and where I had reported bullying, harassment and unwanted behaviour) went into special measures, was closed or the headteacher left! I believe two of the private schools escaped this, but I believe they did give excellent references, as one had promised they would recommend me for any post, in any school, I wished to apply for.

Dinton Occupational Health had already told me that I'd already won against Firlane School, with Whiteland School! HMSI had told me they were going into every school I had left to find out the real reason why I'd left, after the same HMSI team saw me in two different schools within a week. HMSI was totally supportive. Also, both doctors at Sealand Occupational Health and Dinton Occupational Health knew the problem had been management in schools and that the management in the school had been the problem, not me! Dawn helped me to let go of the past and to move on, but it took many years to do that! It took years of talking to Dawn for me to feel better; it took years of talking to me for Dawn to feel better too. I felt so much better talking to Dawn, because

Dawn knew the truth! Dawn cared, understood and we helped each other to see the best thing we could do was to be happy, because bullying is the intention to hurt. My lecturer, years ago, who was also a psychologist, had helped me through this too, with his pearls of wisdom. HMSI also knew the truth, as did Sealand Occupational Health, Sealand Hospital, Dinton Occupational Health and the good headteachers.

Dawn had been to Sealand Hospital and they'd told her, "You haven't lost your marbles as it was the management of Firlane School, including your head of department, that has upset you." I supported Dawn to overcome the acute pain, fear and misery of the bullying, and she supported me. Jack Ashton's (and Angela Rivers') motives were self-preservation and ambition (Forth School), unfortunately. Roberta Oliver and Derrick Tusk's motives were self-preservation and ambition too (Firlane School). The pattern was: identify a problem to management, management then blamed the person who was the victim, because they wouldn't blame themselves! HMSI spoke to me at Granterland School. The HMSI had told me that I had the same job as them, because I was going into different schools and I had my own opinion about them all. Following that, nearly every state school, that hadn't treated me properly, went into special measures, some were closed; the one school that didn't go into special measures had the headteacher replaced (Dinton School)! HMSI helped me to overcome the acute pain, fear and misery of bullying. Dealey School also helped Dawn to overcome the acute pain, fear and misery of bullying. Dawn told me, "It's like a breath of fresh air, working as a supply teacher at Dealey School."

Later, after speaking to HMSI, those schools that had upset me all had their own problems! Many went into special measures and many were closed. Southland School was so awful that no one would take it over. Firlane School was closed and became an academy. Keris School was closed and was taken over by Emmerland School. Forth School was also put into special measures and the headteacher was jailed and two senior members of staff were suspended (this was in the newspaper and the newspaper was left on a table near where I had been asked to sit, for me to read, in one school). Turnerlane School was also placed in special measures and was closed. Undercastle City School also went into special measures, following my conversation with the chief inspector of schools, who told me his team was inspecting every school in the area.

Justice had been served by HMSI! The miscreants had not got away with it, after all!

In schools, the problem really had been about ethos: the schools that I strongly agreed with were some of the best schools in the country, such as Whiteland School, Heartland School and Emmerland School.

Although I continued to do supply teaching and exam marking, I had retired as a permanent teacher and manager. All I found that was that I really did want to be a teacher and it was something I had a vocation for and that never changed! Being a teacher had always been my ambition and it still was!

At Vane Road Primary School the headteacher was a pleasure to work with! Continuous comments were made there too, but they were all supportive! I was praised directly by the headteacher all of the time! This also happened in many other primary schools too!

Comments were continually being made, in schools where I did supply teaching, which were obviously directed at me, by people who didn't really speak to me and were not part of my friendship group. Many comments were made, directed about my family, by people who didn't even know them. This became part of a pattern of bullying, both in school and outside of school. It was done deliberately to upset me, so that I would be upset and would no longer be happy at work, so that I couldn't do my best at work. I felt bullied, harassed and the victim of unwanted behaviour. It all started in this school but continued after this outside of each school! This form of bullying is exceedingly difficult to prove.

However, a pattern was emerging as even younger teachers than me were often ill and off school for a long time. One teacher recently, much younger than me, has been off for months! Another teacher looked ill and in pain when she walked. No wonder many teachers were leaving the profession! They couldn't stand the bullying and lack of support either!

Even the neighbours knew about bullying in schools!

Jane and Mike Grant, our neighbours, knew Percy Banks, who I worked with years ago and they knew he'd left school very unhappy as well!

I met Jacqui Ayre, years later. "I know the children all did what you told them to when I first went to Firlane School; I know the problem was the management. They stopped supporting you at Firlane School! Hugh Percy (head of department, Firlane School) had been asking me questions about what you had said about your family. I told Hugh that I was trustworthy and wouldn't betray someone's confidence! I knew what the management was doing to you! They stopped supporting you because when I first went you didn't have any problems with anyone! They were always asking questions about you but I wouldn't answer them! When I first went to Firlane School, everyone did what you said, and followed your instructions like soldiers!" I had been right all along! I knew it! Dawn knew it! Jacqui knew it! So did Simon! I had been bullied at Firlane School and this was how they'd done it! The management of Firlane School had bullied me, as well as Dawn and a number of others too! Jacqui had also told me, many times, that she'd reported she'd been bullied too and she'd been unsupported by management as well!

The management had then defended themselves by attacking the victim! It was all about power, manipulation and money! The management of the school saved themselves a fortune, by forcing expensive, experienced teachers to leave, because the expensive, experienced teachers were no longer supported by management! These were the same teachers who'd been praised by two HMSI inspections and had contributed to the GCSE results of a "good school". It was appearance and reality. They appeared successful by worldly values but were morally corrupt.

It was a continual power struggle, where they used their power and their friends to stop my professional career, because if I was seen to be successful, then it proved that they were wrong! I wasn't tricked by them at all! It was all mind games! Dawn hadn't been fooled by them either. The solution was to concentrate on being happy and healthy, and to do my personal best in the circumstances! The solution was to concentrate on being happy and healthy, and for Dawn and other colleagues to do their personal best in the circumstances! The solution was to concentrate on being happy and healthy, and for everyone to do their personal best in the circumstances! I was not ill! By doing this, others were not ill either. At the end of life, they can't fool God! They might have won the battle, but they hadn't won the war!

Dawn also concentrated on being happy and healthy too and we found this worked for both of us. However, before we concentrated on being happy and healthy, Dawn had been remarkably close to being extremely ill, but she was saved by her GP and by Sealand Hospital. I had also been remarkably close to being ill but was saved by my GP, Sealand Occupational Health, Dinton occupational Health and Sealand Hospital, as well as HMSI and the good headteachers. Dawn and Richard both thought I had to leave Firlane School because they were both worried in case the management of Firlane School caused me to have a nervous breakdown. We knew their strategy was to bully the staff, one by one, then blame the victim for being ill, because they wouldn't blame themselves.

Another male member of staff, Phil Robson, I met, when I was teaching in a private school, told me, "I retired early. All the older, experienced teaching staff were going on the sick with stress in my previous school!" This strategy was the same strategy as the strategy used at Firlane School; a clear pattern emerged, as the same strategy was used at Firlane School and at Forth School. Phil continued, "The teaching unions have been weakened, because of capitalism and the miners' strike, which they didn't win. Management has been blaming everything onto the individual, so workers have less power, and the whole situation is all about money!" Phil was saying exactly the same as me! He was saying exactly the same as Dawn and many other older, experienced and expensive teachers! Also, he agreed with me, "It's all about money! You just have to look at the delay in the OAP age and the fact that younger workers won't get the same retirement pensions we have, because it'll be based on their average earnings, not their highest earnings." Phil was a similar age to me, short, friendly and a pleasure to meet and to work with! He had short brown hair, with shades of grey.

Another 40-year-old male teacher, Frank Smith, doing supply, told me, "In my school the older teachers left, one by one; they were replaced by younger, cheaper teachers! My wife worked in the Civil Service and said many teachers had left schools and were working as civil servants, instead of as teachers." Frank was also friendly, handsome and tall, with black, curly hair.

A teacher who qualified in July, Emma Raine, told me, "I was working as a teaching assistant! That was the only work I was offered, so I had to take it, or I'd have nothing!" This just shows employing qualified staff, but not paying them according to their qualifications, had become a common pattern to save money. Obviously, it all depended on the management of the individual school!

I met many teachers, with the same story, so it had been a pattern of behaviour! Another male supply teacher, Tony Laverick, with a Ph. D, who was also older, told me the horror story of how he'd been treated! He told me, "Lies were told about me to an agency, and the agency sided with the school, because that's how they earn money." Tony was about my age, also in his 60s; he was short and slim, with short grey hair.

"On supply, I've met many people and I've listened to other supply staff; we can both see that many teachers doing supply have been very unhappy with the way they've been treated by schools. What a waste of talent!"

"Exactly! As they've concentrated on saving money, they've failed to appreciate expensive, experienced teachers. They've certainly saved money!"

"They call it capitalism/ privatisation. We know it as something else."

"We know it as exploiting the workforce and bullying, to save money."

On one Continued Professional Development course a fellow teacher, Amanda Longstaff, and I agreed management had been blaming individual teachers for any problems in the classroom, to destroy teachers, instead of supporting hardworking teachers with a vision! We both agreed the strategy they used was to argue that the teacher alone was responsible, no one else. We both agreed that other Continued Professional Development courses valued the vision of teachers having the right to teach, and pupils having the right to learn. This was the vision I agreed with, when I'd worked in the best schools in the country and the best school in the North East! The problem was really about ethos, vision and values! The best schools agreed with me! I went to ordinary schools as a pupil and wanted to learn; my class (when I was a pupil) went to an ordinary school and wanted to learn too! The schools did not support disruptive pupils at the expense of the teacher and the rest of the class then, so why should they now? Some pupils need more support to succeed, which should be given, so everyone can move forwards in a positive direction; that's what the best schools in the country do!

I don't think anyone should be allowed to disrupt the education of the whole class; it wasn't allowed years ago, so why should it be allowed now? However, some pupils need more support to succeed than others, and in the best schools in the country the disadvantaged pupils are given this support, so everyone can succeed in the school. This contrast was exceptionally clear to me, when working in different schools. In the best schools in the country, the teacher had the right to teach and pupils had the right to learn. However, in these schools, disadvantaged pupils were given the support they needed, so they were learning the value of education. I was not the only one to have this ethos and vision; the best schools in the country shared it too. The individual teacher is not the only important factor, because I wanted to learn at school (when I was a pupil) and I never disrupted lessons. I don't think it's right for any pupil to deliberately disrupt lessons and then to be supported by management! The best schools in the country created an environment where teachers could teach and pupils had the right to learn and everyone in the school was exceptionally clear about these expectations. The schools with these values were the schools which supported failing schools; these were the schools I agreed with and so did HMSI!

I later met Percy Banks! Percy Banks even asked about Dawn! He found the truth out the hard way because the management of Firlane School later made an environment he couldn't work in either! Dawn told me, "I find that incredible!"

I told Percy, "Life is not about status, money and worldly values, but about being a good person, and doing the right thing. Really, we all should have been happy at work and we all should have continued to work as a team! What a shame management didn't listen to HMSI, who had praised the school for this!"

"How have you managed? I never expected this!"

"Sealand Occupational Health was going to support me against Firlane School, and Dinton Occupational Health told me I'd already won against them, with Whiteland School (where I'd contributed to some of the best results in the country)!"

"I didn't know that! Simon Grant was very ill at Firlane School and he left after he'd been off for a long time with stress."

Percy Banks now knew how much they'd upset others as well!

"I met Simon at Heartland School and I've worked with him for years! I know what a lovely lad he is and he isn't ill! I know the problem is the way he's been treated at school."

"You're right but how did you know?"

"I'm from the mining community, so my life, of living through strikes, has prepared me for this! I'm not fooled by them! I'm going to write a novel; my dad once told me there's a book inside everyone. Jesus came for the poor and the outcasts." He now knew the truth too! "When I saw Simon Grant, recently, I didn't recognised him at first!"

"Simon Grant looked ill when I last saw him."

"He's not really been ill, there's nothing wrong with him. The problem is the way he's been treated. He was always happy, as we all were, for many years. Many of us have left feeling bullied; they're not worth the distress they've caused."

Both Percy Banks and his wife agreed, "You're right. He hasn't really been ill, the problem is the way he's been treated! Him and others!"

"Fear and misery are the consequences of bullying."

"They are! That explains why so many left, unhappy." I'd been right all along!

Dawn later told me, "I don't trust Percy Banks at all and I wouldn't even have spoken to him. That's rich, coming from Percy Banks who bullied me!"

As Dawn found out, many criminals used the internet and telephone calls to regularly scam/ steal. "I went straight to my bank to find out if they'd stolen any money! They told me I'd done the right thing, and not to give out any personal details. They said many people had been tricked and had whole pensions stolen! Someone pretended to be HMRC and told people to download an app from HMRC, to prevent scams. They then stole £8,000 and then made 72 attempts to steal money from the same person. Clearly, the man was devastated when he realised what they'd done! Others ring people up, threatening them that money has been taken from their accounts, then telling them what to do! All scams!"

"Criminals are always telephoning innocent people, to trick them out of money, so they become rich, and the innocent people become poor! They prey on people's trust! They tell lies! They destroy people's lives."

"I'm pleased I went straight to the bank, so I don't have to worry about anything."

"Well done! That was much safer."

"We just have to keep our marbles, as we get older."

"That's the main thing now."

Years later, I met Louise Miller at a garage, where she worked. I didn't recognise her but she recognised me straight away. She told me, "You taught me at Firlane School when Mrs Evans was head of department." Louise was now in her 30s, was well made, with brown shoulder length hair and wore glasses.

"I never worked with a Mrs Evans at Firlane School."

"You did, because you taught my class, in year 10, opposite her classroom."

"Do you mean Mrs Oliver?"

"Yes, that's her name! She was my tutor! My name was Louise Carpenter, then."

"I do remember! Your boyfriend ..."

" ... was killed playing chicken. He was knocked over by a bus; you do remember me."

She made many comments about the school, then asked, "Why did you leave?"

I simply explained, "I'd been happy there, for many years. It had been a good school but got worse! I was praised by two HMSIs in the school and the LEA and I left, then worked at Essingland School (in a well-known deprived area) which was far better than Firlane School!"

Louise and her colleague both laughed, "Essingland is one of the worst areas in the country! That's saying something if Firlane School was a good school, then it was worse than Essingland School."

"I then taught at Whiteland School, one of the best schools in the country, and contributed to some of the best results in the country!"

Louise made comments about Roberta Oliver, "She was

worried in case you … but you didn't." She implied Roberta Oliver had been manipulating Louise, and other pupils, against me, so if I'd taken the school to an industrial tribunal, they would have manipulated pupils against me. Louise continued, saying, "We were going to say she did send us out." This implied Roberta Oliver really had been coaching pupils to defend her! Fortunately, Sealand Occupational Health and Dinton Occupational Health weren't fooled by her either!

Clearly, she was defending herself, ready to attack me and was being supported by the headteacher and the management of the school! They must have known I did have a case against them and had planned to defend themselves at an industrial tribunal! I was totally shocked at such unprofessional behaviour, manipulating pupils against a colleague. After those comments I explained, "I'd been praised by HMSI as "best practice" and "as the type of teacher the government wanted to value". I also added, "Sealand LEA had told me I was "excellent". At Whiteland School I contributed to some of the best GCSE results in the country, straight after I'd left Firlane School and Essingland School."

Louise, and the other assistant at the garage, Martin Robinson, both laughed, then both agreed, "It was them!" Clearly, my GP was right, and Sealand Occupational Health and Dinton Occupational Health were right too! Unknowingly, Louise and Martin, the other assistant at the garage, agreed with Sealand Occupational Health and Dinton Occupational Health!

After the change of management at Firlane School, I had reported many incidents of bullying at work! I wasn't the only one! It didn't stop the bullying. They didn't support staff with disruptive pupils, yet, for years, I'd been valued and praised for my work with disruptive pupils! I'd taught some of the most disruptive pupils in Firlane School, with both parents and pupils telling staff I was the teacher they trusted! The problem had been the change of management and a looming financial crash in 2008! The change of management then supported disruptive pupils against staff and manipulated the situation to defend themselves and blame the individual. Everyone could feel fear and misery In Firlane School, which are the symptoms of bullying. Louise just confirmed what had been going on! It was the contrast of the fear and misery after a change of management to the happiness and success before the change of management. All management did was blame the individual; management had created an environment that was impossible to work in, then blamed us for being upset! Isn't that constructive dismissal? Wasn't Sealand Occupational Health correct?

What a contrast to all of the other past pupils I'd taught and met after they'd left school at the shops, restaurants or pubs, over the years! The only explanation for all of this was the change of management at that time! In Firlane School, many pupils had bought me many cards and presents! I taught a past pupil's nephew: his auntie's class held a party for me before I left Turnerlane School to have my first child! The class bought me a beautiful baby shawl, then they bought individual baby presents as well! What a contrast! I'd also worked with other past pupils, who went on to be teachers; they always acted as positive referees for me in the schools I worked in!

In the past, if I went out socially with colleagues from work, past pupils introduced themselves, so I knew who they were! This also happened to Dawn many times, and still does, as she still lives in the area.

I felt awkward and upset after I'd met Louise; this had never happened before with anyone else! It was a problem created by the lack of support from management. To reinforce this, another pupil from Laura's class made a similar comment to a friend of my family member, which was passed onto a family member! This was a total contrast to other comments made by past pupils to my family members, before this change of management! Previously, comments made to a family member were that their GCSE grades were higher for my subject than for other subjects, which was true. Also, other pupils had told family members they loved my lessons the most in the school! Who would admit to this, in management?

After the change in management, pupils were told to leave Firlane School immediately, after they'd left year 11 and weren't allowed to come and see me! They were turned away from the school, when they came to see me, after they'd left year 11! The school office staff were heartbroken to do this, but they had to follow orders from above! The management can tell lies on earth but no one can fool God. I decided to keep my trust in God. Previously, many pupils had come back to see me at school, after they'd left school. Holly Ainsley even brought her first car to show me! Other pupils gave me cuddles and treated me with the greatest of respect after I'd left, and I always felt happy to see them again, such as pupils in my classes who later became teachers, in the same subject I had taught them (I had inspired some of them to become teachers)!

It had been an absolute pleasure to work with Kerry Seasons in two schools! We had a bond and sat together at meetings! Kerry Seasons was also a past pupil of mine, and I had taught her in the same school as Louise Miller (Firlane School)! I had taught Kerry before the change of management and she'd told all colleagues and pupils in Southland School, "Mrs Lowry was my favourite teacher at school, and I wanted to be a teacher, just like her!" We both agreed we had loved our lessons together! The only explanation for this change was the lack of support by the change in management, who just wanted to save money and look after their own careers! Kerry had been the opposite of Louise Miller. Kerry was small and slim, with long brown, straight hair. Her eyes twinkled with fun, as an adult, just as they had when she'd been a pupil in my class! She was always pleasant, polite and smiling! Kerry was always a pleasure to teach!

The problem was clearly the change of management, as they created a miserable environment I couldn't work in, neither could other people! Previously, Firlane School had been a good school to work in, and an incredibly happy school, before the change of management! Kerry Seasons and I were both happy to see each other, and she told everyone, "We all thoroughly enjoyed our lessons together," which was true!

Christine Reeves did the same! I'd taught her at Whiteland School. She was a pleasure to work with and acted as my referee in the school, at Heartland School. Anyone could ask Christine anything about me, because we had had a great time at school! I will always remember the enormous bunch of flowers her tutor group bought me, and they told everyone that they'd loved having me as their tutor and didn't want their original tutor back! I had lots of happy memories with pupils.

Previously, pupils had come to see me when I went out with other teachers on a lunchtime or after school, and they were always really pleased to see me! I'd been right all along! The problem wasn't me: the problem had been a change of management! After the change of management, pupils who came back to see me were told, "You've left and you're no longer allowed in this school!" by staff in the school office, following the instructions they'd been given by Derrick Tusk. Derrick Tusk, the new headteacher (Firlane School) would not allow my past pupils to come back to Firlane School to see me or anyone else! The school office staff were all upset too, as they had to tell them they were no longer welcome in the school, because they'd left! I couldn't believe that had happened!

The contrast was the fear and misery felt under the change of management, which are the symptoms of bullying! I believe that good management is getting the best from your staff, developing each person to their maximum potential and working together to solve problems. My friends, who were also my colleagues, at school believed that good management was getting the best from staff and working together to solve problems; unfortunately, we met Acute Fear and Misery, and felt bullied, harassed and unwanted, after a change of management.

Also, there were continuous comments made to upset me, both in school and outside of school! I reported all comments to the teaching union, which helped me to ignore them! The purpose of bullying is to hurt; ignoring the bullying and smiling annoys the bully more! Dawn took the same approach, and that's how she managed the bullying, harassment and unwanted behaviour too! It's exceedingly difficult to do, but is simple, quick and effective. The more you smile, the easier smiling becomes, then you eventually feel much happier! It's exceedingly difficult to keep a positive mindset through bullying, but taking the moral high ground empowers the victim! Don't lower yourself to their level! Teamwork solves problems: unfortunately, bullying management use this to blame individuals, one at a time, and it is a pattern of weak management, because they won't blame themselves, will they? They did this to individuals who had always worked hard, and had done their best, with proven ability over a period of years. Luckily, they couldn't fool HMSI!

The real issue was money, because they could employ younger teachers for less money. I wasn't the only person who wasn't tricked by them! Dawn wasn't and neither was her doctor or Sealand Hospital! Sealand Occupational Health and Dinton Occupational Health weren't tricked by them either!

Could everyone now learn to work together? Have we learned that people are more important than wealth? Is there now hope that we can all change, for the better? Will this lead to individuals, country leaders and world leaders valuing teamwork, so everyone works together, to make the world a better place for everyone? Good mental health is a self–belief and a confidence in yourself! Some people can do this by themselves, but some people need support to be able to do this. Resilience is the ability to be able to bounce back, to beat the odds, to be determined to keep striving and to bend without breaking! This is what I needed to do! All the years of living in a mining community, through years of strikes and industrial action (I was a child in a family, in an industry, continually on strike), had shown me not to be tricked by others! I had learned something important in life and this helped me to cope and to survive! Who would have thought that I could have learned this valuable life skill, of resilience, in the mining community? The values of safety first and prevention is better than a cure also worked!

My health was more important than money! The problem had been that experienced teachers were expensive! The truth was that staff well-being is important; the happier the member of staff is, the more productive a worker you have! Simple but true! That explains why I'd done so exceptionally well in some circumstances! I have an honours degree and a Commendation on my Teaching Practice; I have been told I was "best practice" and "the type of teacher the government wants to value" by HMSI; I was always "excellent" in Sealand LEA inspections! In addition to this, I had contributed to some of the best results for GCSE in individual schools in the country! How had I done that?

Was it that I had been happy and had an environment in which I could do my best? Surely, enabling all staff to reach their maximum potential at work, is the job of management. I wasn't the problem at all! The problem had been management, as many other colleagues found too! Feeling valued is important! When I felt valued, the school received my best! When I felt frightened, worried and anxious in schools, it was my feelings protecting me! No job is worth anyone's health! Trust your instincts! If you feel bullied, tell someone such as your doctor, your union and the occupational health! Don't bottle up any worry, concerns and anxieties. Identify the problem, then take small steps, one at a time, to solve the problem. This saves your marbles and saves the NHS a fortune!

15. Why Were They So Upset?

The whole experience had been about mental health; it had also been about the distribution of wealth and feeling valued. Look what happened near the financial crash of 2008: many expensive and experienced teachers were forced out of their posts, obviously to save money! News reports showed the same thing happened to many in the medical profession and the police!

OAP was delayed until 66, by the government! The effects on the individual woman, as many had not paid into an occupational pension, so only had their OAP, have been enormous! We were told most of our lives that we would receive our OAP at 60, but then they changed the goal posts at the last minute! I'd been told most of my life that I would receive my OAP in 2019, but this was changed, so I couldn't receive it until 2025, at the age of 66! Dawn received her OAP at age 60, in 2010. Many women of my generation didn't always pay into an occupational pension; many couldn't take an occupational pension early and retire! Men were much better off than women in retirement, so how was that equality?

Dawn told me, "It should've been phased in, gradually, at the very least." How is this equality, when men were not told this, most of their lives? They changed the rules for women of my generation, which affected many women's lives and caused a great deal of worry, hardship and distress for many! Hardship was caused for many women of my generation, as many, like me, had worked part-time; many did not always work full time, because of family reasons; many had no occupational pension or didn't work at all with a family. As they grow older, many must now work full time, while many men have the choice to either work part-time or to retire altogether.

The sum of £42,000 is a large sum of money for an individual to lose! The sum of £42,000 plus (as OAP increases every year) is how much each woman lost, when they had to wait until they were 66, instead of 60! A friend at school, Jane, who is 64, told me, "I'm still working because I live alone and have an interest only mortgage, which I can't afford to pay off. If I'd received my OAP at 60, I could've paid it off, with the £42,000 plus I would've received in OAP."

"We've also lost free bus passes at 60."

Many women were upset by the increase in pension age and took the government to court. They didn't win, unfortunately, but this shows the strength of feeling and distress caused by it! Many women were terribly upset, annoyed and heartbroken. It upset me, but many others were far worse off than me. They wouldn't have been able to do this with private pensions. It shows the problem had been all about money and the distribution of wealth. The OAP was now delayed until 66 for women, instead of 60, so this shows there had been a problem and it had been about money, as the news and the newspapers reported daily! Would our group of women ever receive any financial compensation for the unfair way it was administered?

This all created problems about money, because the OAP was not given to women at 60 when we'd been told most of our lives that it would be. We now they had to wait until we were 66, another six years! The issue was money! Many women in their 60s felt upset, cheated and betrayed! Many women didn't have full occupational pensions, because of childcare arrangements and many dreaded having to work full time until they were 66! This was where the inequality was: more men had occupational pensions, so they didn't have to work full time until the age of 66. They had more money than women, in the same age group. How was this equality?

In the newspapers, a 39% rise in homelessness was reported in the over 60s. What a disgrace, in one of the richest countries in the world! How had this happened? How had I paid into an occupational pension for 20 years and received an occupational pension at 57, and paid into my OAP for over 40 years, but couldn't get my OAP until 66? I found it unbelievable that my occupational pension was so much more than my OAP! Yet, on the news they kept defending themselves, by using phrases such as: "Pensions are now triple locked." Would they really keep this triple lock or try to avoid paying it? Time would tell.

They defended their actions of raising the age of the OAP for women to 66 by saying it would cost £181 billion to pay it! No one cared that reports showed women had less pension than men! That fact was quietly forgotten! The OAP in the UK wasn't even a living wage anyway and was one of the lowest in Europe!

Also, in 2015, there was a change in the way pensions were organised. Previously, pensions for teachers had been based on one's highest earnings, now they were based on average earnings, therefore teachers would receive less pension in the future! From 2015, the government was paying teachers' pensions on the average wage, whereas our pensions were based on the highest wage we earned. It just showed the real problem was all about capitalism and money, not looking after the majority! From 2015, teachers would be much worse off, when they collected their pensions.

I could see what the government/ management had done! They'd been taking people's jobs and money off them: miners, steelworkers, teachers, police, the NHS and others, instead of paying big pensions and wages. Then, people were employed who were younger and cheaper! It had been a pattern and it had been done on purpose! They made Ruthlessness look like a saint. How many Martin McVities have been driven to suicide by this form of management? How could anyone ignore the many messages of the importance of mental health and drive employees to suicide?

This was how I survived their cruelty and injustice; I analysed what they'd done, coldly; this was how I survived! I realised they win when I'm upset; I win if I remain happy and analyse what they did. I analysed my distress and the causes of my distress. Bullying is the intention to hurt. It was really about power, money and ambition. All I could do was to pray to God, for the strength to carry on and to be happy and healthy. I was always very happy when I was younger, so obviously, someone or something had caused my distress! I was determined to follow truth and honesty and to do the right thing, in the face of this adversity. It was the instinct of survival! The management that had upset me, and others, wasn't worth the distress they'd caused, and neither were their jobs! Compensation for constructive dismissal would have been a better solution, as identified by Sealand Occupational Health, but at the time I put my family's safety and mental health first! We'd just won one court case and didn't need the stress of another one!

Dawn admitted, "I've continued to have horrendous nightmares over the people who'd upset both of us at Firlane School! The nightmares are horrific! My doctor diagnosed post-traumatic stress (PTSD), so I now feel lucky to be alive; my doctor is lovely and he's saved my life! When I'm awake, I feel lucky to have survived their cruelty! My doctor had known I'd been bullied at work and all I could do was to leave, to save my health. My doctor had been right! Dr Phips supported me and helped me to cope with the depraved, corrupt control I'd endured at work. Afterwards, he told me, "I knew you were being bullied at work." I now, very clearly, understand the pain we've both endured while working under the change of management, and the pain of bullying management, which had been driven by power, money and ambition."

"I still feel incredibly sad to lose what we had! I think we've all lost something incredibly special, as we'd been happy at work for years. Your doctor knows the truth about what had upset you and so do I, so you're not alone! Sealand Hospital also knew the management of Firlane School had upset me, and the doctor at Sealand Hospital had told me, "Teachers! It's your profession who has done this to you". You know how much the management of Firlane School had upset me too, and so did my doctor; Sealand Occupational Health and Dinton Occupational Health. They all knew who was behind my distress too! Dinton Occupational Health also knew the management of Forth School had threatened my whole family and had upset me too. They also knew that Beatrice Milton had threatened me too. Thank goodness for the medical profession! Thank goodness the Crown Prosecution Service and the jury saw that Angela Rivers really was a liar, manipulative and untrustworthy, and sentenced her to jail for eight years!"

"Thank goodness we both left when we did, or it could have been even worse!"

"You're right there!"

"Many others are even worse off than us."

"Recently, all of one of my year 10 classes had seen many homeless people; I was shocked and could only say, "I didn't see any homeless people at Newpalace when I was young." They couldn't believe the change! One lovely, pleasant, polite and well-mannered pupil was so shocked when I said that I never saw homeless people in the city when I was young, she asked, "Mrs Lowry, did they have phones in those days?" This lovely class was shocked when she asked me this. Another lovely pupil told her, "You shouldn't talk to her like that! This is our favourite teacher! She taught all of us when we were in year 7." They were shocked at my honest answer, that most people didn't have a telephone in the house and there was just one telephone in a red telephone box in the street, which was all hundreds of people had, if there was an emergency. No one had mobile phones then, but we didn't have an abundance of homeless people either."

"How terrible that people's lives have deteriorated so badly, that in the 21st century, there's more homelessness now that hadn't been years ago! Many people are much worse off than us and we've been very upset." Dawn advised, "I've overcome many problems in my life, and work was just another problem! The years have sharpened my will to survive and to overcome any difficulties that life throws at me! My survival instinct is razor sharp."

"We need the British bulldog fighting spirit, to overcome this, and any other problems in life! Talking about this problem helps us to eventually change the distress to anger, which is much easier to deal with. I know we have to channel this emotion into a positive outcome! After all, Angela Rivers has gone to prison, I haven't, because I wasn't the criminal! Poetic justice has been served! HMSI has helped me to cope with it all too!"

"We have enough to live on, which is the most important thing."

"We're both now far happier and healthier. I think concentrating on being a moral person, doing the right thing and treating others the way I would like to be treated is a better way forward. I'm just not going to be fooled by worldly values, by power, deceitfulness and manipulation! I pray, so I can cope and think about what is really important in life, because we can solve problems by thinking about the cause of the problems, then making a plan to solve them, step by step."

"We're important, so we don't need to worry about them anymore."

"People are important in life, not possessions. I think surviving has been a personal achievement."

"We've done amazingly well to survive everything and this in itself is an outstanding achievement!"

"Being a moral person is more important than worldly values of success, money, power and status!"

"We've been an inspiration to each other."

"I want to help others. I hope to inspire others who've been treated badly in life. I hope to show it's alright if things go terribly wrong in your life."

"You then have to persevere and overcome all problems. You just need to survive."

"You just need to do the best you can in the circumstances. You just need to do the right thing."

"Looking around at life, we're incredibly lucky compared to others."

"It's the acute feeing of injustice. We both have enough money for food and bills, and our mortgages are virtually paid off, so we're incredibly lucky compared to others, but it still doesn't stop the pain and the sense of injustice!"

"Many others are even worse off than us."

I understood why other countries had mass demonstrations. I was comfortable, compared to many others. I couldn't change what had happened, but I could decide to enjoy the sunshine and nature, which made me happier and less stressed. Working less hours had its advantages! I no longer had to put up with rude, disruptive children, with no back up. I could choose which schools I worked in! Every cloud has a silver lining!

Concentrating on being happy and healthy and looking well after each other works! I had found a simple, free solution to solve problems! Working together to solve problems works. People are important, not the pursuit of power, wealth and status. Kindness and Continued Professional Development for all are the answers at work! Better employers and better management in public services and private services, to improve life standards and happiness levels for everyone, would solve problems for many. Continued Professional Development, concentrating on good mental health and valuing your strong friendships and family could solve problems for many people. Dawn and I had kept each other mentally healthy, which was worth more than money. Having a positive can-do attitude to solving problems works! If you have a problem, think about the cause of the problem, then think about how to solve the problem, step by step! It works!

I couldn't have managed a day, without my wonderful family! They made every day a pleasure and were all pleasant, polite, kind and considerate people! They didn't deliberately hurt other people; they were too positive and too concerned with channelling their energy in a positive direction! Following their dreams and ambitions was a pleasure every day; they were always busy, which kept us happy and healthy too! Most importantly, they were good, decent and moral people! Good people are invaluable; you can't buy a wonderful family in a shop; the best things in life are free! Helping others also helps yourself to well-being and happiness!

Failure is not about things going wrong in life: you must move on and walk away, to keep safe, as prevention is better than a cure, if you can't solve the problem. Solve what you can, but if you can't, you must move on and solve your own problems. Solve what you can but have the wisdom to walk away, to live for another day, if the situation's impossible. Health and happiness are more important than being bullied and tricked by worldly values. Stay happy and healthy, put safety first and follow prevention is better than a cure: simple advice, but it can save health, money and lives. Don't be tricked by others, who don't have your best interests at heart. It's appearance and reality. Many appear successful by worldly values but are morally corrupt.

I found a few schools used agencies to upset me! Some agencies were offering work for one hour, but I knew schools were behind it! What a disgrace! It was the travelling time, the petrol and a waste of my time. Also, schools offered less money for half a day with different agencies! What a cheek! It was all about money! Also, different agencies offered me different amounts of money for the same school! Schools would employ me with one agency, then try to employ me with a different agency, for less money! I didn't go, so they had to send someone else! Evidence: it was about money; it was not about me as a teacher. The way I'd been treated at work had been ruthless and had really been about saving money. It was exactly the same for many other colleagues and for many other workers. It was capitalism: making as much money for the business as possible, with a disregard for the employee. It was a pattern of behaviour; fortunately, others could see it too, which saved my mental health! My GP, Sealand Occupational Health, Dinton Occupational Health,

Sealand Hospital, HMSI and the good headteachers, in the best schools in the area, all knew the truth too!

As well as still being a teacher, I became an expert exam marker, in this country for more than one GCSE, and internationally! Dawn also enjoyed doing private tuition and working with university students. However, my concern remained about the distribution of wealth in this country and across the world; what about the homeless, the people in high rise flats and the people relying on foodbanks? Why was this now worse than when I was younger? Who was responsible for this? Who wanted to admit being responsible for this? Anyone?

16. How Can This Be Solved?

Dawn solved all problems with a cup of coffee and a slice of cake: a modern-day detective!

Dawn listened to hospital advice: "You're not losing your marbles; you're not mentally ill. The problem is the way you've been treated." This was solid evidence from the hospital! I believed Sealand Occupational Health and Dinton Occupational Health who'd both supported me, as well as HMSI! My teaching union was also incredibly supportive, so I knew where to turn to, if needed. I wrote everything down and reported it to my teaching union, so I had constant support and my mind was cleared each day, so I could cope. I found the more I talked about it and wrote the problem down, the better I felt, because then I was then very sure about what had really upset me! By looking at the big picture, I realised it had happened to others too; this was how I found the inner strength to cope. It took a long time, and a lot of talking to Dawn, even though we went around in circles! It was a constant merry go round! It was repetitive! It was also free! It saved our mental health!

It was the same pattern in so many schools: older, experienced and expensive teachers found they had an environment they could no longer work in, so felt forced to leave. When they went for interviews for permanent posts, many found the posts went to inexpensive, newly qualified teachers! Many police, staff working in the medical profession and civil servants found the same! It was a pattern of saving money at the expense of older, experienced and expensive staff! Talking about the problem with other teachers helped! It was a pattern of behaviour and identifying the problem helped, so I, and others, didn't feel alone! It was not nature causing the distress; it was nurture! Seeing the overall problem and how to solve it, step by step, helped! Sarah Smythe, a friend who I met on supply kept in touch, "I feel so upset, I find every day at school difficult. I applied for a permanent post in the school I'm now working in as I enjoy working here, but they've given the job to an NQT."

"Everyone else is finding the same! It isn't you, the problem's really about money."

"You're right there! In every interview I go to the job goes to the newly qualified teacher, or to the student who will qualify at the end of the year."

"Everyone else I know finds the same. It all depends on the management of each school, that's why you haven't got to let them upset you. Just enjoy working there while it lasts."

"That's my struggle! I find it difficult to do my best now, because I feel so upset."

"Smile, relax and do your best. It's their loss if they haven't employed you."

"That helps! Just having someone who understands how I feel helps."

"Concentrate on you being happy and doing your best every day."

"Yes, that will solve it! It's the moral support that helps."

"You're not alone! The real problem's money; they're not worth the distress they've caused."

"That's what the problem is! I love working here and I'm loved by the children and the parents."

"That's why it's their loss!"

"Then they upset the teachers they've employed and that's why so many teachers are leaving the profession."

"Exactly! We can see the problems, which are money and the way they're treating teachers. It all depends on the management of the individual school."

"I love working at the school I'm at now."

"So smile, relax and enjoy every day, by doing your best."

"I just feel much better by talking about it all."

"That's how we can help each other! Keeping a positive, can-do attitude works."

"Yes, I'll keep doing that."

"The real problem is the social injustice and exploitation of supply teachers."

"That's the real problem! It's not us at all."

"That's why we must look after our health and happiness, without allowing them to make us ill."

"How can we stop the exploitation?"

"At least we've identified the problem, which is much better than letting them make us ill. I know what they've done because years ago I did day to day supply and was paid according to my payscale."

"We're not now."

"That's how I know it's social injustice and exploitation of the workforce. When I worked for a term in a school, doing supply, I was paid according to my payscale and received my Teacher's Pension."

"The problem is they don't pay me according to my payscale; they always employ someone much cheaper and I don't have a Teacher's Pension."

"That's why I'm writing novels: to highlight the social injustice and exploitation of supply teachers."

"That's a good start. We'll have to work out ways to change this, but it's very difficult because the agencies make a profit and charge the schools more than they pay us. It's still cheaper than schools employing expensive and experienced teachers."

"We know the problems are money, social injustice and exploitation."

"It's just very difficult to try to change it because we don't have the power to do it."

Talking about the way teachers were being treated in schools and thinking about my new hobby, writing novels, saved my marbles! Helping others, helps yourself too: think about the many people who are worse off than you and appreciate everything you have. Look well after yourself, and then look well after others too, so everyone is happy and valued. By talking and writing about what had upset me, it helped me to move on and to help others too. I had saved the NHS a fortune by talking with colleagues; I had been analysing everything that had really happened. Hindsight is a marvellous thing: putting everything into perspective had helped me, Dawn and other colleagues, such as Sarah, to cope, without being ill. We had saved ourselves; I hoped to save others too, by writing novels. I acted as a detective and worked out their motives behind it all! All I found out, at the end, was that Mary, my friend at Firlane

School, had been right, at the very beginning! She had warned me not to be fooled by management, who wanted everyone to think they were everything; Mary told me they weren't and for me to concentrate on looking after my family and my health, not them! Before she'd left, she told me how ruthless management in the school really was and not to be tricked by them! Wasn't she right?

Dawn looked years younger and was much happier now that she'd retired. She had financial security, friends and a wonderful life now! She had holidays that she'd never had before! I'd always enjoyed holidays, which I continued to do. I also had a much better life, but still didn't get my OAP until 66, which affected my retirement plans! Dawn did get her OAP at 60, but I didn't, simply because of the year when we were born. I concentrated on being happy and healthy, every day, and encouraged all colleagues who also felt upset to do so too! It worked!

I enjoyed walks, the outdoors and nature. I enjoyed living in the moment, and looked forward to the future, so I didn't worry about things in the past and the things I couldn't change, but talked about them, so I could enjoy life and move on. These simple strategies helped! Being happy and healthy is much better than being tricked by capitalism and the pursuit of wealth. People are important and we are all people too! You can fool some of the people some of the time, but you can't fool all of the people all of the time. Dawn felt, "They should feel very guilty and ashamed, but they'll never admit it publicly!"

"Of course not: they don't want to pay compensation for constructive dismissal and loss of earnings and pension! Sealand Occupational Health had been right all along, when they'd assured me they would support me against Firlane School for loss of earnings and loss of pension! If I hadn't had my family to consider, this would've been a better solution! At the time, I felt I needed to put their needs first, as we'd already been the victims of a car accident and didn't need any more stress!"

"We used to be so happy at work for years. I can't believe what they did to a staff that had been so successful and had done so well for the school in HMSI inspections. No wonder so many staff left so unhappy; I saw them all at Sealand shops! It's their own fault they went into special measures and then had to close and reopen under a new name."

"I appreciate the happy memories I have from then: the pupils, friends, parents, the excursions, the concerts and the shows! I can certainly see the contrast in the change of management!"

"So can I, so can we all, but they'll not admit it."

"I'm not alone in seeing the real problem!"

"Without working, we wouldn't have our occupational pensions or any OAP."

"I'm still waiting for my OAP! We can treasure the friends and the happy memories we have."

"We were so happy then, every day."

"It's true when they say you don't know what you've got until it's gone."

I was always pleased to see Dawn, Andrea, Jacqui, Lilly, Amy and Tonia when working in other schools! Lilly told me how they all saw a pattern in the department I had worked in, at Firlane School! Lilly told me, "We could all see what was happening, because staff left your department, one at a time. One left, then another one left, then another one left …"

"We worked together, for years, and it was always a pleasure to organise the SATs together, for years!"

"I saw the change of management, then I saw one teacher, at a time, leave from the department you'd worked in and it went on for years, well after you'd left."

"It was a pattern of behaviour by management, not one individual person!" Lilly gave me lots of cuddles and that made us both feel much better!

Also, working with past pupils, who treated me with respect, and who acted as a referee for me, helped me and past pupils helped Dawn as well. It was an absolute pleasure for me to meet Keeley Sanders again. I worked with Keeley in two schools, "I always tell everyone I always loved your lessons, which was why I went on to become a teacher and to teach the same subject as you."

"We had fun every lesson, didn't we?"

"I still love Shakespeare and Jane Austen and I get paid to do teach them now."

Wasn't that lovely? I worked with Christine Roper, a past pupil, who also said exactly the same as Keeley, but in a different school. Being valued by Whiteland School, Emmerland School and Heartland School, which are some of the best schools in the country also helped me! Also, Dawn was loved by Dealey School. It had been a pattern of divide and conquer! It was the difference between heaven and hell!

At Bishop School, Amy Walters and Tonia Golightly, both teachers who Dawn and I had worked with at Firlane School, asked, "How's Dawn getting on? I haven't seen her for years."

I told them the truth, "Dawn looks years younger, more beautiful and is much happier now!"

"It was Firlane School then! Everyone's happier after they've left!" Tonia laughed.

"It's lovely to see you both again!"

"We used to be happy, sitting together at breaks and lunchtimes," Amy added.

"We made good friends at Firlane School."

Amy Walters and Tonia Golightly both gave me a big cuddle whenever they saw me! They were both in their 50s now but I had known them from when they were in their 30s! They were both about my height (not very tall!) and slim. They both had brown hair and were still friendly, pleasant and polite! We all knew staff who'd now died from Firlane School and concentrated on our happy memories, which were many! Meeting up at Bishop School always brought back happy memories for all of us!

The management had been deceitful hypocrites in Firlane School and in Forth School!

There was a television programme about Dinton police, which showed the management of Dinton police praising themselves, "We saved money by getting rid of older, more expensive staff and by replacing them with younger, cheaper staff."

Another police force commented, "We will not be using Dinton's approach!" I had no doubt that this was what had been happening in schools too!

I was highly fortunate to have a wonderful family to nurture, protect and to encourage! By putting others before yourself, life is easier to cope with! Their needs were greater than mine! Religion helped every day too! Treating other people the way you would like to be treated and putting someone else's needs first was a simple, efficient and effective solution! It worked! All of my childhood and adulthood, I'd gone to church! All I found was that religion was right! My parents were right! Before my father died, he told me and my brother Oliver, "Look after your mam and the bairns." This excellent advice helped me to cope with his death and with everyday problems. Looking after others was more important than looking after myself! It brought its own rewards and happiness, which are things money can't buy! The best things in life are free!

The solution is to have a work/ life balance! If there's a problem in one aspect of your life, try to do everything you can, to solve it; if not, walk away and concentrate on other aspects of your life, so you're always channelling your energy in a positive direction.

17. Has This Happened Before?

A documentary about Hitler showed a link with power, deceit, manipulation and lies! Ruthless, unscrupulous people pursuing power by deceit, manipulation and lies had all been done before. There has been a pattern throughout history of greed, unfairness, bullying and war. As older teachers, we should have been treated with respect all of the time. Luckily, Dawn and I had supported each other, and the main thing was that we didn't become ill. I couldn't believe it when I watched documentaries about the two world wars; I couldn't believe the link between money, power, lies and deceit. A quick solution is to trust your own instincts and to keep yourself safe. Simple! This solved it for me, for Dawn and for others. The documentary showed the link between power and manipulation: Hitler justified himself and blamed everyone else! Doesn't that sound familiar? The soldiers and the ordinary people didn't know the truth either. Hitler lectured on the evils of the world! During the war it was all about propaganda: the authorities only let the public know what they wanted them to know.

The solution, then and now, is to do the right thing and not to be blinded by power, wealth and worldly values! Following a simple life, of kindness, fairness and compassion, along with doing the right thing, is easier and less stressful! If it doesn't feel right and you don't have the power to change it, walk away and keep yourself safe! Follow safety first and prevention is better than a cure! Follow honesty, ethics and always do the right thing. It might not earn you money, power and worldly success, but at least you can sleep at night, with a clear conscience.

I could see a pattern of power, money, manipulation and social class. The mafia in another country thrived when there was poverty or a crisis, because people needed money, then many people in poverty felt tricked into doing things they perhaps wouldn't really have wanted to do. Throughout history, there has been conflict over power, money, status and the distribution of wealth.

Will we all ever learn? The problem now and then has been power, wealth and the distribution of wealth and privilege; the current government also believed in capitalism, not socialism. Was this a contributory factor? A later report blamed the management of schools, as they made the decisions in schools, not the government.

However, life doesn't have to be a them and us attitude; we could all work together, for the benefit of us all. The problem, then and now, has been about manipulation. We know the truth: it's all happened before, throughout history. It's about appearance and reality. Many appeared successful by worldly values but were morally corrupt.

A quick solution for all of us: trust your personal instincts and stay safe. Simple! This solved it for me, for Dawn and for many colleagues and can solve many problems for others too.

Sealand Occupational Health had been correct. They repeatedly assured me they would support me against Firlane School, because I'd always been highly successful as a teacher, and the problem really had been the management of Firlane School. Sealand Occupational Health identified the issues, which were my loss of wages and my loss of pension, and Sealand Occupational Health knew that Firlane School had known what they were doing! Even after I'd left, Sealand Occupational Health repeatedly reassured me they would support me against Firlane School, but I was worried about the effects on my family, as our family had just won one court case, and I didn't want additional stress for my family. However, the bullying, harassment and unwanted behaviour continued in every school, even 14 years later! Our GPs were right, Sealand Occupational Health and Dinton Occupational Health were right all along. As politics and politicians have shown us throughout history, conflict and injustice are easily created. The medical profession had been right! All that happened was that at the end, I was more annoyed than upset, which is much better than being depressed.

The whole situation had been about money, power, inequality and the distribution of wealth. A recent UN report showed the UK did have increasing social problems, with worse poverty and homelessness than many poorer countries. There must be something drastically wrong when people at the bottom end of the social scale don't have enough food and a roof over their heads, in the fifth richest country in the world! This problem had been caused by man's greed, injustice and inequality; capitalism had made money for businesses, without valuing the workers; this was certainly ironic, almost 100 years after two world wars! Many people expected another war, but a different type of war, showing the problems of money, power and the distribution of wealth.

Years later, talking about mental health became popular. No wonder! Management in schools had caused problems for many older, more expensive and more experienced teachers! Mental health issues were constantly in the news: talking about problems was recommended! Dawn and I had supported each other through thick and thin and it had cost us nothing! We both talked to other teachers too, so we could all see common problems and how to solve them. It was now politically correct to talk about problems and how to solve them! Clearly, I felt it was much better to be safe than sorry at work. Finding another job was clearly better than staying in an environment where I felt bullied, harassed and the victim of unwanted behaviour! Good mental health and concentrating on being happy and healthy is always much better than fear, misery, feeling afraid and depression, which are the symptoms of bullying. It is totally legal to concentrate on being happy and healthy, to talk about problems and how to solve them! Our GPs were right, so were Sealand Hospital, Sealand Occupational Health and Dinton Occupational Health, along with HMSI and the headteachers in the best schools in the area!

The more I thought about what had been upsetting me, and the more I put it into words, the happier I felt, but I kept concentrating on doing the right thing. I understood how they'd upset me and others, and I understood the truth about what they'd really done, but I knew they would deny it. Dawn knew the same! My other colleagues knew the same too. I knew they would defend themselves and they would always blame others, because they wouldn't blame themselves, would they? Dawn knew the same! Other colleagues knew the same too!

I found writing things down helped to keep positive mental health and a can-do attitude. I wasn't ill. I was just terribly upset by the way I'd been treated. Dawn felt the same! Other colleagues felt the same too! Friendship had been invaluable and had saved us, because who else would have believed we were all telling the truth? My family saved my mental health too, because there was always something to do or an event to attend! I had a family to care about and their feelings were more important than my own! Having a family saved my mental health too! I decided health and happiness were more important than worldly status, but it took me years to say that! Dawn decided health and happiness were more important than a job, but it took her years to say that too! My other colleagues found the same, as their doctors had also told them to leave if they felt bullied. All of that distress over management! What a waste of time and energy! This is what had upset me and others and getting over this distress had been the problem! Our GPs were right! The hospital and two occupational healths were right too, along with HMSI and the headteachers of the best schools in the area!

All that I found, years later, after being on a constant merry go round of worry, was that my GP was right, and so were Sealand Occupational Health and Dinton Occupational Health! It was now fashionable to look after your mental health! Dawn felt revenge was a dish best served cold. Other colleagues felt being positive, with a can-do attitude, and finding another job was much better than being afraid, fearful and depressed. Many of us still wanted to be teachers, so many of us kept teaching but many teachers left the teaching profession, finding it wasn't worth the stress, bullying or manipulation! Many young teachers left too, as they couldn't stand the way they'd been treated any longer! It all depended on the individual management of the school! Fortunately, the medical profession and HMSI saved my mental health, as they knew the truth too! Some of the best schools in the country also knew the truth and they saved my mental health too!

Waiting and thinking about something is a much better response than acting while upset! I felt being morally right, without acting incorrectly, was a much better response, than making serious mistakes or being driven to suicide!

18. Survival

Survive and strive to achieve the important values in life and do the right thing. No one would like to be treated the way we'd been treated, yet many people lived in much worse circumstances and couldn't escape their glass prisons. Surely there must be a way for everyone to escape. Surely there must be a way for honest people to escape. Surely there must be a way to escape poverty for everyone. Do some people need to curb their all-consuming greed? Persevere and overcome problems; become inspirational role models. Life and people are important, not worldly values. Save yourself and save others, write a novel! (Writing things down helps to relieve the stress!) Concentrate on your own happy memories from when you were young. Concentrate on being happy every day. Write problems down, so you're not ill. Talking about them to someone you trust and solving them, one by one, can save your mental health. I felt much better for writing things down; it released the chains, the handcuffs and the boulders!

This was a simple, quick, free and effective strategy, which worked! If it worked for me and it worked for others, then this simple, quick, free, effective strategy (of writing problems down) could help others too! Through this, I felt less devastated, less afraid and less miserable, which was releasing me from the prison, torture and confinement of bullying. This simple process, of writing problems down, helped me to focus on solutions to the problems; this simple process, of writing problems down, could help others to focus on the solutions to their problems too.

Martin Smythe, Andrea Tweed, Simon Coyles, Jacqui Ayre, Dawn Sinclair, Carole Renwick and I, and others, all left Firlane School feeling there was a problem with the change of management, and that they had created an environment we couldn't work in! The office staff also left! It was a pattern of behaviour. Does austerity mean getting rid of many experienced and expensive teachers, and many other experienced and expensive members of staff, to save money? In the newspapers, they reported there would be a shortage of 50,000 teachers in five years' time. Is anyone surprised?

Talking to Dawn and to other teachers helped me to cope with problems at work, so I wasn't ill and I could solve my problems. My family helped me to cope, so I wasn't ill and this gave me time to think and to solve problems! Discussing the problems at work, with Dawn and other supply teachers, helped us all to cope and to be resilient, instead of being ill. We all found we were victims of social injustice, as we were all qualified teachers, no longer paid according to our payscale when I had been, years ago, being a supply teacher! It was the same job as years ago, the difference was the 2008 financial crash, which led to the birth of agencies running the supply teacher train to save LEAs money! I wasn't born yesterday! Talking about the problem, on a merry go round, saved our mental health! It didn't just happen to one person!

Grit and determination, to overcome problems, and reliance were the skills I now needed! I had always had these skills, after all, I had watched many super hero films and tragedies on TV! Surely, I had learned these skills before? Every super hero has a villain to overcome! Every novel and every film have problems to overcome!

That was how I coped; I identified problems and then tried to solve them, step by step, so I wasn't ill! Solving problems is always much better than being weak and anxious. The perpetrators of the corrupt regime could get their just rewards, sooner or later, without my help. They couldn't escape HMSI, who also knew the truth! They couldn't escape their own consciences and they couldn't escape God. How could they sleep at night? I'm better off in good health, without them.

Dawn told me, "I feel no sympathy at all towards the management who has acted so appallingly towards us. Staff shortages in the future are a direct result of short-sighted actions in the present."

"No wonder so many people are less well off than years ago! Others are paid much less than us, and live in poverty."

"Others are much worse off than us."

"They are! Many are working full time and claim benefits because they aren't paid enough."

"That's disgraceful!"

"That's how the rich grow richer and the poor grow poorer."

"The people in power know what they're doing!"

"The employer grows richer and the taxpayer picks up the bill for the low wages, by paying for the benefits."

"The way women in your age group have been treated is disgraceful! I was lucky to receive my OAP at 60."

"You were lucky! I live in hope that someone gives us something."

"So do I, but I don't think they'll part with the money easily."

"No. I still can't believe they really did it. I always thought they would give us something. It isn't a benefit, it's something we've paid into all of our lives. They wouldn't be allowed to do that with private pensions."

"As we can see, with our Teacher's Pensions."

Working together, to heal ourselves, worked; my father had always told me that there was a book inside of everyone! Now, I could enjoy every day, by concentrating on being happy and healthy; it was a quick and simple solution that costs nothing. Our attitude of we will survive, saved us. We weren't the problem: the problem was how we'd been treated! The underlying problem had been money and the distribution of wealth; some people have, and some people have not!

My happy memories of our good group of friends, for years, saved my mental health! Luckily, Dawn and I were friends for life, not just at work, which saved our mental health. I missed what we'd all previously had at work! You never know what you have until it's gone. Many left feeling upset! I reconnected with my friend, Kerris Harris from higher education, and she commented that I hadn't changed, which I was pleased to hear! I was happy every day when I was in higher education. Kerris was now a primary school teacher, working part-time, as she too had retired from full-time teaching. When I told her I was writing a novel, she was totally impressed. She knew my mining background; she knew my novel was a logical follow-on from my student days!

My motto now is to appreciate every day and to concentrate on being happy and healthy; keep everything in perspective: health and happiness are more important than being bullied and harassed, where the bully will blame the victim because they won't blame themselves, will they? Mutual support, with Dawn and other teachers, was invaluable yet didn't cost a penny and saved the NHS a fortune! It saved my mental health. Concentrating on being happy and healthy is much better than being depressed and ill. Our doctors were right! Sealand Occupational Health and Dinton Occupational Health were also right! The medical profession had known what was going on, as could be seen in the report on Ceiling News, about the number of teachers on the sick with stress.

Identifying the problem helped me: I was no longer being treated the way other people would like to be treated themselves; the same thing happened to many others, and some, like Martin McVitie, ended up taking their own lives. With kindness, fairness and developing everyone to their maximum potential, lives and mental health could have been saved!

I, and others, should have been treated professionally and treated with respect and valued, with effective Continued Professional Development working in an environment where I, and others, could reach our maximum potential. The problem was the change of management! Although I was successful in supply teaching, we lost wages and pension, even though we were doing the same job as other teachers in the school! The vice-principal of Undercastle City School knew that I knew what management in schools had done and he told me, "We've tried to make teachers think if they were doing supply, it was a lesser job, but you know the truth! We've all done it to save money; all schools have been doing it. Although your contract was with us for a year, we still need you to do supply, so we'll pay you at the same rate, which is higher when you are paid directly by the school than through an agency. You do know the truth."

The schools that paid me directly, even though I did the same job as doing supply, paid me more than when the school paid me through an agency. Sealand Occupational Health had been correct. Dinton Occupational Health had said I had already won against them, which helped. However, I am still waiting for my compensation! Fortunately, the teaching unions knew the truth too and were trying to support all teachers! All teachers must be qualified! The teaching unions were also shocked at how supply teachers, who are qualified teachers, are treated now, compared to years ago! I was also treated with respect years ago and I wasn't bullied! I knew this was true, as at the beginning of my career as a teacher I was a supply teacher and was paid more, years ago, than I am now! I wasn't bullied at work either!

However, not everyone who was paid directly by a school was paid according to their payscale and Teacher's Pension! Others weren't as lucky as me! All I found, and all others found too, was that it was up to the individual school.

Dawn was still waiting for her compensation. Others were still waiting for their compensation too. In our new careers, as supply teachers, we were doing the same job, but working in more than one school! I was also an exam marker and enjoyed writing novels too, which certainly helped me to survive. Save your health and the health of others: trust your instincts and stay safe, don't be fooled by others.

I was lucky to have a wonderful family; they kept life in perspective! Protecting my family was the most important job I would ever have! I was lucky they were a pleasure every day; yes, they were time-consuming but they kept me busy! Every day I had important things to do, by being a mother and a wife! We were so lucky to be their parents because you couldn't buy them in a shop! Our three children were excellent role models to the world! The rest of the world could learn a great deal from them! All they had to do was to keep being marvellous people and to continue to be an inspiration to others! They were already wonderful people, who always wanted to help others and to do the right thing in life! All we all needed was to live a simple life and to concentrate on doing the right thing! All that glitters isn't gold! Don't be fooled by worldly values! All I found was that the values of Christianity solved all problems! Simply being a good, moral and kind person were important things in life, which may not be appreciated by wealth and status, but are far more important!

Dawn's memories of singing Christmas carols, every morning in the build-up to Christmas one particular year, while driving on the way to Dealey School, showed the contrast! Dealey School was marvellous to Dawn! A past pupil worked there and made her cups of coffee! The headteacher came into her classroom, unannounced, and was totally supportive of how Dawn was approaching the work she'd been given to do and how she approached working with difficult pupils. Dawn had also enjoyed working with university students. She was highly successful at private tuition and thoroughly enjoyed it. She was happy again, and eventually laughed lots again! This helped to save Dawn's mental health.

I was happier in my 60s because I could then see the pattern: in the media, other teachers, doctors, nurses, Amalane (an internet company), and other workers also suffered from stress! It was clearly not just us as individuals, but a pattern of management. I could see how others had become rich. I felt it was more important to do the right thing, than to be tricked by worldly values. I could choose supply teaching, exam marking or private tuition or do all three! Due to age and my family, I knew why I hadn't taken a permanent teaching post in a school when offered by the chair of governors, but I still valued the offer! The point of social justice is that I should have been paid the same rate as a permanent teacher, whether I worked in a school as a supply teacher or permanently! I was doing the same job and years ago I had been paid according to my payscale, whether it was supply or a permanent teaching post. It was the principle of social injustice that I wanted to highlight, discuss and solve.

Exam marking at home was peaceful and therapeutic. A quick and simple survival strategy was: don't be tricked by the worldly values of power, deceit, manipulation, worldly success, money and status; concentrate on health and happiness, instead of allowing the fear and misery of bullying to rule!

Finding proof on the internet saved my mental health! I found HMSI reports 2000, 2009 and 2014 and they proved beyond a shadow of a doubt that I'd been right! I'd been right all along! When I looked on the internet, I found the worst schools which I had reported to my teaching union for bullying, harassment and unwanted behaviour had all gone into special measures and many had been closed! This happened after the HMSI team had spoken to me, when I had been in Sealand LEA. HMSI had previously praised me for "best practice" and the" type of teacher the government wanted to value" and I was doing "the same job" as them, as I was "telling schools what I thought of them too". How ironic! I certainly hadn't expected this, but this was true too!

I concentrated on economic necessity, which was to get another job, and then I concentrated on being happy and healthy, which seemed easier and much better than being ill and was less stressful for my family than trying to prove it in court. You need to wait until you have enough evidence to win! Sealand Occupational Health knew the truth, and they would have supported me, but at the time I put my family first, to protect them. It was only because I had had a family that they got away with it! If I hadn't had others to consider, I probably would have taken the offer made by Sealand Occupational Health. People are important. I put my family first, so they didn't have to live through the stress of another court case!

We'd won the previous court case, which was why we didn't need the stress of another one! I knew the devious things that they'd done to try to destroy us as witnesses; I knew they'd hired a series of private detectives to follow us! Their intention had been to discredit us in court, to present us as liars! In the end, their evidence inadvertently supported everything we'd been saying! They hadn't expected that, had they? The truth was: I was happier and healthier away from the people who were bullying me! They weren't worth the stress they'd caused. I now felt vindicated! I was feeling happier and healthier, but the feeling of being followed, threatened and intimidated was there. I reported everything to my teaching union and concentrated on doing the right thing, to keep myself safe, my family safe and my friends safe. This empowered me to cope and to survive, because I had my evidence ready for court too!

Actions cause reactions! They were deliberately trying to upset me, so if I made a mistake, they would blame me! With Dawn's support, my reaction was to ignore the bullying and to smile at them; that would annoy them the most anyway! Bullying is the intention to hurt, so smiling was not letting them see the pain they'd caused; their intention had been to cause pain, distress and fear! Dawn had smiled consistently to Pauline Laserton and Pauline Laserton had been furious!

I tried to smile, but it was very difficult at times!

Krystal Welsh, who had always been friendly, had distanced herself and told me, "Don't tell anyone I'd checked your lesson plan and I'd agreed with it." She kept with Susan Stone, who was clearly supporting Roberta Oliver against everyone! This was a management issue as they'd deliberately isolated me, to create an unbearable environment to work in! The management had picked us off, one by one, which showed it was done deliberately and ruthlessly. Percy Banks joined in with this management style and made Dawn's life a misery at work. Unfortunately for Percy, they later made his life a misery at work, and created an environment he couldn't work in either! It was appearance and reality. They appeared successful by worldly values but they were morally corrupt.

My strategy to cope was to write everything down, so I could see the problems in front of me. This strategy also stopped problems from being bottled up. It just meant I kept writing about the same problems, which was, on reflection, a coping strategy! It was better than living in fear and misery! Good friends can support each other with problems and solve them! Dawn and I helped each other to cope; I found this made life easier and more solvable. A can-do attitude solves problems instead of crying over them and being crushed by others. Trust your instincts and don't be tricked by others. Be a moral person and treat others the way you would like to be treated. Pray or think about what is really important in life, because that helps you to cope: remembering that people are important in life, not possessions, also helps. Having a wonderful family certainly helped too! Just keep writing the same problem and solution down, to relieve the stress and anxiety. This simple strategy could help others, to save their mental health and prevent suicides.

Trust in God or in goodness, because that releases stress, so you don't feel alone, and so you feel as though there will be justice at the end of the bullying tunnel. Don't let bullying, harassment and unwanted behaviour destroy your light. Stay alive and stay safe. We can see what happened to Martin McVitie; it's happened to many others too. If we don't need to worry about the people in power, we feel happier! Believing in God could take all of the worry about their worldly actions and their power away; that leaves us with happiness; if you don't believe in God, believing in goodness and doing the right thing also helps! When I had felt empty of happiness and full of sadness, I prayed for the Holy Spirit to help me, and then I no longer felt alone! My happiness returned, and suddenly, worldly values no longer felt important; I was important, not worldly values, and I felt much happier! Was it the thought of not being alone that saved me and gave me strength? Was it the thought that someone cared and there would be justice at the end of life? Was it the thought that my parents, and other family members, would care and were in heaven, where I hoped to meet them again? It didn't matter if I couldn't prove anything, just believing someone was there and cared had saved me! Would just knowing someone cared help save others too? Would identifying problems and then solving them, step by step, help others too?

There had also been a common problem of capitalism, austerity (in other sections of society) and stress in other jobs, not just with individuals. There was now expected to be a shortage of teachers in five years' time, of approximately 50,000. Doctors were also under stress at work, as were Amalane workers. Many social problems were now being caused in the UK. There had been a rise in homelessness in recent years in the UK, and a necessity for food banks and heating problems for many people, as many had to choose between buying food or paying for heating. In a recent UN report, the UK, the fifth richest country in the world, had more homelessness and poverty than many other less well-developed countries, so the continuing problem was the distribution of wealth. I was not alone in feeling upset by the way I'd been treated, but others had been treated far worse than me! I was very disappointed to hear the government denied the UN report, which looked extremely accurate to me! Why did they continue to deprive OAPs of the pension they had worked for, even though the UK's OAP was much lower than other countries in the EU?

I wished I'd been able to prove the way I'd been treated at work in court, but I couldn't at the time, because of family reasons; I had a family to protect, who didn't need to live through the stress of another court case. However, it was all too fantastic not to be true! I put my trust in the hope that the pen was mightier than the sword. Truth is stranger than fiction; it's all too fantastic not to be true!

Keep a can-do attitude and strive to overcome all problems in life! Grit, determination and resilience are excellent qualities in adversity! That was how two world wars were won!

19. Meeting up at Newpalace

Meeting up in Newpalace was therapeutic because Dawn and I discussed all problems, and then felt better! On reflection, my teaching union's advice had also helped: enjoy your time with family and friends. Together, we found that discussing our problems with others, who were trustworthy, helped us to resolve problems in the best way possible.

Newpalace was the biggest city near us; it was alive, friendly and bustling! Newpalace had many restaurants, shops and pubs, so there was something for everyone! There were also free activities for children and special events all year round! It was always a pleasure to walk around, to see the many markets and quaint shops. It was a pleasure just to see and to hear the chatter and the music and singing, played live, in the many streets! Newpalace laughed, smiled and joked with everyone who went!

"It's taken us both years to recover from the bullying we endured, to deal with it and to cope," Diane confessed.

"Years later, we can see clearly what they've done, and how much they've upset us."

"Of course we can! It's all totally logical!"

"It was really the basis of a court case! All I've found is that Sealand Occupational Health was correct, and so was Dinton Occupational Health!"

"My doctor and Sealand Hospital were also right!"

"We can now see the problem was really lies and bullying, which they would've denied! The clear pattern was to isolate the victim, and then to blame the victim, for being upset. Fortunately, the medical profession wasn't fooled! The management at Firlane School and at Forth School had been telling lies and using their power to manipulate events!"

"Look what happened to them!"

"They both went into special measures, after HMSI told me they were going into every school to find the real reason why I'd left, and both eventually were closed."

"Serves them right! You can fool some of the people some of the time, but not all of the people all of the time."

I decided to show the lies and the truth, by writing everything down, about where I used to work. Dawn felt, "We need to expose their lies and tell the truth, about how we were treated at work." I decided to expose the devious and underhand exploits of dishonest people, who really thought they would succeed in their corrupt intentions. I'd reported events to the medical profession and to the teaching union, to protect my mental health! It worked!

It clearly had been a change of management and mental health advice and mental health courses have shown that it's best to appreciate or concentrate on other areas of your life if there're problems in one area of your life that you can't change. Protect your mental health on a daily basis, for example with family, friends, community and finances. I believed the real problem was money, because that had been the continuing problem in the news, in government debates and in elections. The intention by management to destroy staff was bullying and psychological warfare, because it had been done deliberately, to staff, one at a time, destroying a large friendship group. No wonder Firlane School went into special measures eventually! Firlane School had been a happy school: "Good," by HMSI with "good management". The change was in the management, which did not value the staff, which had been valued by the original headteacher, HMSI and Sealand LEA. It had been about mental health; it had also about the distribution of wealth and feeling valued.

I'd always been valued and happy and able to work to my maximum potential, until there'd been a change of management! I had no doubt that the root causes had been money and ruthless ambition! It obviously wasn't my ability, because I'd always been so successful! I hadn't been a career person or ambitious, after I'd a family! Yet, I was still at the top of my payscale and a manager at school, as well as a teacher! I did earn much more money than younger, cheaper teachers! Was that my crime? Was it that I had raised a concern with a primary school, when a family member was sleepwalking and worrying about a weekly spelling test, when the list of spellings was too difficult? Was it that I had reported bullying by pupils in a secondary school to the school, and then to the police, when the school failed to protect the victim? Both actions might have been enough to begin this chain of bullying, as I was the victim of this witch hunt. Both Beatrice Milton and Chloe Crispin had told me this was the real reason for the way I'd been treated. As loss of wages and loss of pension had happened to many others too, was it also about money and the financial crash of 2008?

Bullying is the intention to hurt: I had been the victim of mental cruelty with the comments made to me at school, the shops, the bank and the building society. The comments outside of school stopped after we took our money out of the Huddersland Building Society, following a complaint I'd made about the unacceptable customer service I'd received. The senior management agreed with me and gave me financial compensation, which I put into a different bank. This complaint stopped all comments being made outside of school at the shops, the banks and the building societies. It didn't stop all comments at schools, which was why I continued to report everything to my teaching union, and why I still report all comments to my teaching union. It's to save my mental health and to provide evidence, if needed, for a court case.

I had no doubt that school management was doing this because I had evidence against the schools and the LEA, so they did this to undermine me as a witness. I knew why: they didn't want to pay compensation, the same as the insurance company, who hired private detectives to follow me, and my husband. At the time, my husband and I felt someone was watching us, but we couldn't prove it, until the other side had to disclose their evidence to the court! My teaching union told me this pattern of comments had happened to others as well; my teaching union representative advised me to concentrate on being happy with my family and friends. He was right! This stopped the fear and the feeling of powerlessness. Concentrating on what made me feel happy and healthy was another simple solution! It worked!

I knew the management of schools was behind the comments, the bullying, harassment and unwanted behaviour. I knew it was their management because different people kept making the same type of comments independently, so it had been a pattern. Jacqui, Carole and Percy all made comments that I hadn't kept in touch with anyone from Firlane School; I didn't mention Dawn's name at the time, as I was afraid they would bully her too. I tried to protect Dawn. Carole was always fishing for information about Dawn, and about me. She even went to see one of my family members at work, to ask her questions, but the family member told me, and didn't give her details either! Carole Miller also did the same to Dawn. Jacqui told me she'd kept in touch with Terence and Krystal; Dawn was shocked because she had thought better of her. Jacqui ended up doing supply, the same as us, as did Carole, as did many others. Krystle also left under very unhappy circumstances.

Carole Renwick had also made a comment that I'd been waiting for my pension, which was more lies spread by management! Denise Marsey made a comment, "They were going to say it was because you'd stayed in the one school, but they can't say that now." The same comments were made at different places, trying to cause conflict with my family. I now know this was just a strategy of management, to try to divide and conquer, so they would win! The simplest solution was to ignore it all and to report it to my union, so I had evidence against them! My friends, such as Dawn Sinclair, Amy Walters and Tonia Golightly who had left Firlane School, with no contact to their management, didn't make these comments!

I'd been happier at Heartland School and Emmerland School because they had the same expectations regarding behaviour as me! Also, I was valued as a teacher by Diana Dobson, head of department at Heartland School and regarded as the expert in the department for the paper I marked for the exam board by her and the headteacher, Keith Gibbon. The behaviour at Heartland School was much better than other schools. I was now only working on a supply basis, to prevent the continuing bullying, harassment and unwanted comments, which had been going on in schools and out of schools! The continuous comments outside of school only stopped after I removed our money from the building society and transferred it to the bank and complained about the unacceptable customer service! I really did appreciate the financial compensation I was awarded, but where was the financial compensation from schools? Also, as I was growing older, supply teaching suited me more than a permanent post; I could be flexible and fit around the needs of my family more (I was more tired so I couldn't do it all).

Dawn, a modern-day detective, had also worked it out! All

the fictional detectives would have been proud of us! "We'd worked well at school and we'd been happy. We'd been praised by HMSI and Sealand LEA and management hadn't liked it!"

"They were annoyed that I was identified as "best practice" by HMSI and "excellent" as a teacher by Sealand LEA, when management hadn't been! On reflection, this was also where the problem lay, along with money! They were jealous! Jealousy is a green-eyed monster! We'd been happy at work and we'd always done our best!"

"Happy workers who are treated fairly are happy to do extra and to keep doing their best. Unhappy workers, who are unfairly treated and work in fear and misery, cannot do their best and are more likely to work to rule."

"Some unfairly treated workers could do the absolute minimum, as history shows us repeatedly." Years of talking about it, together, took away the fear and the misery of the bullying; it was the realisation that they didn't have the power to hurt us anymore; it was the realisation that we didn't have to be frightened anymore; it was the realisation we could be happy again and laugh lots again! Then, we felt much better because we'd got to the bottom of what they'd done to upset us.

They had inadvertently forged a friendship through thick and thin; Dawn and I had needed each other and had found happiness in valuing friendships and in valuing our families. This was all free, yet invaluable; it saved our mental health! We weren't fooled by them at all now. Dawn and I both knew what they'd done. Dawn and I both knew we had better health away from them! They were just not worth the distress they'd caused! Working together, to solve problems, made a difference to how we felt, which was much better than feeling weak, powerless and anxious. This helped us to feel mentally strong, rather than feeling like weak victims. It was appearance and reality. They appeared successful by worldly values but they were morally corrupt. Friendship is invaluable, yet costs nothing! Sharing the feelings of fear and misery, the feelings of being bullied, and concentrating on solving problems was far better than being unhappy! It worked!

Years later, we both felt much happier and more rested. Dawn then told me, "I now feel safe. I never felt safe there at the end."

"Management revelled in promoting a climate of fear and misery, at the end."

"One basic mistake they made was to assume we wouldn't talk about it to others, who we could trust. They totally underestimated us. How arrogant! Did they think they were invincible? The higher they climb, up the ladder of dictatorship, the harder they fall. How arrogant of them to think there would never be a day of reckoning."

"I wonder how many of them keep in touch with each other."

"Richard always says that people like Pauline Laserton end up very lonely in their extreme old age."

"Feeling afraid, feeling in danger and feeling unsafe was exactly how I'd felt at Firlane School too, at the end! I've left the day of reckoning with HMSI, the unions, the healthcare profession and with God. Talking to others, who have also felt upset in schools, has helped as well!"

"We don't have the power to stop them."

"We don't have the wealth either. I didn't take it further and did supply teaching to protect my family from the distress they didn't need! Another court case would've been very stressful."

"That's how they get away with it."

"As it's a common problem: supply teachers not being paid to payscale and not receiving Teacher's Pension, along with other agency workers, it's also a union problem."

"The unions don't have the power to do anything either."

"Not since the miners' strike in 1984-1985."

"The police made a lot of money but the miners lost."

"And look at what's happened since then."

After meeting Dawn, I felt much better and felt as though I could now smile and laugh, because I felt marvellous. I could totally see they'd been planning each person's downfall and that it was bullying. Fortunately, Dawn knew I had reported bullying to the headteacher, Basil Wight, as had Jacqui Ayre and so had Simon Coyles! Basil Wright had threatened Simon Coyles, "If you ever go to the newspapers about this, I'll make sure you never work again!" Many others had also reported bullying. All that happened was that when a person reported bullying they were bullied even more and had to leave to protect their mental health!

I felt as though I, and others, should've had the confidence to continue to climb high and to conquer the world, instead of being so frightened, afraid and anxious. By talking and writing about it, it helped me to appreciate my wonderful life; I felt I could laugh and be happy again, and that the weight of the world had been removed from my shoulders. Having a friend who also knew the truth had given us both the strength to see what they'd done and to move on. I just hoped my pearls of wisdom would help others, to stay safe and to protect their health, which was why I wrote novels.

The truth is, they would deny it all and attack me and every other person who reported bullying! I felt much happier talking about it and everyone commented on how Dawn looked years younger!

In the news, a heartbroken girl, Claire Forbouy, committed suicide, which is awful and why we're all much better off saying what has upset us, solving problems and concentrating on our health and happiness. There are many Martin McVities in the world; there are many Claire Forbouys in the world. Talking had cost us nothing, yet had saved the NHS a fortune. Dawn and I had appreciated each other through thick and thin, over problems at work, and that had saved our mental health. Talking about problems is always better than staying upset, yet I could see the problems of talking leading to a court case, which is why I reported everything to my teaching union, so I had evidence in court, if needed.

I'd very felt upset, devastated and betrayed that my trusted friend, Beatrice Milton, had crushed my trust and confidence in her, as had Chloe Crispin. However, 20 years later, I still felt upset by Beatrice Milton, because she'd threatened me and then lied, by denying it! Beatrice Milton had once been my friend; we'd done our homework together; we'd taken our dogs for walks together; we'd been friends for years! I still felt broken hearted by her betrayal, but I knew she had been manipulated, as had Chloe Crispin and Carole Renwick. However, I was better off without the stress, distress and anxiety the bullying had created! My main comfort was that they could tell as many lies as they wanted, but they couldn't really lie to their own consciences or to God.

It was the same pattern of bullying, harassment and unwanted behaviour shown by Jack Ashton, Beatrice Milton and Chloe Crispin. They'd all been working in Dinton LEA. Dinton

LEA was where the primary school was which had left so much to be desired for my children! These teachers had all been working in Dinton LEA so, obviously, the management of at least one faith school in Dinton LEA was involved in the bullying, harassment and unwanted behaviour, as told to me by both Beatrice Milton and Chloe Crispin! They attacked me, to defend themselves! The bullying would be difficult to prove in court. Both Beatrice and Chloe had threatened me! Chloe had threatened me, by saying, "If you ever tell anyone who the person is behind this, the headteacher of the secondary school she works at, they'll make sure you never work again! They're protecting their friends, the faith schools. Percy Mullaney is behind it all, because he's sticking up for Ruperton School." Did they all have a handbook on bullying teachers? This was the same threat that had been made to Simon Coyles!

Sealand Hospital had told me that my teaching job was mixed in with any problems my children met in schools! The doctor at Sealand Hospital told me, "Teachers! It's your own profession who're treating you like this. It's teachers who're treating your family like this. It's teachers who're doing this." They were certainly right, weren't they? I hope the teachers concerned, and staff, have read about the person who'd been driven to suicide! I had had a lucky escape, as had Dawn! We were not ill; we'd been terribly upset; we were far happier away from them! They wouldn't like anyone to treat them like this, so they shouldn't have treated me, and others, like this. They shouldn't have treated my family like this, but now, I could see it was part of a pattern, of how management treated not just the one victim, but whole families! Wasn't it strange how the police stopped the bullying by pupils in school against a family member, by issuing police cautions and warning of prosecution through the courts! Why did the police care but the faith schools involved only defended themselves?

Dawn told me to smile at them because that would annoy them the most! Bullying is the intention to hurt, which was why they were so annoyed if we smiled. Smiling and being happy were more difficult in those circumstances, because it was psychological bullying. I loved Dawn's idea of smiling because that annoyed them the most, but, when feeling afraid and miserable, it's extremely difficult to do! Their intention had been to hurt, so, outwardly, smiling was the best solution. One of my lecturers, who was a psychologist, had told us all that looking away from a bully, then smiling, was the best way to deal with bullying. It sounds simple, but it's actually very difficult to do! This strategy helped me; it could help other people and cost the NHS nothing. Don't retaliate, because they will then blame you because they certainly won't blame themselves, will they? It took years to get over this, but I now hope to use this experience to help others, by writing novels. Would this end the social injustice and exploitation of supply teachers and others?

Dawn was certainly right about smiling being the best strategy to cope with them, as was my psychology lecturer!

Previously, Dawn's doctor had told her to go back to see him if the working environment grew worse! My doctor had told me to leave my post and to find another post! Independently, both doctors told us to leave; both doctors told us to get another job. Independently, Andrea Tweed had been told exactly the same by her doctor too, as had Carole Renwick and Jacqui Ayre! We all, later, did supply teaching. The strain of oppression gradually lifted over the years; we all now looked and felt younger than we did years ago.

I found the solution to bullying was to concentrate on living a long and happy life; that was the best way to manage it, as they wanted to hurt! It was a waste of a life worrying about them because they wouldn't admit they had anything to do with causing someone to be unhappy, ill or dead!

Dawn had both pensions, her occupational pension and her OAP, so life was marvellous, eventually! It had really been about power, manipulation and money; he who laughs last, laughs the longest! I can laugh now, because I know the truth of it all: my life is happier now and I can laugh more now! My main problems were behind me, or so I hoped! I could enjoy every day now, by working in the best schools in the country: Whiteland School, Heartland School, Emmerland School, Deighton Alana School and Dinton High School. Both private schools helped, as they had the same expectations of pupils' behaviour as me, so I felt relieved! Why else would they employ me? Also, I was highly valued in these schools.

The issues in schools had really been about expectations and being a valued member of a team. When I went to school as a pupil, everyone was expected to work in lessons and to have a work ethic! Whiteland School, Heartland School and Emmerland School still expected this! I felt so much better, because three of the best schools in the country, and two private schools (Dinton High School and Deighton Alana School) had the same expectations as me! Others had been deliberately bullying and had been trying to manipulate events to save money, and to use their power to show they were right. How strange that this coincided with a world financial crash in 2008!

Many older teachers around the country found themselves feeling bullied and victims of constructive dismissal! The management was lucky, because due to a wish to protect my family, I simply found another job! On reflection, if it hadn't been for these family circumstances, I might have allowed Sealand Occupational Health to support me against them! The union later said it would've supported me, if they'd known what Sealand Occupational Health had advised me to do. Sealand Occupational Health even rang me many times, after I'd left, to offer this support. Again, I tried to protect my family from distress. Dinton Occupational Health told me I'd already won against Firlane School, with Whiteland School! Was that why they were so annoyed and tried to make my life a misery?

Diana Dobson made a comment near me, but not directly to me, "They didn't expect you to work here; they now know who we are because I've spoken to them." Diana was in her 30s, beautiful, friendly and short! She had long, blonde, straight hair. Heartland School was one of the best schools in the area, and I agreed with their expectations and they agreed with mine! Along with my successful colleagues, I should've been supported by management, with disruptive pupils in every school. I didn't have any (or at the very least exceedingly rare) disruptive pupils at Heartland School, because the headteacher told me to tell pupils he was my personal friend and he wanted to see anyone who wasn't excellent and a pleasure to teach! No one wanted to see him at all! When I had been at Whiteland School and Emmerland School, I knew I would be totally supported by management, and the pupils knew it too, so no pupil wanted to be in trouble!

When I first started teaching at Turnerlane School, I'd been regarded as a disciplinarian and during my first Christmas in the school, the headteacher came to my classroom and laughed when he saw the amount of Christmas cards I'd received from the pupils, saying, "How have you got so many more cards than everyone else in the school?" The management at Firlane School had tried to trick us all, but then, everyone else who'd praised us and valued us would have been wrong too! Dawn was right when, at Firlane School, she said, "Pull the other one; it has bells on!" This was Dawn's answer to anything the management at Firlane School tried to do when she knew they were trying to defend themselves, while attacking others.

I found concentrating on being happy, valuing my friends, staying safe and trusting my instincts worked. A friend in need is a friend indeed! I knew I would never forget Dawn's kindness, when I was so upset and Richard was noticeably upset, when he heard me speak on the telephone, because I was so frightened. He told Dawn to ring me back straight away. We solved all problems together. Concentrating on positive mental health, identifying the problem and taking small steps to solve it, worked!

I'm now looking forward to the future. Writing novels has been good for my health and it has given me closure, which is priceless. I hoped to support others in distress too. Writing problems down was a positive outlet, as writing things down released the distress, the upset and the stress, so I felt happier. I didn't want to lose my marbles! The worry had been my loss of wages and my loss of pension, because everyone needs money to live on! Wasn't Sealand Occupational Health right all along? It was compounded by not receiving my OAP until six years later than I had expected all of my life; I now had to wait until I was 66!

Sometimes, a simple solution is easier: you are simply better off without the people who upset you too much! Live a happy, healthy and peaceful life, instead of being upset by them! After all that, Dawn's doctor was right, when he advised her, "Stay with the people who make you happy and keep away from the others!"

I was very lucky to have a supportive family! My family was my priority! I already had a busy life and knew I'd done the right thing to protect my family from further distress. They were important: I could still be a teacher, an exam marker and an author! Having an amazing family is something you can't buy in a shop! People are more important than possessions! My family was far more important than money! We had enough money and I didn't actually need more! I didn't need to be greedy over money because my family gave me pleasure and pride every day! How did they all turn out to be such marvellous, kind and considerate people? It wasn't my family that went around deliberately hurting others.

Bullying causes fear and misery, which is why some people commit suicide! The perpetrators defend themselves and blame their victim! They can defend themselves as much as they want to, to other people, but they can't lie to themselves! Deep down, they know what they've done. How do they sleep at night?

Ms Price, the Home Secretary, had been accused of bullying at work. Her reply was, "I have been following the policy of paying less to senior (that means older staff) to save money. I have been following the advice given by management: "… pay policy which aims to reduce senior salaries …" I'd been right all along! A senior civil servant was taking a member of the government to court, for bullying at work. It was exactly the same cycle of behaviour!

Will they not learn? The government was also responsible for the distribution of wealth and had openly believed in capitalism, not socialism. They made Ruthlessness look like a saint. There are many Martin McVities in the world, ordinary people who just couldn't bear to live their lives any longer. There were many vulnerable people and many people driven to suicide by others, in the 21st century.

It didn't have to be a them and us attitude; why couldn't we all work together, for the benefit of everyone? The people who drive people to suicide or do nothing to prevent unnecessary deaths try to blame others, even though they know the truth themselves. The whole situation had been about manipulation and how people treat other people. I now knew the truth: it had all happened before, in history, and would continue to happen in the future, unless everyone cared more about the effect of their actions on others. If every individual cared about others, and kept being an honest, trustworthy and caring person, who helped others in society, perhaps more people would be happy and healthy and this would save lives. Don't let anyone destroy your light! Always strive to be the person who cares about others and who helps someone to solve problems, because something as simple as caring could save lives.

The lower expectancy age for people living in poverty and in deprived areas can't be disputed. However, everyone should have a happy and healthy environment, where everyone can reach their maximum potential, not just the privileged few. Some in the UK are given a life of privilege and luxury, while others are poor and homeless. Some people have been treated very harshly in life. Life is unfair for many and many are a lot less well off than others. I felt lucky not to be made mentally ill; others were not so lucky. However, Dawn and I both felt that was the intention of the management at Firlane School was to hurt; I thought the same of the management at Forth School! Angela Rivers was an unusual case, where she was sentenced to jail for eight years, for her lies, deceit, manipulation and for breaking the law. She hadn't expected that, had she?

Teamwork solves problems and saves mental health! Our GPs saved our mental health; Sealand Occupational Health saved my mental health; Dinton Occupational Health saved my mental health and Sealand Hospital saved my health and Dawn's. Simply talking to Dawn saved my mental health; Dawn talking to me saved her mental health. Talking was a simple solution, but it was effective! Identifying the problem and then taking steps, however small, one at a time, to solve the problem, saves mental health!

Pensions, as people grow older, such as the occupational pension and OAP do make a difference to the quality of life of older people. All I could now do was to try to live a long time and enjoy them (when I eventually receive my OAP six years late!) and look after my family, as well as I could! When you're retired you're your own boss. I looked forward to the day when I would eventually receive my OAP. Where was my compensation for not receiving it at 60, when I'd expected to most of my life?

However, some people lived in luxury while others lived in poverty. Remember: care about everyone, as people are more important than possessions. Bullies might be in a position of worldly power but it doesn't make them morally right! The real issue had been bullying and the solution was overcoming bullying by talking about problems, solving them, step by step and by concentrating on being happy and healthy!

20. The Future

I now felt mentally strong as I knew the problem was management at work, not me! So did Dawn! She wasn't the problem at work either! Andrea Tweed hadn't been the problem at work either! What a long list of people who'd left; it was bullying because it was a pattern of bullying older, experienced and expensive teachers, to save money! I could now spend my time supporting other teachers, who felt bullied at work and depressed! Once I had identified the problem, I could work to help others, individually and as part of humanity!

What a contrast! Being happy was much better than being afraid and miserable; fear and misery are the symptoms of bullying! I now felt strong and happy. Having a family and a friend who knew the truth too, as well as two occupational healths, HMSI, and the best schools in the area, had helped. Talking about bullying and feelings, of being afraid and miserable, is the first step to solving it! I now appreciated how much better life was without the people who'd upset me, and moving away from them had worked! It was much better than being ill! This was a simple solution, which could help others too! Solving problems is much better than being ill! Safety first and prevention is better than a cure. Living a happy life is much better than being upset and miserable. Quite simply: help others when they're upset! Don't walk away; show you care. Always be the person others can turn to, if they have a problem and need help! Always be reliable, trustworthy and kind. Always help others to overcome problems, so they are happy, healthy and alive! Kindness, support and constancy, in the face of adversity, and being there can save lives.

Caring and kindness are the answers, as well as having a can-do attitude to survive and to overcome all problems! I now concentrate on being happy and healthy every day, which is a much better answer than living in fear and misery, and helping others to do the same. Tell your GP and the Occupational Health, if you're worried about work. My problems were behind me, not in front, so I could laugh again and enjoy life, every day. My family, friends, doctor, HMSI and the best schools in the area had all saved me! This was much better than hospitalisation and medication tablets! I was simply far happier and healthier away from the people who were upsetting me. It had taken me years to appreciate what I have now, emotionally and mentally. Keep a positive mental attitude; have a can-do attitude; have more determination to solve problems. Find a new hobby, for good mental health, which I did, writing a novel! Family and friendship are free, yet saves the NHS a fortune!

Look well after your own health, by keeping both mentally and physically fit, if you possibly can! It's much better to be safe than sorry! Prevention is much better than a cure, as I've seen! You can't buy good health, so if something doesn't feel right, trust your instincts, because your instincts will protect you! It's appearance and reality. Many appear successful by worldly values but are morally corrupt. Have a clear conscience and keep away from bullying, harassment and unwanted behaviour. Have a clear conscience and keep away from crime. Have a clear conscience and do the right thing. Recognise your own individual achievements and strengths! Help others: by helping others, you also help yourself because you feel happier!

The solution to my anxiety had been talking and solving problems. I'd now proven the fight or flight advice to be correct, so I now knew how to help others. Solve problems if you can but have the wisdom to know when you don't have the power to solve a form of conflict, and walk away so you stay safe. My main problem was how to deal with bullying management; Dawn's main problem was how to deal with bullying management; other colleagues' main problem was how to deal with bullying management. The school management had deliberately made an environment we couldn't work in; I know what they've done; they know what they've done; others know what they've done too.

The solution is to accept how you feel, so you can see the problem. Once you know what the problem is, you set up a plan to solve the problem, using small steps. Once you manage to complete one small step, you can move onto the next small step. This is how to solve problems. In addition to this, you must identify your own achievements and personal strengths, to protect yourself, so you have the power and energy to solve problems. Labelling your feelings, and recognising your negative thoughts, is a step to solving problems! My parents had always told me to be kind, to help people and to never do anything back if anyone was unkind! "Two wrongs don't make a right," my father had always told me! I already had the tools to solve this! Keep being a kind, helpful person and don't retaliate to bullies! "Always do the right thing," my father had always advised! Didn't this seem a simple, quick and efficient way to solve problems? I could still use this advice and use my experience to support others! Kindness was a better solution than living in fear and misery!

Even though my father had been dead for years, he could still help me every day, in my heart and in my thoughts! At his funeral, the priest had told me (and everyone in the church), "When I met Michael, I met Jesus our Lord, at the same time." What a lovely thing to say! I kept trying to do the right thing at all times! I didn't need the stress those bullies had caused and I was much happier without them! My health and happiness were what was really important. A very simple solution was to walk away! A second solution was to use this experience to support others in distress!

I found solving the problem had made me much happier than feeling powerless, fearful and miserable. Talk to others about your problems, so you can work out a way to solve problems! Feeling powerless, fearful and miserable are the symptoms of bullying. My GP and the Occupational Health (at Sealand and at Dinton) saved my mental health, as did HMSI! So had my father, even though he'd died many years ago! My mother had always advised, "They can stay like that, if they're unkind; you don't have to join them." Their kindness and goodness, along with prayers, saved me!

Dawn's nightmares continued for many years, even after she'd retired; Dawn couldn't stop the post-traumatic stress; her nightmares centred around Pauline Laserton. No one can escape God, so I've put my trust in God. Religion has helped me and others too. I've been incredibly lucky in life, compared to many others; life has been even worse for many people! Take the moral high ground and have a clear conscience, because you can't lie to yourself and you can't lie to God. Moral integrity, simple values and a simple life lead to peace of mind, which is better than being bullied, harassed and being a victim of unwanted behaviour. My motto for a road to happiness: live a moral life, because having a clear conscience means you're at peace with yourself.

The failure is not about things going wrong in your life; the solution is to stay safe and to solve problems. Solve what you can, but if you can't, walk away, so you stay safe and stay alive. Solve what you can but walk away to live for another day, if you can't solve the problem. You may not win that battle, but you can still win the war! A good employer would've solved all of the problems, for me, for Dawn and for my colleagues and the problems of many others. Write things down if you're upset, so you don't bottle things up, and then you can see the problem in front of you: this helps you to solve problems because you can see them in front of you. For me, solving problems has been working through the distress, to see why I'd been so upset! I was always happy when I was younger, so someone or something must have caused my distress later in life! My happy memories, my happy childhood and my happy life, before I had been bullied at work, saved my mental health! Be honest with yourself about what others have done to upset you, even though they would never admit it!

It was now very clear, the problem for me, the problem for Dawn, and the problem for many of my colleagues, was proving what headteachers and management had done in court; these senior leadership teams knew the problem was proving it in court and would have known that most people don't go to work for such conflict! I know I didn't follow that route, simply because I wanted to protect my family from more distress. Children in full time education, with crucial examinations in front of them, do not need that distress. If I could take them to court now, I would, as my children are all older now! Sealand Occupational Health was right when they said the issues were my loss of wages and my loss of pension. Dinton Occupational Health told me I'd already won against Firlane School, with Whiteland School. By doing this, they saved my mental health!

Dinton Occupational Health also told me I had been threatened by two people (at the time I'd forgotten to tell them about Chloe Crispin) and they'd told me that other teachers had had the same problem, in the same school, with the same headteacher (Angela Rivers). It was poetic justice and situation irony when Angela Rivers went to jail! The way I, and many others in the school, had been treated really had been the makings of a court case, but no one really wanted such conflict with employers! My novel was a different solution: a solution they never would have expected! Have they now seen the error of their ways? Will they now change? Is there hope for them in the future?

They hadn't expected HMSI to find the truth, had they? No one had expected HMSI to go back to the schools to find out the truth and to write the HMSI reports that they did write, did they? I knew why these HMSI reports had been written, but they didn't, until they read this novel! I ended up as a teacher, an exam marker and an author.

Smile!

Be joyous: enjoy every day and treat other people the way you'd like to be treated, to make the world a better place. Start with yourself to make the world a better place and be the best you can be, and appreciate your family, friends and the essentials in life, for everyone. He who laughs last, laughs the longest. I was happy, without any major problems.

I hoped, at the very least, after Covid-19 (the Coronavirus), a virus which was beginning to circulate around the world, that employees would now be valued; the world is a better place when everyone works together, to solve problems for everyone. Together, everyone achieves more.

Hopefully, the world will realise that people are more important than possessions and wealth. I'm relieved to be happy and healthy and now appreciate everything I have today! Today should be happier than yesterday. Today is precious. Tomorrow should be happy too. Enjoy every day, concentrating on being happy and healthy. Treasure people, because people are more important than status, money and wealth. Appreciate every day. Don't waste your time being upset by others who take delight in upsetting you and spoiling your happiness. Fortunately, you can look after your own happiness and help other people too, without hurting others. Dawn was right when she said, "Pull the other one, it has bells on," as her reaction to the way management in Firlane School had upset her. This still makes us both laugh, years later!

I felt relieved to escape the fear and misery of bullying. Laughing and solving problems, to make the world a better place, is much better than deliberately hurting others. Would everyone ever learn that every single person is important and equal to everyone else?

Everyone now has a blank page in front of them, every day, and we can all do what we wish in the circumstances, so long as we are safe and don't hurt others. Perfect! The world is our oyster, for me, for you and for everyone. Enjoy time with family and friends. Value your friends and family; value your friends for life. Appreciate everything you have, every day; concentrate on the things that really make you happy as an individual, not merely the pursuit of power and wealth. Concentrate on good mental health and value your strong friendships and family; we can keep each other mentally healthy, which is worth more than money. Have a positive can-do attitude. Walks along nature are free, yet protect our mental health! Fresh air and exercise are free! Every day is better for me now than years ago. Smiling, being happy and good times are here, if I can keep my positive, can-do mental attitude! I have now left the past behind. I can remember my many happy memories because no one can take them away from me. I can enjoy the present now, and look forward to the future, because I was happy in the past.

The whole saga had been about mental health, the distribution of wealth and equality. A friend in need is a friend indeed. "A trustworthy friend is worth his or her weight in gold; a new friend is silver, but an old friend is gold," my mother often told me, years ago! Being happy and healthy are the most important things in life. Look well after yourself, then look well after others too. My GP, Sealand Occupational Health and Dinton Occupational Health were proved to be right, because I listened to their advice and to the mental healthcare advice given by Continued Professional Development, which was free and provided to all teachers by our teaching union. I've had a lucky escape from mental illness caused by bullying, greed and manipulation. Luckily, my GP wasn't tricked by them, neither was the hospital, neither was Sealand Occupational Health, neither was Dinton Occupational Health, neither were HMSI (her Majesty's School Inspectors) and neither were the headteachers of the best schools in the area! Luckily, I had also trusted in my instincts and I was right too! I would have been ill if

I'd been tricked by them! Luckily, the medical profession saved me!

The medical profession certainly wasn't tricked by them! They insulted our intelligence, the teaching unions' intelligence and the medical profession's intelligence! Good mental health is talking about problems and solving them. It's good to learn from mistakes. Wanting to do the right thing helps, so people can move on and learn from mistakes, to improve themselves, their lives and to help others. It's good to keep doing things and to keep learning new things. On the news and on the television, there's always advice for people to look after their mental health and to tell their friends about problems, so they're not alone. Moral support to solve problems costs nothing! A problem shared should be a problem halved. Does everyone now value everyone equally, caring for the mental health of every other person?

Trust your own instincts and stay safe; it's much better than relying on prescription medication. In the press, it was reported, by medical experts, that almost 12 million people are being prescribed potentially addictive drugs by GPs, and women are more likely to be prescribed them! I think you must trust yourself about what is upsetting you, because, as we see daily in the news on the television and in newspapers, other people continually defend themselves if there's a problem! Solve problems and ask for help if you need it. Identify what's upsetting you and solve the problem. Believe in yourself and trust your own instincts about why you feel upset and don't be tricked by power, wealth and status. Do you always try to be honest, trustworthy and reliable?

Management of schools, businesses and services should be looking into the causes of mental health problems at work, to protect their employees, because prevention is better than a cure! Safety first is much better than illness and prevention is much better than a cure. The government and the world should be looking into the causes of mental problems, because prevention is better than a cure. Walk away from bullies, bullying and from bullying management and report it, because all they will do is attack you and defend themselves. This would've been the cause of the problems of stress, depression and mental health for me, if I hadn't walked away and saved my health. This would've been the cause of the problems of stress, depression and mental health for Dawn, if she hadn't walked away and saved her health. This would've been the cause of the problems of stress, depression and mental health for my colleagues, if they hadn't walked away and saved their health. For me, for Dawn and for my colleagues, the problem had really been the ethos and mindset of some employers and people in a position of power who didn't care about their employees, and who would have defended themselves and attacked their victim! Trust your instincts: there's a reason why you don't feel safe at work. Have you enough evidence to win in court? Do you as an individual care about the mental health of the people around you? Whiteland School, Emmerland School and Heartland School were the three best schools in the whole area and they'd saved my mental health too, along with HMSI! No one had expected that, had they?

All of that distress was caused by something simple! All of that distress was caused by a lack of social responsibility! All of that distress was caused by management, not only for me, my colleagues but for other employees in this country. A problem shared should be a problem halved; a problem shared should not be used to bully the person who is asking for support. Everyone should support you, to overcome problems, so problems don't overcome you. Working together solves problems; defending yourself and attacking the other person is the basis of a court case. Luckily for me, for Dawn and for my colleagues, the medical profession wasn't tricked by these employers, neither were HMSI (Her Majesty's School Inspectors). Do you care when someone else is upset, anxious and is trying to do the right thing?

Concentrate on good physical health and good mental health! You can't buy a person in a shop! Value every person because every person is equal and is unique!

Follow the concept of self-help and help each other, friends, family and neighbours. Also, talking with people in the same position is a strengthening bond, and helps us all to move on. A friend for life can help you through thick and thin. The problem at work for me, for Dawn at work and for my colleagues at work, was poor management. Management should've been developing their staff to their maximum potential and working together, to solve problems, but really, if we'd been supported and valued, none of us would have left. Why did they ignore HMSI who praised me and the whole staff of Firlane School? Why did they ignore HMSI who had praised me at Forth School? Why didn't both schools value an expensive and experienced member of staff?

I hope there will be a change in the future, so everyone can enjoy working in their chosen field. I hope to change the world for the better! Are you listening? Do you want everyone to be happy and able to reach their maximum potential?

Tell a friend about your problems and your feelings, so you don't bottle things up and solve problems, in a positive way! We all had friends, pupils and happy lives at work, but we just hadn't realised it at the time. It just shows you don't know what you have, until it's gone! Count your blessings in life. Concentrate on being happy and healthy; it keeps people out of trouble too! Value the people in your life who are trustworthy, honest and reliable. All that I've found, at the end, is that the best things in life are free! Having a family, a trustworthy friend, moral people in your life and good neighbours are a real treasure. Moral support can help us to overcome our problems.

Telling someone how you feel could save a life and avoid illness, depression, anxiety and suicide. Focusing on your own social status won't save lives. Can you use your position in life to help others? Can you lead by setting a good example? Can you inspire others to do the right thing? Could you be a good listener if someone is upset? Could you allow someone to explore their emotions/ feelings and then help that person to devise a plan to move forward, taking one small step at a time? Could the plan include progression, so that once one person reaches one step forward, they know what the next step forward is? Could you help someone to identify their strengths and achievements too?

You only have one life, so you should enjoy it. Enjoy every minute, because if you have the right environment, you can have the power to reach your maximum potential. The truth is: my life is much better now but what about other people? Life is lovely again and I can smile again; I can laugh again, but what about other people? I've stopped being upset by other people's bullying, in the past, but what about other people? How can we help others, so everyone is happy, healthy and enjoys life?

We can all concentrate on being happy, healthy and doing the right thing! Be in charge of your own conscience because, at the end of the day, you have to live with your own conscience. Saving your health and happiness gives you riches beyond measure. Walk away if you don't have the power to solve a problem, because the people who're upsetting you aren't worth the distress they've caused. Are you happy and healthy?

The management thought they'd got away with it, until they read this novel! They didn't expect to see it in print, did they? They now know why I've waited until I'm practically retired before I've published this novel! The pen is mightier than the sword. Truth is stranger than fiction. I did know what had really gone on. I know it's all too fantastic not to be true. Can we all try to make the world a better place?

Time has also shown how many pressed the self-destruct button for themselves! Management tried to trick as many people as they could, but I knew the truth, the medical profession knew the truth and HMSI knew the truth too! Dawn, other colleagues and their medical teams also knew the truth. The courts need enough evidence to prove the truth. Everyone has the chance of redemption, but first, you must accept what you have done wrong, be sorry, and then try to change. Has management now learned from the past? Can management now change in the future? Do they now seek redemption? The individual can change for the better, a group can change for the better and the world can change for the better. Who will make that decision?

There's always hope for the future. Has management learned it's a better place if each individual tries to do the right thing? Has management learned it's a better place if we all help each other? Has management learned it's a better place if we all work together? Will individuals learn that everyone should be valued equally? Will countries learn that everyone should be valued equally? Will the world learn that everyone should be valued equally? Laughter is healthy! The system is that everybody needs enough money to live on, so everyone should have the right to earn money, legally. The problem is everyone has basic needs to live, but there isn't enough wealth in the world for everyone's greed. Have people learned to care about others now? Will they remember this? Will everyone share with others? Is the will for change here?

I live in the hope! I hope everyone strives to make themselves better, to make the country better and to make the whole world better. If everyone strives to make themselves better, to make the country better and to make the whole world better, working together to solve problems and to resolve conflict, would we all be happier?. If there's a problem, can we all work together to solve it, to save mental health, so people don't feel weak, anxious and powerless? Do we need a fighting spirit for justice, truth and equality?

Hope for the best but prepare for the worst!

Good management in schools is developing both staff and pupils to their maximum potential, without allowing disruptive pupils to rule.

A new war descended across the world! It was another Invisible War. What was this war? What would the consequences be? How would the UK cope? Good management by the government is to develop the population to their maximum potential, without allowing the thugs to rule. This Invisible War highlighted how people had been very upset in life, by the way they'd been treated by others too. Education, I hope, is for everyone in the UK, where everyone should be allowed to develop to their maximum potential, without preventing the learning of others. Would schools still be open in the Invisible War? Equality is vital in education and in the UK, to make the communities, the country and the world a better place. Education, and the whole of the UK, should uphold the values of truth, honesty and equality for everyone, to end conflict, to end poverty and to end racial discrimination. Would the UK show these values in the face of the Invisible War? Would the UK survive the Invisible War?

Printed in Great Britain
by Amazon